"A historically accurate and entertaining mystery series."
— *The New York Review of Books*

PRAISE FOR THE
LOUISA MAY ALCOTT
MYSTERY SERIES

Louisa and the Crystal Gazer

"In *Louisa and the Crystal Gazer*, Louisa continues to grow as a character. . . . This self-growth and self-awareness help keep the book from becoming simply another historical cozy. . . . By relying on her own personal strengths and those of family and friends, Louisa has the ability to find the criminal, regardless of the circumstances."   — Reviewing the Evidence

Louisa and the Country Bachelor

"Louisa May Alcott makes a wonderful narrator, whether observing the foibles of those around her or addressing the reader with gentle humor. . . .Fans of historical mysteries will find much to enjoy here."   — The Romance Readers Connection

"Maclean's latest cozy is entertaining and has a fascinating mystery and a healthy dose of humor. The author's attention to historical detail adds realism and depth to this page-turner."
— *Romantic Times*

"The generous mix of oddly assorted characters and the village setting make this a pleasantly diverting outing. Fans of Alcott and period mysteries in general will enjoy it."
— *The Historical Novels Review*

continued . . .

"Anna Maclean has created an entertaining period piece around Louisa May Alcott and her adventures as an amateur sleuth before she becomes a well-known author. . . . Those readers who enjoy mysteries set in the past, like the Irene Adler series, will want to add this series to the list of their must reads."   —Roundtable Reviews

Louisa and the Missing Heiress

"This thrilling mystery reads like one of Alcott's own 'blood-and-thunder' tales. The colorful characters and long-held secrets will keep you guessing until the final page."
                        —Kelly O'Connor McNees, author of
                            The Lost Summer of Louisa May Alcott

"An adventure fit for Louisa May Alcott. A fine tribute to a legendary heroine."
                        —Laura Joh Rowland, author of the Adventures
                                        of Charlotte Brontë series

"Your favorite author takes on a life of her own and proves to be a smart, courageous sleuth."
                            —Victoria Thompson, author of
                                the Gaslight Mystery series

"Charming and clever amateur sleuth Louisa May Alcott springs to life."
                        —Karen Harper, national bestselling
                            author of *The Queen's Governess*

"Maclean has a wonderful grasp of the history, language, and style of nineteenth-century Boston . . . enough plot twists to keep me entertained until the satisfying conclusion."
                                            —The Best Reviews

"It was perhaps inevitable that Louisa May Alcott, the pseudonymous author of so many blood-and-thunder tales, would, herself, take up sleuthing. This tale of dark secrets, mysterious men, and heiresses in distress will please any reader who has longed to pursue Jo March's 'sensation stories,' those lucrative tales that allowed Beth to go to the seashore, but of which the good Professor Bhaer so stoutly disapproved. As Jo herself might say, a thumping good read."
—Joanne Dobson, author of *Death Without Tenure*

"This novel reveals that my great-great-aunt had a secret career that none of us knew about. It's great fun and a page-turner, and it uses the morals and mores of the time and place to delightful effect." —John Pratt, heir to the Alcott Estate

"A great debut that's appropriate for all ages." —*Mystery Scene*

"Great fun. . . . Maclean has done a wonderful job of capturing Alcott's voice and style. . . . I suspect the real Alcott would have liked it and wished she had written it herself."
—Women Writers

"Readers will find themselves enthralled with the details of Louisa's life, family and friends, as well as with the expertly crafted mystery." —Romance Readers Connection

"Mystery and suspense abound in this first-person fictional account of Alcott's amateur sleuthing. This well-crafted debut novel should help garner fans for her series." —*Romantic Times*

"Louisa's forwardness makes the story very accessible for the average reader of today." —*The Historical Novels Review*

Other Louisa May Alcott Mysteries

Louisa and the Missing Heiress
Louisa and the Country Bachelor

LOUISA
and the
CRYSTAL
GAZER

A Louisa May Alcott Mystery

ANNA MACLEAN

AN OBSIDIAN MYSTERY

OBSIDIAN

Published by New American Library, a division of
Penguin Group (USA) Inc., 375 Hudson Street,
New York, New York 10014, USA
Penguin Group (Canada), 90 Eglinton Avenue East, Suite 700, Toronto,
Ontario M4P 2Y3, Canada (a division of Pearson Penguin Canada Inc.)
Penguin Books Ltd., 80 Strand, London WC2R 0RL, England
Penguin Ireland, 25 St. Stephen's Green, Dublin 2,
Ireland (a division of Penguin Books Ltd.)
Penguin Group (Australia), 250 Camberwell Road, Camberwell, Victoria 3124,
Australia (a division of Pearson Australia Group Pty. Ltd.)
Penguin Books India Pvt. Ltd., 11 Community Centre, Panchsheel Park,
New Delhi - 10 017, India
Penguin Group (NZ), 67 Apollo Drive, Rosedale, Auckland 0632,
New Zealand (a division of Pearson New Zealand Ltd.)
Penguin Books (South Africa) (Pty.) Ltd., 24 Sturdee Avenue,
Rosebank, Johannesburg 2196, South Africa

Penguin Books Ltd., Registered Offices:
80 Strand, London WC2R 0RL, England

Published by Obsidian, an imprint of New American Library, a division of Penguin
Group (USA) Inc. Previously published in a Signet edition.

First Obsidian Printing, February 2012
10 9 8 7 6 5 4 3 2 1

For all the generous and helpful volunteers at Orchard House, who help preserve Louisa's legacy

Acknowledgments

Thanks to Ellen Edwards for her support, ideas, and professionalism; to Alison Lurie for her inspiring conversations about Louisa; to Jan Turnquist for her wonderful work at Orchard House; to Steve Poleskie for the patience and love; and to Tiffany Yates for the close reading she gave this work. To quote Louisa, I can never thank you enough for the patient sowing and reaping you have done.

LOUISA

and the

CRYSTAL

GAZER

Gentle Reader,

In December of 1855 I found myself in Boston temporarily separated from my beloved family in Walpole, New Hampshire, and facing a Christmas, that most wonderful of seasons, without the comfort of my loved ones.

But drudge a living I must, for I was not yet the rich and famous author I later became. My stories, when they sold, earned little, and so I had sought employment and received an offer from Reverend Ezra Gannett, who wished me to complete an order of a dozen winter shirts for him, all to be finely seamed, buttonholed, and finished with pleats and embroidery.

I was an unenthused seamstress at best, but his payment would allow me to purchase Christmas presents for my family, so I accepted his offer, and a second one besides, for a dozen summer shirts of lighter fabric to be completed by April. These matters are relevant to my story. Trust me.

My dear friend Sylvia Shattuck was also in residence in Boston, fortunately, for more than ever I counted on her steadfast and amusing companionship. Sylvia, however, was in a strange frame of mind, one that set into motion a course of events that would involve us in murder, faithless lovers, and sad deeds of a dark past. Beware of boredom, gentle reader. It can lead one down dangerous paths.

"I miss Father," she sighed one morning as we took our

walk along the harbor. It was a misty, cold day, and the harbor waves were tipped with frosty white.

"Unfortunately, your father passed away when you were a child," I answered gently. "You barely knew that long-enduring man, so how do you now claim to miss him?"

It was unlike Sylvia to yearn for any family member, dead or alive, and I had a vague presentiment that she was to introduce yet another faddish custom into my life. Sylvia lived in vogues, and had just relinquished Confucianism, which had not brought the enlightenment she sought. No use to explain to her that philosophers spent years at that task; Sylvia tended to give three months and then move on.

"My point exactly," my companion responded, turning upon me bright eyes filled with a passionate melancholy. "I feel the need for a masculine presence in my life, and would like to converse with my father. I will, with the assistance of Mrs. Agatha Percy. Please come with me to one of her sittings!"

I groaned and jammed my hands deeper into my pockets, despite the stares of several passersby; a lady did not put her hands in her pockets. She did if they were cold, I thought. Ship rigging creaked in the wind and bells chimed the start of a new watch, and I pondered Sylvia's statement.

Mrs. Agatha D. Percy was the newest fad in Boston, one of the recently risen members of that questionable group of individuals known as "spiritists," or mediums. One must feel a very heavy burden of ennui to wish to spend time at that dubious amusement, I thought.

"Oh, it will be such fun, Louisa. All of Boston goes!" Sylvia persisted.

"Then it must be quite crowded," I rejoined, walking at a faster pace to try to dissuade Sylvia from this topic.

But she turned pink with enthusiasm and fairly raced about me in circles, imploring that I join her in this new activity. "Please come with me, Louy; say you will! I have an invitation for you from Mrs. Percy." Sailors in their blue overcoats turned in our direction and grinned.

"I can think of better ways to spend time and money than sitting in the dark and watching parlor tricks. I would much rather, for instance, attend one of Signor Massimo's musical evenings." The signor, a famous pianist, was touring the United States from his home in Rome and had decided to winter in Boston. He was giving a series of performances—performances I could not afford, since the tickets were as much as three dollars apiece, even when they were available, which wasn't often, as he preferred private homes and small salons.

"Mother tried to get tickets and could not. She was furious," Sylvia said. I could understand; women with Mrs. Shattuck's family name and wealth were not accustomed to hearing no.

"Look, there is ice in the harbor," I said, putting my hand over my eyes to shield them from the glare.

"I will have your answer," Sylvia persisted.

I introduced several new topics of conversation, hoping to distract Sylvia from her mission—Jenny Lind, the Wild West, a newly published travel book about France that was flying off the shelves—but each topic she cleverly rejoined and detoured back to Mrs. Percy. Jenny Lind, accompanied by her American manager, P. T. Barnum, had visited Mrs.

Percy. Mrs. Percy had published a "memoir" from a spirit who had visited her from Oklahoma. Mrs. Percy had toured France the year before and had been received by their umbrella-carrying Citizen King.

"Don't you see?" Sylvia sighed in exasperation, pulling at my hand to prevent me from taking another step. "The spirits themselves wish you to visit her. They put those very suggestions in your mind!"

"Then they should put a plot or two in my mind," I said, remembering the still-blank sheet of paper before which I had sat that morning at my desk. Being between stories was an unpleasant state for me, when no plot or story threaded the random thoughts of everyday imagination, no characters spoke to me in my head as I swept the parlor or stitched linens.

"They will," Sylvia said complacently. "I hear they become quite chatty and friendly in Mrs. Percy's parlor. You might use the scene in one of your 'blood and thunder' stories. Think what fun it would be to write about Mrs. Percy!"

"I am unconvinced that 'fun' is the correct word to describe an hour of sitting in the dark, pretending to speak with the dead," I said.

"Spirits," corrected Sylvia. "The dead don't like to be called dead. Such a harsh word."

Neither of us was yet aware of exactly how harsh that séance would become.

"I will think about it," I promised. "But now come with me to Tremont Street, and let us look in the windows and begin to think of Christmas presents, and what we will give our families."

"I know what Mother wishes," said Sylvia. "A son-in-law."

"I have an easier shopping list," I laughed. "A ream of writing paper for Father, new Berlin wools for Auntie Bond, something frivolous for Marmee since everyone else is certain to give her sturdy handkerchiefs." Marmee, my beloved mother, was also known as Abba, but more and more in my imagination she was Marmee, and she was already the center of a story I had yet to write but often thought about, a story about four daughters, one named Jo, and their wise, generous mother. "A pair of gloves for Anna in Syracuse, and Faber pencils for Abby." Abby, the youngest Alcott girl, was the artist of the family.

"You've forgotten Lizzie," said Sylvia.

"No, I haven't." Lizzie was a musician, a quiet, shy girl who asked for little and was content with all she had, which was little enough. "But what can I give a sister who deserves a grand piano, a gift out of the question? I am at a loss."

"You'll think of something, Louy. You always do," Sylvia assured me.

CHAPTER ONE

Mrs. Percy's Parlor

AFTER MY PERAMBULATION with Sylvia I returned to my rooms and was greeted somewhat distractedly by Auntie Louisa Bond, a kindhearted woman of middle years with a long and close connection to my family who had offered room and board to her "favorite young person" while I (that favorite young person) was separated from my family.

"Oh, dear, your nose is quite red, dear Louisa," she fussed, wiping my face with her handkerchief as if I were seven years old, not twenty-three. "Must you go walking in this cold? Your mother would be distressed." She flitted about like a butterfly, her lace collar and cuffs flapping as she helped me off with hat and coat.

"Mother would not be distressed." I laughed. "She believes in the power of daily exercise in all weather. Shall I help with the dinner, Auntie Bond?"

"The stew is ready whenever you are, my dear. Set a plate for yourself, because I have eaten. I have friends com-

ing over for a round of cards, so we will be in the front parlor."

Auntie Bond was a good and generous soul, but with a single vice: She liked to gamble, and although it was pennies that were wagered, she turned beet red whenever she announced that her friends were coming over for a round of cards.

I thought it harmless enough; many women, especially those past an age for attending dancing parties or rowing picnics on the Charles, played cards these days, though they dreaded being gossiped about. Cakes and buns came from the bakery, the newfangled carpet sweeper made it unnecessary to spend all of Saturday taking up the rugs and beating them, and every household except the poorest had a servant or two. What were the ladies to do with their time?

Go to crystal gazers, I thought. Father would say they have too much free time when others have too little.

"I will take a tray upstairs, then, so as not to disturb you." I gave Auntie Bond a kiss on the cheek to reassure her.

Living in rooms felt strange, for my hardworking and practical mother had always, even in the most penurious times, found a way for our family to live together under the solidified roof of that species of establishment known as home. "Rooms" signified something entirely different, something somewhat daring. I was on my own, and I awoke each morning with a strange flush of excitement.

The excitement soon turned to a less exalted emotion when my eyes beheld the pile of shirts I had agreed to sew for Reverend Ezra Gannett. The reverend was an energetic preacher, and often left the pulpit with a torn seam or ripped buttonhole, and so his wardrobe was in constant need of renewal.

Next to my sewing basket was a pile of papers—my stories, my openings and experiments for "blood and thunder" stories about damsels in distress, evil suitors, and dark family secrets.

But my writing had come to a standstill, as it sometimes does, leaving me prey to a mood so somber as to be called despondency, for fear that the part of my imagination that created stories might never awaken again. Always it feels so. I am thankful it has never proven so.

I stitched seams long into the night, listening to the crackling of the fire and the occasional muffled burst of laughter from the downstairs parlor, where Auntie Bond and her friends played cards. I could hear their voices but not their words, and the indistinct sounds added a dreamlike quality to the winter night. The flames cast shadows about the room, and my fatigue made me see movement in dark corners, though I knew nothing moved there. How easy it would be to pretend that there was something of the supernatural in that room, where voices floated in from nowhere, where shadows danced. It was the kind of dreamy mood that allowed one to think it possible to converse with the dear departed.

As I sat over my sewing, I wondered what kind of woman would choose to take advantage of that weakness of the heart and mind and set herself up as a crystal gazer.

Mrs. Percy and her activities had filled many newspaper columns in the three months since she had taken up residence in Boston. Most of the reports were unfavorable, yet her client list grew daily.

I tried to imagine Mrs. Percy, thinking of nothing as superficial as hair color but of the state of her soul and her disposition.

Instantly, as I pushed my needle in and out of the fine linen shirts in the dim candlelight, there came a voice in my imagination. "I was poor and plain, with no accomplishments or charms of mind or person, and yet Philip loved me," it whispered. I do not know the source of these voices, only that they lead to stories, and I follow.

And since the story was already begun, I knew I would go with Sylvia to the séance room. It would be amusing, and perhaps Mrs. Percy would inspire and help create the story begun that evening in my imagination.

Sleep came easily that night, after my two hours at my desk—I used to sleep so well, when those pages were filled!

Sylvia and I met the next day, at five o'clock in the afternoon, in front of Mrs. Agatha D. Percy's house on Arlington Street. It was already quite dark in that late-winter afternoon and very atmospheric, with snow sliding down the sky in front of the gas streetlamps and the carriage horses in their striped blankets, their breath steaming before them. I suppose very few mediums meet with their clientele in full daylight, I thought.

"This is to be a very select group," Sylvia said with satisfaction. "I understand it is by invitation. She does not receive just anybody."

"Sylvia," I said, "you sound remarkably like your mother."

"You see, Louy?" Sylvia said. "I do need a masculine presence to bring balance to my life."

Mrs. Percy's home was a modest brick structure in a good

neighborhood filled with similar brick establishments. Her house showed signs of recent improvements, though the building itself was not old. The green shutters were new and designed to exclude all light when pulled shut. A brighter-colored brick on the west side showed that the little sunroom had just been added—perhaps, I thought, for unexpected entrances of "phantoms." Broken vines and rose canes indicated some adjustment had been made to the east side as well. I decided to take careful mental notes and describe it in a letter to Mother, along with the events of the séance, for her opinion.

Sylvia rang the bell, her eyes as wide as a child's at Christmas. A servant answered the door and showed us into a little waiting room.

The maid, a pretty girl of nineteen or so, wore an expensive white lace mantilla held in place with a garnet hatpin, rather than the usual lace cap of the parlormaid. Instead of a sensible brown frock, she wore red petticoats with a purple apron over them trimmed in glass beads. From the numerous sausage curls hanging beside her unnaturally rosy cheeks and the excessive swaying of her skirts as she walked, it was plain the girl needed a mother's stern guidance. Here was the perfect project for Abba!

"Your name?" I asked.

"Suzie," the girl replied saucily. "Miss Suzie Dear."

"Indeed," said Sylvia, studying her with interest.

"Mrs. Percy begs your patience," said the maid with more pomp and circumstance in her voice. "She has not yet achieved the exact quietude required for summoning the spirits."

"You mean she is behind schedule," grumbled a man who

sat before the fire warming his hands. "Bad policy. Should never keep a crowd waiting." He half rose and nodded in our direction. Mr. Phineas Taylor Barnum, the greatest showman on earth himself!

Who would not have recognized him, with that broad forehead, tightly curling black hair just starting to turn gray at the temples, those piercing gray eyes, and that firm chin? His image had been before the public on an almost daily basis for many years, in the papers, broadsheets, and books, including as a frontispiece in his own hugely successful autobiography published just the year before. Oh, how that book had sold! Some twenty thousand copies in just months. I admit to envy. Would I ever write anything that sold as well? (Many years later, you realize, my own *Little Women* outsold him by many hundreds of thousands, to my perpetual delight.)

But what, I wondered then, could the wealthy, prosperous Mr. Barnum want of a crystal gazer?

The famous—or should I say notorious?—showman was dressed in a dark suit and would have been indistinguishable from any number of somewhat corpulent middle-aged men of business, except that his face was so very well-known. The quickness of his gaze bespoke an extraordinarily active imagination, but there was a furtiveness in his manner, a hesitancy of movement, an unexpected sliding back and forth of the eyes, that indicated all was not well with him.

"At your service, ladies," he said. "Mr. Phineas Barnum." He extended his hand.

"Miss Louisa Alcott, and my friend Miss Sylvia Shattuck." I sat on a settee opposite him.

"Alcott, Alcott," he mused, plucking at his velvet lapels. "Is your father the philosopher Bronson Alcott?"

"He is."

"Well, then." Mr. Barnum screwed up his mouth and looked into the distance, then returned his gaze to me. "I am a man of quick decision. I have a proposal for him. I have heard of his 'conversations.' I would like to introduce events of significance, not just entertainment, to the American Museum. Would your father be interested in exhibiting there?"

Father, kind reader, earned a dollar now and then by giving private lectures in homes to discuss issues of public morality and personal conscience.

Sylvia's mouth twitched. For a moment I allowed myself the luxury of imagining my noble philosopher father onstage, next to perhaps a lion and tamer or an acrobat, discoursing to the crowd on abolitionism or the progress of the soul.

"I will mention your idea to him," I answered demurely, "but I think such a large and very public arrangement might not suit his method of education."

"Of course, of course," muttered Mr. Barnum with a downcast expression, and I saw I had given offense, despite the gentleness of the response. "I am not having a lucky year. Signor Massimo also declined my offer to appear at the American Museum."

Mr. Barnum seemed so forlorn that I felt I should make amends somehow. "I've heard that Signor Massimo will not play for large crowds in public," I said. "He has the same philosophy of performance as Father, that smaller groups benefit more."

"I, too, am an admirer of the philosopher of Concord," spoke up a second middle-aged gentleman who had stood upon our entry and waited, patiently, for us to acknowledge him. "I am Mr. William Phips."

"Phips of Canton?" asked Mr. Barnum, excited and recovered from his disappointment over Father.

Mr. Phips bowed. "At your service," he answered modestly. I studied him as closely as the dim light in the reception room allowed. He was tall, solidly built, and well muscled in spite of his fifty or so years. An outdoorsman, I thought. One who rides every morning, and bathes in cold water even in winter. He wore a dark suit of thick cloth cut in military fashion, with crossed-over lapels and tight breeches. He wished people to remember his military service, his clothing said. But his smile was ingratiating.

"I am amazed, sir, to meet you!" said Mr. Barnum. "As true a hero as ever lived!"

"Well, life requires boldness, sir," said Mr. Phips modestly. He seemed not at all bold to me.

"What is Canton?" asked Sylvia.

"Why, this man is a champion!" boomed Mr. Barnum. "In 1839, single-handedly, he fought off a hundred Chinamen! The story ran in the papers for weeks! Enthralled, sir, I was enthralled!"

"A mere dozen, not a hundred," said Mr. Phips. "And not single-handedly. My friend August Pincher was with me, though he did not make it out, poor boy." Mr. Phips shook his head sorrowfully.

"Who was August Pincher?" I asked.

"A friend, Miss Alcott. A friend unlike any other, who fell in battle." Then his face brightened, and, seeing Sylvia's and my confusion, he deigned to enlighten us.

"I was a private guard with the East India Company, protecting the Canton traders," he said, pulling on his lapels and puffing out his cheeks.

"Ah. The East India Company. I believe Father owned some stocks in it," said Sylvia. "We have a curio cabinet filled with Indian silver vases. They are very lovely."

Barnum smiled indulgently. "Dear girl," he said, "your vases are the proverbial tip of the iceberg. England's empire and wealth were built by that company."

"I wish they had stopped with vases," I said. "The company's importation of opium from India to China was wicked. They encouraged the Chinese to partake in a habit that is deadly."

"But the trade imbalance had to be righted," Barnum said. "The opium trade helps pay for that English tea you drink in the afternoon."

That, dear reader, was exactly what Father had said when the Opium Wars began, and why the Alcott family began drinking sage tea grown in our own garden.

Mr. Phips cleared his throat and returned to the telling of his tale, having stood as long as he could the usurpation of his limelight by Mr. Barnum. "When that tyrant Lin Tse-Hsu decided to end the opium trade, he besieged our headquarters and sent assassins. I discovered a plot to murder Lancelot Dent, the most important trader of the Chamber. Lin sent a dozen men, all armed, to kill that one man. But August Pincher and I foiled him. We fought off the assassins and saved Dent, though August was mortally wounded."

"A true hero!" Barnum repeated, and I began to find his adoration a bit trying. It was a cruel and unfair war, Father had proclaimed of those events years before.

"You were wounded—" Mr. Barnum stopped in midsentence. In his face shone the enthusiasm of the hero-worshiping young boy, though the enthusiasm was now crowned with wrinkles, and strands of gray grizzled his thick black curls.

Mr. Phips held up a hand in protest. "We must not discuss war injuries in front of the ladies. So, you are our famous philosopher's daughter?" He focused on me, returning the conversation to the topic of my father.

"I heard Mr. Bronson pontificate one evening last year in Concord," spoke up a woman who had been sitting primly in a deeply shadowed corner of the parlor and observing us silently.

Sylvia and I turned in her direction. It is a rare personage who can occupy a room and so completely prevent my knowledge of her till she wishes to be acknowledged. This woman was an expert at secrecy.

She was a year or two older than myself, I guessed, about twenty-five, and very pretty, though she had worked hard to downplay her native beauty. She had dressed entirely in an unflattering shade of brown and wore a plain bonnet with no lace or floral trim. Until she leaned forward and let the fire reflect on her fair complexion and pale hair, she was a shadow within the shadows.

"Miss Amelia Snodgrass," she said in almost a whisper. "Did I hear that you are Miss Alcott? Just last month I read the *Flower Fables* to my little nieces. Such a charming book, Miss Alcott. Will there be others?"

"Thank you. I hope there will be many others," I answered. I had worked all summer on a new collection of woodland fables, hoping for a Christmas market for the book, but had yet to find a publisher.

"Have you come for the séance?" asked Sylvia.

"Why else? I wish to see her with my own eyes," said Miss Snodgrass.

If P. T. Barnum was famous for his very public life, Miss Amelia Snodgrass was equally well-known, in certain rarefied circles, for her very private life. She was a member of one of those numerous Boston families that are rich in history but poor in funds, people who live quietly behind somewhat dingy lace curtains, using their grandmother's silver plate and their great-grandfather's furniture, and speaking, when they spoke, of events a hundred years old. Such people never die; they simply fade quietly away till one day one notices they are no longer shopping at Waterstone's linen shop.

Miss Amelia Snodgrass had recently, though, made herself an exception to that familiar biography. Her mother, for whom she had spent the past decade caring, had passed away, and she had announced her engagement to Wilmot Green, the eldest son of Green and Green Shippers and Importers. Once wed, she would be well able to replace those aged curtains and furnishings.

But why, I wondered, does she dress in such unattractive manner? She is in a costume of sorts. What tableau is she playing?

We had just finished exchanging pleasantries when Suzie Dear returned to the parlor, carrying a brass tray of teacups and tiny biscuits folded in a strange manner.

"Cook's a Chinawoman," she explained with distaste. "We had noodle salad for supper yesterday. Imagine such a thing."

Suzie stood in the doorway, and over her shoulder I saw a

small woman dressed in blue brocade trousers and tunic, peering in at us with evident curiosity.

"Chinese? Is she, now?" asked Mr. Phips, interested. He rose, but as soon as he moved the woman in blue turned and fled, her long black braid swaying against her back. Mr. Phips sat back down, and Suzie passed the tea and biscuits.

"Orientals!" exclaimed Miss Snodgrass with disapproval. "I suppose it is because it is so very difficult to acquire decent help these days that so many are resorting to Irish and Orientals. We are late. When will Mrs. Percy receive us?" This question was directed to Suzie Dear.

"Soon, I expect. More people are coming for this séance. A Mr. and Mrs. Deeds, and an Eye-talian, a Signor Massimo, have been invited." Suzie put the tray on the table and left with a toss of her curls.

Signor Massimo? Meeting the great pianist would be almost as wonderful as hearing him play. Now I was pleased I had come.

"Oh, late, late!" trilled another woman's voice. I looked up and saw two other people standing in the doorway, led there by buxom Suzie Dear.

Miss Snodgrass shot Suzie a look of repugnance, of hatred almost, if I may use such a strong word.

The newly arrived woman who had trilled was fanning herself furiously and leaning against the doorjamb as if she would faint. "Oh, my, my," she exclaimed. "Late, late!"

"Yes, she is," boomed P. T. Barnum's deep voice. "Bad policy, keeping customers waiting."

"I referred to myself," said the woman petulantly. "Have I delayed the séance?"

"You have not," said Sylvia. "Mrs. Percy has delayed us. And Mr. Massimo, who is not here yet."

"Oh, my," trilled our most recent arrival. She turned to the man at her side. "We have not delayed them. Isn't that fortuitous, Mr. Deeds, isn't that fortuitous?"

"Indeed," he replied. "But I thought we were not to speak names here?"

Really? No one had informed Sylvia and myself of that requirement. Or perhaps the Deedses wished even more privacy than Amelia Snodgrass, who cringed in the shadows away from the light.

"Oh!" And the creature, Mrs. Deeds, fanned herself even more vigorously. "Do forgive me, dear!"

"Too late," boomed Barnum. "We have made introductions all around."

"Rude to do otherwise, rude," said the new arrival, clicking her fan shut with a practiced gesture. "I am Mrs. Deeds, Mrs. Ezra Deeds. My husband."

Jack Spratt and wife, I thought. She was as large as he was thin. Middle-aged, matronly, overdone with lace and floral corsages, and rings glittering on all her fingers but her thumbs. A huge diamond brooch flashed on her bosom, and about her throat she wore a thick collar of pearls from which was suspended a large diamond surrounded by emeralds. It was an evening piece, most inappropriate for daytime, but even so, it was beautiful.

Miss Snodgrass stared at the new arrival as if stupefied, her mouth open but no sound coming out of it.

"A lovely necklace, Mrs. Deeds," said Mr. Barnum, tilting his head closer to see it better.

"A new piece in my collection," said Mrs. Deeds.

"On loan, not yet paid for." Mr. Deeds sighed. "There is a disagreement over its price."

Mrs. Deeds pinched his arm—"Men will speak of such matters!" she protested gaily—and her husband moved quickly into a corner of the parlor, taking a place next to Amelia Snodgrass and becoming a second shadow within the shadows.

An uncomfortable silence settled over the room. I gazed at my hands in my lap so that I would not stare impolitely into faces; Sylvia studied the wallpaper. Mrs. Deeds glared covetously at the new-fashioned mantel clock, a large, carved affair with much gilding and chiming of bells on the quarter hour. Mr. Barnum had sunk into his chair, deep into his own thoughts, and Mr. Phips sat as upright and patient as granite, his face stiff.

Some ten more minutes passed in this manner, till finally Suzie Dear returned and announced that Mrs. Percy would now receive us.

Sylvia squeezed my hand in excitement. I admit to feeling a thrill myself, and hoped I would remember as much detail as possible and get it scribbled into my notebook before any of the things I noticed disappeared into the depths of irretrievable memory.

"I wonder what dear Papa will have to say to me!" Sylvia whispered in my ear.

"That you have wasted good money," I whispered back. "Though the company amuses." It would have amused even more if Signor Massimo had kept his appointment.

CHAPTER TWO

The Dear Departed Speak

THE ROOM INTO which we were led was paneled in very dark, carved wood, and was windowless. Since it was not an interior room but one built on the west side of the house, I assumed that Mrs. Percy had covered the window, perhaps with that hugely looming armoire on the west wall. It was drearily, suffocatingly dark.

The ceiling was somewhat lower by perhaps six inches than the ceiling in the hall and was ornately painted in the new style, with trellises and posies and Egyptian repeats. These details are not without significance, gentle reader. Bear with me.

A large round table occupied the center of the room, and at that table sat Mrs. Percy, her eyes closed, her face, illumined by a single candle, tilted as though she listened to music we could not hear. She was dressed in swaths of black lace and fringe, with bells and sequins covering much of the strange, Gypsylike costume.

Mrs. Deeds stubbed her toe trying to find her chair in the darkness. She giggled nervously. Mrs. Percy did not move, but continued listening to that inaudible music until we were all settled.

Mrs. Percy greeted us all one by one, by name, and when my turn came she gave me a long gaze. "More than the philosopher's daughter," she said. "A solver of crimes. Welcome, Miss Alcott."

"Welcome," she said more loudly, this time to the room at large, lifting her hands in a gesture similar, I suspect, to the one used by Moses to part the sea; it was that grandiloquent. When she returned her hands to the table, her many heavy silver and gilt bracelets clinked noisily. She was an interesting middle-aged woman with a firm double chin, a full head of unnaturally dark hair (probably padded), and more than a touch of powder and rouge on her face.

"One is missing," said Mrs. Percy, displeasure in her voice. Suddenly she slumped in her chair, put her hand to her forehead, and groaned deeply. "Such a headache," she said in a bass, almost masculine voice. "Ah!" She sat up again and smiled. "Signor Massimo is not well. He cannot attend, but sends his regards," she said.

That's one way to account for a shortage in the audience, I thought. Invent their excuse for them.

"Oh, too exciting, too exciting," said Mrs. Deeds.

"I greet the spirits. You must now be silent," said Mrs. Percy to Mrs. Deeds.

"The spirits are here so quickly? I thought they needed to be summoned," said Mr. Barnum.

"You have attended other séances?" Mrs. Percy shot him a suspicious look.

"No," said Mr. Barnum. "Indeed, I have not. I merely speculated."

Mrs. Percy glared. Then her face softened. It was a handsome face, highly colored, and lively with curiosity and cunning intelligence. She looked about her with benign interest. "I remember that diamond brooch you are wearing, Mrs. Deeds. Lovely," she said.

"Mrs. Percy and I share a common interest in jewels," said Mrs. Deeds in a small voice, and I thought I could hear Miss Snodgrass make a choking sound.

A candle flared and sent strange shadows dancing about the room. "Mr. Barnum," Mrs. Percy said. "The spirits wish to begin with you. I have several messages. But first we will hold hands. Ladies, if you would remove your gloves."

Mrs. Deeds giggled.

"Must we?" protested Amelia Snodgrass in a little voice.

The rest of that afternoon, reader, I will put down here as it happened, without adornment or commentary.

We joined hands and closed eyes, though the room was already so dark we could barely see one another. Amelia Snodgrass sat on my right; her hand in mine was dry and light as fine parchment. Mr. Barnum sat to my left. His hand was moist, and he gripped me with some strength. Sylvia sat one chair over from me, next to Mrs. Deeds, who sat next to her husband.

Once we were arranged and Mrs. Deeds had stopped giggling, Mrs. Percy gave a loud, strange sigh, then slumped in her chair. A kind of nervousness filled the dark room.

Several minutes passed in this manner, we sitting in the dreariness holding hands, and Mrs. Percy sighing and muttering as if asleep.

Suddenly there was a loud rapping sound, three times, and Mrs. Percy sat up, her clouds of black lace making a kind of whispering sound as she moved.

"Are you there?" she called in a rapturous voice.

The rapping sounded again.

"We will use the spirit alphabet," Mrs. Percy said. "One tap is A, two taps are B, three are C, et cetera. If the answer is yes, there will be two quick, light taps. If no, there will be three quick, light taps. Spirits, are you present?"

Two quick, light taps.

"To whom do you wish to speak?"

Two taps. B. One tap. A. Eighteen taps. R.

"Is it Mr. Barnum?"

Two quick taps.

"Shall I write for you?"

Two quick taps.

Mrs. Percy removed a heavy cloth off something that had been placed on the table before our arrival, and I saw that it was a writing tablet and an inkwell. Dreamlike, she dipped the pen in the ink and began to write with a slow, scratching sound, her bracelets jangling. This exercise occupied several minutes. Mr. Barnum's hand in mine was perspiring.

"You may read it," said Mrs. Percy, when she had replaced the pen in its stand. "My eyes are blurred with visions of Summerland."

Summerland, kind reader, was the newly fashionable

phrase to describe the afterlife, as if heaven, hell, and purgatory did not adequately cover that territory.

Mr. Barnum released my hand and dragged the tablet across the table. He tilted it this way and that to catch the light from the single candle on the table.

"Out loud, please," said Mrs. Percy. "There are no secrets in this room. We here are blessed by the spirits with trust in one another."

As I've promised to avoid commentary on this particular scene, reader, you must believe that the following observation is accurate rather than imaginative: Several shocked "Oh!"s and clearings of throats followed the medium's pronouncement, including one in Miss Amelia Snodgrass's small, high voice.

"Well," said Mr. Barnum. "The spirits could do with lessons in penmanship. I will do my best. It says, 'Forgiveness rather than vengeance. Women are easily led astray and used'—no, perhaps it is 'abused'—'by those with power.'"

"Is there a signature?" asked Mrs. Percy, for Mr. Barnum had stopped.

"There is," he acknowledged. "It is signed, 'Dorcas.'"

Judging from the power of his grip as he again clutched my hand in his to complete the circle, this message had not pleased him.

"May I ask this Dorcas a question?" Mr. Barnum asked. His voice was icy.

"You may," said our crystal gazer, "but there is no assurance that she will answer."

"Does Dorcas apologize for another woman present? Will she come forward?"

There were several long moments of silence.

"It seems not, Mr. Barnum," said Mrs. Percy.

Mr. Barnum breathed heavily, as if his collar were suddenly too tight. I thought for a moment he would rise and leave. He did not.

Mrs. Percy's head lolled forward once again, and she made her strange groaning noises.

I felt a breath on my face, as if someone had passed close by in that encompassing darkness.

"My husband." She sighed. Her voice sounded girlish. "Is he here for me? William? Are you here, dearest? Mercy, mercy, save, forgive. Oh, who shall look on thee and live?"

Mr. Phips cleared his throat and spoke. "Is it you, Emily?" His voice trembled with emotion.

"William," Mrs. Percy whispered. "I forgive you, William. I know there was another before me, but I forgive that you did not wait. Go in peace, dearest husband. Peace." The voice trailed off.

Now there is safe prophecy, I thought. How many women could utter those same words? Hundreds, thousands, in Boston alone.

"Emily?" Mr. Phips called again. "Don't go yet, Emily; we must speak." But the candle quivered, we heard a sound like a door slamming, and a cold draft washed over us. I looked over at Mr. Phips and saw his eyes, wide and glistening.

"Someone else is among us," Mrs. Percy said, her voice deepened now. She sounded alarmed; her head bobbed up and down, from side to side, as if someone invisible had taken hold and were wrestling with her. "A restless spirit, unhappy, oh, so unhappy!" shrieked Mrs. Percy. "No, not a spirit, an ether soul, still in the body but wishing to give a message. A woman. No. A girl. A child bride. M. Why, child, do you keep saying M? Ah. Michaela? Mickey. Is that it?"

Two quick taps filled the room.

"Mickey, who do you wish to speak with?"

"Most ungrammatical," Sylvia whispered to me.

We received a stern glare from Mrs. Percy, who then repeated, "Mickey, for whom is your message?"

Silence.

"Are you still afraid, Mickey?"

Two quick taps.

"Have you a secret?"

Two quick taps.

"Oh, my," said Mrs. Deeds. "This is exciting. I've shivers on my arm."

Mrs. Percy's head lolled like a broken doll's; then she sat up quite straight. "You mustn't speak," she reprimanded. "The spirits like silence. If one keeps silent, then the spirits are not destructive. Mr. Deeds, have you a question?"

"No," said that meek man, "only considerable confusion. Are you saying that this unknown personage has a message for me?"

"She is unclear on this. But in my experience, when the soul's ether is so unwilling to make itself known, it desires only continued secrecy. There is a cost. Am I understood?"

"Not at all," protested Mr. Deeds.

"Very unpleasant," said Mr. Phips, who seemed frightened.

"Someone else is crossing the spirit border!" Mrs. Percy suddenly choked, and when she finished there was a creak, a whoosh, and a trumpet fell before us, dangling just above the center of the table. The polished metal glittered in the dim light and revolved slowly as if held by an invisible hand. We watched in amazement as it slowly disappeared again into the darkness of the ceiling. Mrs. Percy pulled a black cloth from an object in front of her and revealed a crystal ball, one small point of light reflecting on its surface from the flickering candle.

"I see a woman," she said, passing her hands over the ball. "Tall and white-haired. She wears a cape trimmed with ermine. She weeps. 'My daughter,' she sighs over and over. 'Why will she not wed?'"

"That would be Mother, I believe," whispered Sylvia. "I know the cape."

"Obviously Mrs. Percy does, too," I whispered back. "She probably met her at a milliner's shop or some such place, and listened to her complaints."

I spoke too loudly for Mrs. Percy's acute hearing; she looked up and glared at me. "Have you something to say, Miss Alcott?" she asked in an imperious voice.

"Nothing," I said, feigning contrition.

"Sylvia! Sylvia! Daughter!" Mrs. Percy called in a deep, husky voice, now flailing her arms and making as if she would stand. "Oh, it is a masculine spirit, coming through from Summerland!" she exclaimed.

"Father?" asked Sylvia, sitting up straighter.

Two quick taps.

"Ask him a question," spoke Mrs. Percy.

Sylvia tilted her head to one side in thought. "How might I please you, Father?" she asked.

The medium again reached for the tablet and the pen, and wrote something slowly, laboriously. She pushed the paper to Sylvia. The message was brief, a single word.

"Marry?" Sylvia said aloud.

Miss Amelia Snodgrass laughed. "My dear. You say the word as if it were poison."

Mrs. Percy grew very agitated, pounded the table, coughed and sneezed as do older gents who still have the habit of taking snuff—as had Sylvia's father in his later years, according to Sylvia's mother. She began to mutter, almost chant, in a deep, singsong voice: "Marry in haste, repent, repent, marry out of your station, woe, woe. But marry well, and prosper after. None will know."

"Marry?" repeated Sylvia, still dazed and unwilling to believe her ears. "I must admit this is the first time I know of when Mother and Father agreed upon something."

"Perhaps the wrong spirit came forward," I suggested, already fearing how this message would affect my suggestible companion.

"The tablet, quickly," said Mrs. Percy, her voice returning to normal. "I've the strangest voice in my head. I have never spoken with this spirit before. It is a message for you, Miss Alcott." The medium's head fell forward, and she began to mumble. "So lovely, so very lovely," she said several times, with great sighs between the utterances. "All peace and love. Happy. Very happy." Mrs. Percy laughed, then sighed again. Then she picked up the pen. She wrote slowly, her bracelets clinking all the while, and when she had finished, she pushed the tablet toward me.

"'Reminder,' no, 'remember me,'" I read aloud. "'Dottie.'"

Dottie, patient reader, was the name of a friend who had died the winter before, victim of a cruel murderer. I glowered at Mrs. Percy, and she was perceptive enough to discern my very great skepticism and disapproval.

"Quickly," she panted. "The tablet. There is another voice. Another message." She scribbled a message, changed her mind, crossed it out.

"She would not give a name," said Mrs. Percy. "When a spirit does not give a name, she prefers the message spoken rather than written. It is an in-the-body spirit, rather than one who has crossed over, and she is in much distress, and on her way. The voice kept saying, 'I am on my way.' Are you expecting a visitor, Miss Alcott?"

"I am not," I answered.

Again, the medium's head lolled forward, which gesture was followed by a stern, upright posture. Her voice, when she spoke this time, was puzzled.

"There is no one here for you," she said, looking in Amelia Snodgrass's direction. "Why have you come? You were not invited to this circle."

At that exact moment the already dim gas lamp on the wall went out completely. We sat in absolute darkness. There was a noise, as of a window or door creaking open. A current of cold winter air, the sound of breathing. We turned in the direction from whence came that otherworldly respiration and saw a figure, all in white from head to feet, as in a burial shroud, hovering against the west wall of the room. The figure moaned. It raised a ghostly hand and through its shroud pointed at Mrs. Deeds.

"The necklace!" it shrieked.

Mrs. Deeds clutched her throat.

There was a metallic crashing noise in the hall and we turned instinctively in that direction. When I turned to look again at the ghostly white figure, it had disappeared.

Mrs. Percy screamed. We stood and rushed to her, but her hands came up and pushed at the air before her face, as if brushing away wasps.

"It is over," she said with a final clatter of her heavy bracelets.

CHAPTER THREE

The Visitor Arrives

"WELL, NOW DO you believe?" asked Sylvia when we were outdoors again in the invigorating air. It was snowing heavily by then, and the spiraling white flakes were cheerful after the darkness of that parlor.

"My beliefs have not changed," I said. "And you, Mr. Barnum?"

"Have you a good memory?" asked the showman, pushing his top hat down over his thick hair. He seemed shaken.

"It serves me well," I said.

"Then let us meet next week and discuss this."

"An hour before our second séance, at MacIntyre's Inn on Boylston Street," I agreed.

"You are returning?" asked Sylvia with delight.

Mrs. Deeds came out of Mrs. Percy's front door just then. She looked pale, and her hand still clutched the pearl collar around her throat. She leaned heavily on her husband's arm and looked, as the saying goes, as if she had seen a ghost.

"Most astonishing, most astonishing," she repeated several times, fanning herself despite the cold of the early evening. "Who is this Mickey? Have you a past, Mr. Deeds?" she asked in an unpleasant voice.

"Never, my love!" he protested, quaking. Even as their carriage drove off, we could hear her voice, loud and demanding to know who his trollop was.

"Poor Mr. Deeds." Mr. Barnum sighed. "Thank heavens my own wife, Charity, has not a covetous nature." He heartily shook my hand and trudged off into the night.

Mr. Phips was the next to leave, having been detained, it seemed, by the considerable number of buttons on his overcoat.

"My sincere regard to your father, young woman," he said to me. "It was a pleasure to make your acquaintance, though I fear this séance was a disappointment."

"You had a message from your wife," Sylvia pointed out.

"I doubt it," he said. "Emily was never so brief in her statements. No, this has been a great disappointment. The past should be buried with the dead, not bandied about for a game." He seemed angry, and when he turned down the sidewalk he was muttering.

Miss Amelia Snodgrass was the last to come out of the house. She said not a word to us as she glided by in her brown hat and coat.

"Marriage," whispered Sylvia to herself as we began our walk home. "Father wishes it," she said to me.

"Don't you require a beau first?" I asked, teasing.

"Quite right, Louy."

Louisa and the Crystal Gazer

Boston, Dec. 2, 1856

Dearest Father,

I am well and happy and earnestly going about the business of earning my living. Independence suits me, though I miss my own beloved family, and count it a good day when the activities of the hours bring you foremost to my thoughts. Today was such a day. Sylvia and I (she sends her regards) attended a séance given by Mrs. Percy of Arlington Street. Fear not, kind parent, I have not succumbed to this new pastime but went as a protector of Sylvia, to see if I might mitigate the effects of this, her newest occupation— speaking with the dearly departed.

Mrs. Agatha Percy, our crystal gazer, has trained well for this calling, and I suspect she is not unfamiliar with the dramas between Sylvia and her mother in the Shattuck household, for her one-word message to Sylvia was this: Marry! And I am to have a surprise visitor.

None of this will be of interest, of course, to a man whose intelligence is of the highest, who knows "humbug" when he hears it. Humbug introduces my next little piece of information. I have met Mr. Phineas T. Barnum, who was at the séance, and he spoke so highly of you, our own philosopher! He asks if you will consider appearing at his American Museum. I did not encourage him in this expectation.

I am wearing the birthday pin you gave me, and send a heart full of love to its giver.

Good-bye, from your ever-loving child,

Louisa

I stitched at the reverend's shirts the next morning till my back ached and I longed for fresh air. I allowed my mind to wander over the events of the previous day, thinking of modest Miss Snodgrass, blustering but jovial Mr. Barnum, the loud Mrs. Deeds and her cringing husband, and the heroic Mr. Phips. What an assorted group Mrs. Percy had gathered!

A running stitch allows you to place six stitches at once on the needle, thus saving considerable time and speeding the work. My seams that morning were all running stitches, though they are not as fine as French stitches. I was impatient with the work and eager for life, for activity and event. I was bored, kind reader. Sewing is a fine activity, but not for me. And so I let my mind wander back to that character who had spoken to me yesterday, as soon as Sylvia gave me that interesting name, Agatha. She spoke again:

When the knowledge came to me that I was dear to a human heart, it was like a magic spell changing the cold, solitary girl into a fond and hopeful woman. Life grew bright and beautiful. The sad past seemed to vanish, lost in the blissful present.

So my new story was to be a love story!

I went for a walk that afternoon through Boston Common, admiring the frosting of snow decorating the ancient oaks, and laughing at the children skating upon the pond, as they tumbled and shrieked and worried their proud mothers with the speed and skill of their activity. It seemed as though this new character, Agatha, walked beside me, and I felt her sadness and her terror and her passion. She was not one to wait for the legitimacy of vows. When her Philip declared her

face was charming, her singing sweeter than any he had ever heard, she gave him all her love freely.

Oh, Agatha. Foolish woman! Do you not know that men often least desire that which is easiest won? Hers would be no simple love story, I decided. There would be a terrible crime.

That led me to think about the woman who had inspired my new character, Mrs. Agatha Percy. I admired her skills at playacting, for there was more of spy work in her pronouncements than tidings from the deceased. Certainly it had required only listening to gossip to determine what message would most make Sylvia alert. Her mother had been pleading with her for four years now to accept one of the many men who had promised their hearts. Sylvia disdained their offers, suspecting that her railroad shares were more of an attraction than herself. As for my surprise visitor, certainly that was a common pronouncement at such circles and no great risk to state. So much, I thought, for crystal gazers.

During my walk I passed the shop window of Mr. Crowell's Music Store, a favorite place of my sister Lizzie, and it reminded me that I had not yet selected a Christmas present for the musical member of the family.

The window was adorned with a gay green silk wreath and filled with sheets of music, metronomes in handsome mahogany casings, tuning forks, and the other paraphernalia enjoyed by Apollo's tuneful children. But what caught my eye was a handsome portfolio, bound in red leather, of new piano pieces by Liszt.

Liszt, gentle reader, was one of Lizzie's favorite composers. I entered the shop, the doorbell tingling merrily, and found Mr. Crowell at his counter, making a small arrangement of little boxes of violin strings.

"Ah! Miss Alcott!" he greeted me in friendly manner. "How is Miss Elizabeth?"

"Well, and in New Hampshire with Mother and Father," I said. "And Mrs. Crowell?"

"Well, and in the back room, making plans for a party." He sighed and grinned. "A party! In my shop! I never thought."

"For Christmas?"

"For Christmas, and for the lottery. I've an announcement, Miss Alcott, one you may want to pass on to our Elizabeth. I've purchased three lessons, an hour each, from Signor Massimo, and I'll hold a drawing to find a winner for those lessons. Isn't that a fine idea? He takes so few students, and it is such an honor to study with him!"

Signor Massimo? The very same artist who had not arrived at Mrs. Percy's séance?

"Has he been ill, our Signor Massimo?" I asked Mr. Crowell.

"Not at all. He's in fine health."

Then he is sensible as well as talented, I thought. He rejected Mrs. Percy's invitation. And wouldn't it be fine if I won those lessons for Lizzie? She could come to Boston for a week, and then return to Walpole.

"May I purchase a ticket for the drawing?" I asked Mr. Crowell, inspired.

He sighed and lifted his hands, palms up. "Tickets cannot be purchased," he explained. "There will be only twelve issued, one to each of the persons who buys one of the new Liszt portfolios."

That situation suited me even better. Should I not win the

lottery, I would still have that beautiful portfolio to give Lizzie.

"And the cost of the portfolio?"

"Five dollars." He saw the expression on my face upon hearing that amount and patted my shoulder, as if to give me courage. "I know that is very expensive, but it is bound in calfskin, with gold letters, and a very small quantity has been printed." He waggled his eyebrows.

Five dollars was three dollars and twenty cents more than I had. It was more than I had planned to spend on all the presents for my family that year. But I was already determined that Lizzie would have her portfolio, and if luck was with me, those three lessons from Signor Massimo. There could be no finer gift for her in all of Boston.

"May I put down fifty cents?" I asked.

Mr. Crowell sighed even more heavily, then spoke in a whisper so that his wife, who was more stinting than himself, would not hear. "You may, but with no guarantee. If it comes to the last portfolio and I have a customer, cash in hand, I must sell it. Your deposit would be returned, of course. It's the missus. Set her heart on a new wallpapering for the house, and it doesn't come cheap."

"I understand." I gave him two quarters and walked home light of heart, convinced that I could finish the reverend's shirts and purchase that portfolio for Lizzie in time. Wouldn't she be pleased! I missed her very much, perhaps even more so than my other sisters at that moment, for the approach of the Christmas season always awoke a passion for music in our home, with Lizzie singing or, when we had one, playing piano for hours every day. If I won the lottery, would Lizzie be willing to come down to Boston from Walpole? She was very happy there in her quiet country abode.

A surprise awaited me. When I arrived home at sunset, chilled but exhilarated from my long walk, Auntie Bond greeted me at the door, flustered and smiling. "You have a visitor," she said, pointing up the stairs. "A surprise visitor."

Upstairs, delicate steps rushed forward and my sister Lizzie's sweet face peered over the stairwell.

"Oh, Louy, I am so glad to see you!" Lizzie, as soon as I reached the top step, flung herself into my arms. She was still in her plaid travel costume, and her valise and hatbox were piled on the floor.

"Dear, whatever are you doing here? You are supposed to be in Walpole with Mother and Father! Is something wrong?"

"Yes," said my younger sister in a dark and dreary voice. "Cousin Eliza was planning a social afternoon for me. A party!" With her placid round face and gentle gaze she looked so angelic that her timidity seemed appropriate. What angel wishes attention?

Reader, if you are unfamiliar with my family, know that of my three sisters, Elizabeth, known as Lizzie, was the shyest. Even school had terrified her, so she had been educated exclusively at home. So it was that she murmured the words *a party!* with all the loathing other girls would have reserved for a trip to the toothpuller.

"And Marmee said we must go along with it and not give offense. Louy, dear, I have run away! Don't make that face, Louy. I left a note on the kitchen table and took the mail train. They know I am here with you. I may stay, mayn't I?"

"Of course. We'll have Auntie Bond bring up the camp bed. There is plenty of room. Oh, Lizzie." We hugged and danced a bit till I tripped on her valise and we both tumbled to the ground.

"Like when we were children," said Lizzie, leaning deeply into my embrace.

"Except then you had your lessons," I said. "What will you do here?" Oh, how tempted I was to give away my surprise for her!

"Auntie Bond has a piano still, doesn't she? I thought so."

"At your disposal, dear child, at your disposal!" called up that good woman, who had witnessed our reunion.

"I will practice, Louy." Lizzie grew dreamy eyed, thinking of new études and sonatas. And then a more practical look entered those pretty blue eyes. "And I will sew with you. My stitches are finer and faster, and I can take some of your work to leave you more time for writing."

We set about unpacking her travel case and chatted cozily, as sisters do, about Marmee's health, Father's expectations, the news from Anna, who was nursing in Syracuse, and of May, the youngest, also known sometimes as Abby, usually in those moments when she most resembled our mother, Abba. She, still at home with Mother and Father, was our artist in the family and was painting lovely watercolors of the gorges and ravines of Walpole, where we had all summered.

A different thought soon preoccupied me.

"Lizzie, did you tell anyone of your surprise visit to Boston?" I asked when the many folios of her sheet music had been brought from the bottom of the old cloth valise.

"No. Else how could it be a surprise? But wait." She frowned, making a tiny wrinkle between her pale winged brows. "I may have said something to Uncle Benjamin's housekeeper. I did. She packed me a lunch for the train."

Had Agatha Percy made a lucky guess? Or had she access to our very private household in Walpole? The thought made me uncomfortable.

I slept well and woke early. Quietly, without waking Lizzie, I sat at my little writing desk and opened the inkwell.

Boston, December 4

Dear Marmee,

Walpole's loss is my happy gain. Lizzie arrived safely last night, and both Auntie Bond and myself opened our arms to her. We are to share a room, and sweet Lizzie has offered to share my work as well. Auntie Bond's music room is open to her, and our angel shall practice scales and études to her heart's content. Do not fear for her; she is in a loving home and shall be well cared for. I admit, a sister's company helps ease my own ache for you and Father, and May, and Anna.

I am sure Father has shared my letter with you, and so you are informed of Sylvia's most recent enthusiasm, attending séances. I rather wish she had persevered longer with her Confucianist phase, but Sylvia is Sylvia. I do have a question, Marmee. Would you ask Uncle Benjamin's housekeeper to whom she might have mentioned Lizzie's secret plans for departure? There is no problem; I am merely curious.

Love to all of you there in Walpole. I am writing quietly, as our dear Lizzie still sleeps. Do you wish any supplies sent up from Boston? Good-bye, from your ever loving child,
Louisa

I placed a kiss on the paper, sealed it into an envelope for the post, and then lifted the volume of Dickens that served as paperweight to my barely begun story.

I was poor and plain, with no accomplishments or charms of mind or person, yet Philip loved me.

I had written before the séance. Now, having met Mrs. Percy, her imagined presence took firm hold in my mind. Her voice grew more assured as I imagined a story to fit the face and personality. Mrs. Percy, judging from her face powder and padded hair, knew the arts of adornment, yet even in the dim light I had seen the wrinkles about her eyes, the dry thinness of the skin on her hands. She spoke again, even as I dipped my pen into the ink.

Years of care and labor had banished all my girlish dreams. I never thought to be beloved, but tried to stifle my great yearning for affection. So when the knowledge came to me that I was dear to a human heart, it was like a . . .

I stopped and frowned, thinking.

. . . like a magic spell changing the cold, solitary girl into a fond and hopeful woman. Life grew bright and beautiful. The sad past seemed to vanish, lost in the blissful present.

"Are you writing a story, Louy?" Lizzie sat up in her little bed and rubbed the sleep from her eyes. Her lace sleep cap was askew.

"Yes, dearest," I said, putting down my pen and going to her. "It is still early. Why don't you sleep longer?" She looked pale. I put my hand to her forehead. It was warm. "Spend the entire day in bed," I suggested. "Travel has exhausted you." I tucked the covers around her and closed the curtains to dim the light. I would write downstairs, in Auntie Bond's dining room. So down I took my pen and inkwell and pages and carefully laid them over a mat of thick newspapers, to protect the fine polished table.

Martha, Auntie Bond's housemaid, came in. She was an efficient woman of some forty years, round in shape and cheerful in manner. Moreover, she had acquired this position through my mother, who a year before had helped find employment for some of Boston's unemployed women. "Up so early! I'll get you some coffee and porridge, Miss Louisa," she said with great enthusiasm, and before I could say, "No, thank you," she headed to her kitchen and returned a minute later with a tray for me.

"Eat up," said Martha, standing over me with hands on hips. I pushed my story aside and ate. Later I would ask Auntie Bond if I might clear a space in the attic for my worktable. Perhaps, reader, it sounded inconvenient, but the thought cheered me. I had my sweetest sister with me, friends about me, and a voice whispering that new story to me. Attics are fine places to work, and the days would pass quickly. I, who had joined the first séance with great reluctance, now eagerly anticipated the second, to satisfy my growing curiosity about Mrs. Agatha Percy.

Walpole, New Hampshire, December 6

Dear Louy,

Thank heavens, and I mean that with all sincerity, as you can imagine, that Lizzie arrived safely and is now under the sheltering wing of her older sister. Your cousin Eliza should have known better than to suggest a party for shy Lizzie without letting me first prepare her for such an announcement. Our sweet Lizzie, our angel! Make certain she dresses warmly, Louy.

I questioned Uncle Benjamin's housekeeper, and she says she told no one of Lizzie's plans to depart, that in fact she did not know of such plans, believing as she did that the travel hamper was to have been for a picnic. She did, however, mention the hamper of food to elderly Dr. Burroughs, who was shopping for fishing line at the same time that she was purchasing castor sugar at Tupper's General Store.

Have you a story I might see, or even some new journal entries you wish to pass on to your doting Marmee? I miss your imagination, my dearest. Walpole seems to have emptied of mystery since you left.

Speaking of leaving, you did not by any misadventure pack my soup strainer in your trunk, did you? It has gone missing, and you know how your father dislikes lumps in the cream soup.

Tell Lizzie she must write me every day. Sending you both all the love a mother's heart can hold.

> *Marmee*

Walpole, New Hampshire, December 6

Dear Daughter,

How fares the battle against Mr. Gripeman, a schoolmaster in Love-gain? I hope you have not forgotten our conversation, im-

mediately before your departure, wherein we further discussed Pilgrim's Progress and I used those metaphors to encourage you to see life, and your writing, as a spiritual experience rather than one in which you try to gain as much as possible of worldly wealth and fame. Remember how the Schoolmaster in Love-gain (which is a market town in the county of Coveting) taught the little souls in his care the arts of flattery, lying, and violence to attain their ends. Be not like them, but pure of heart and intention.

Mr. Barnum asked after me? A weaker man would be flattered, I suppose. I avoid the impulse to believe I am as well-known as he would suggest. Ask for more details about those appearances he mentioned, in particular my rate of reimbursement.

Your mother continues to bloom like a rose in the country air. Walpole has done her good, especially now that no more deceased bodies have made an appearance in our peaceful lives. She does try to smuggle chicken and even beef into our soups and then insists the lumps are unmashed potatoes.

Control your temper, eat lightly of vegetarian fare, and bless the Creator daily and nightly for the important gifts of this world: a family that loves you, your health, your mind.

This, from your loving father, is sent with a fond embrace.

P.S. Your mother says that Lizzie is in Boston? When did she leave? I had not noticed her absence, but then your mother is usually right in these matters.

Two days after Lizzie's arrival, when I knew she had settled in and was happily practicing an étude in Auntie Bond's piano room, I left the pile of shirtsleeves in my workbasket and my new story on my desk in the attic (Auntie Bond had

cleared out an old nanny's room for my use) and took an afternoon off to do some research on the art and performance of
crystal gazing. I visited the public library and the private
Atheneum. I stopped for a long chat with the woman who sold
greenhouse carnations at Constitution Wharf. I visited with
a Mrs. McGillicuddy who had been born in County Cork
and now ran a day home for children whose mothers worked
in the mills. When I returned home, many hours later, I wrote
up my notes and thought and thought.

Seven days after the first séance with Mrs. Percy, Sylvia
and Lizzie and I were at MacIntyre's Inn on Boylston Street,
enjoying warm glasses of eggnog—without brandy, of
course—and waiting for our plates of haddock to arrive. Mr.
Phineas T. Barnum was with us, having sent a note earlier in
the day reiterating his invitation to an early dinner before our
second séance.

Lizzie was impressed by MacIntyre's white tablecloths, ornate gas lamps, and black-uniformed waiters, and she ate with
her elbows tucked closely at her side, rarely even looking up.

"More raisin bread?" Sylvia asked Lizzie, passing the
plate to her.

"It is fine," said Lizzie, timidly taking a second piece.
"More like cake."

"My daughter, Caroline, also prefers cake to bread," said
Mr. Barnum. "We shall order a fine layer cake for dessert,
with a cream frosting," he boomed. "You remind me of her,
Miss Lizzie. Quiet, but quick-witted."

"You miss your family," I said. "It must be difficult, traveling as much as you do."

"It is, but Charity is a fine mother and helpmate, when her

health is good. A father must provide for his children, and my business requires that I wander the world seeking its marvels." He buttered a piece of bread and ate it in three bites, as do men who are often in a great hurry.

"Is that why you wandered into Mrs. Percy's parlor, seeking marvels?" I asked.

He looked in much better spirits than when we first met in Mrs. Percy's waiting room, where he had seemed to me somehow devastated, despite his shiny brassiness of behavior. In fact, this afternoon he looked robust and overly splendid, dressed in a bright suit with an even brighter tie, with many diamond rings glittering on his fingers, and checked spats over his shoes. He looked, well, like what he was: a showman who adored attention and intended to get it. He had been snapping at waiters and winking at the coat-check girl since his arrival, and he spoke in a large voice, as if trying to fill an auditorium. He had even gone to the trouble to arrive late and make an entrance. Father would not have approved of this; nor did I.

He did not answer my question and instead distracted us by asking Lizzie if she preferred lemon or strawberry ice, as his other daughter, Pauline, favored lemon. Our fish arrived, and for the next hour we ate well while Mr. Barnum, between generous mouthfuls, entertained us with highly amusing tales of his travels through Europe with General Tom Thumb, describing how Queen Victoria had set the diminutive man on her knees next to her lapdogs, and how King Louis Philippe of France let Tom Thumb, in his miniature carriage, lead a royal procession down the Champs-Élysées. Mr. Barnum was a fine storyteller. He and Father had qualities in common after all, the strength of their voices and their insistence on being heard among them.

When the plates were cleared and Lizzie was finishing her second piece of cake, Mr. Barnum cleared his throat and gave me a long look.

"Well, Miss Louisa, you seem an extraordinary young person of quick intelligence. What did you make of Mrs. Percy's séance?"

I put down my teacup and returned his long look.

"I think the trumpet was a clever touch, though easily seen through. It appeared, and then disappeared again, through a hinged panel in the ceiling," I said.

"No!" protested Sylvia. "Really, Louy, you think you are so clever. Even if there was a hinged panel, someone must be upstairs to pull the lever or whatever, and Mrs. Percy never left the room."

"Of course," I said. "That is one of Suzie's chores, I assume."

Sylvia's mouth opened into a perfectly round O of surprise.

"And the phantom I recognized, despite the white powder and gauze," Mr. Barnum said. "It was Fannie Adelon, a dancer from the Old State Theatre. She can do a bit of juggling as well. She must be down on her luck, participating in such a charade."

"No!" Sylvia protested again, her eyes wide.

"Sylvia, you didn't believe any of that silliness, did you?" I asked, giving her a chance to redeem her credulity.

"It could not have been all silliness," she said gloomily. "I had a message from Father."

"The handwriting of my message," Mr. Barnum said. "Now that was a neat trick."

"You know a Dorcas, then?" I asked.

He paused. "I do. She was childhood nurse to a relative of mine. The relative has proven a great disappointment, and Dorcas, before she died last year, sent me several letters asking for my patience and forgiveness, on his behalf. The handwriting on the slate board was very like." His voice sounded strained. "Women are softhearted, but business is business." That aside was something I would consider often, after later events.

"He knew a Dorcas, and that was Dorcas's handwriting. Does that prove nothing, Louy?" Sylvia asked determinedly.

"Of course it does," I said. "Mrs. Percy is talented. Sylvia, you are wearing a bracelet now, are you not?"

"You see that I am," she answered.

"On your left wrist. Because you are right-handed. Women always wear heavy jewelry on the less active hand. Mrs. Percy wore her bracelets on her left hand, and she wrote with her left hand."

"Meaning?"

"Forgers sometimes train themselves to use the less active hand to disguise their own true handwriting. I have that on expert authority." The flower woman at Constitution Wharf had been jailed for just that crime in her youth. Moreover, I had taught myself to write with both hands, so that I could write for longer hours without wearying, and remarked how one hand differed from the other in quality of script.

"Mrs. Percy forged Dorcas's handwriting?" Sylvia put down her fork of cream cake and brooded.

"She is a forger," Mr. Barnum agreed, "among other things."

"How did she know about Lizzie's arrival?" Sylvia demanded somewhat crossly.

Mrs. McGillicuddy of Cork had informed me about that method. "She simply asked questions," I said. "I suspect she learned of Lizzie's departure from Dr. Burroughs in Walpole. A simple telegraph to a conspirator in the area would have provided such information, and a woman of Mrs. Percy's national reputation would have assistants in many places, I suspect. Even so, Sylvia, who does not expect, or at least hope for, a surprise visitor on any given day? Do you yourself await one?"

Sylvia blushed. Had she been eyeing the bachelors of Boston, casting about for a presentable young man who would enable her to fulfill her dead father's request?

"That would mean that . . ."

"You don't have to marry. Not right now. Not unless you seek merely to please Mrs. Percy, who invented that message probably after making inquiries about your mother."

"I was on the verge of inviting Jimmy Baldwin for dinner with *Maman*, and you know how he slurps his soup and then drinks too much brandy. But if all that happened in Mrs. Percy's parlor was . . ." Sylvia paused, searching for a word.

"Humbug," supplied Mr. Barnum.

"Humbug," said Sylvia, "then why are we returning this afternoon?"

Writers, dear readers, are often faced with questions of this nature. And there is only one answer: Because it might help my story. But those who do not aspire to live by the pen often do not understand that simple reply, so I substitute another: "Curiosity," I said.

"This is all very interesting, and I am disappointed with Uncle's housekeeper, who seems to spread family news all over New England. But where is my promised third piece of cake?" spoke up Lizzie.

CHAPTER FOUR

A Body Is Discovered

"YOU'LL NEVER CONVINCE me it was all a sham," insisted Sylvia when we arrived back at Arlington Street. "I have been dreaming of Father, and had conversations with him since the séance. Mrs. Percy has opened a door for me."

"Then knock harder, so that this one may be opened," I said when our initial rapping had gone ignored for several minutes.

"My experiences in life have convinced me that real merit does not always succeed as well as 'humbug,'" said Mr. Barnum, taking the door knocker in his gloved hand and giving it a hard bang. "The public loves to be fooled, and the more you fool them the more they love it."

Suzie Dear opened the door to us once again. This time she was dressed all in green, like a woodland fairy. The girl seemed to enjoy playing at dress-up. Perhaps her mistress encouraged it, to add further "atmosphere" to the séances.

"You're early," Suzie complained. "I ain't dusted off the sitting room yet. Don't you dare complain if you sneeze!"

Susie was agitated and breathless. Perhaps we had caught her napping and she had run down the stairs. Her exotic headgear, a lace mantilla rather than a maid's cap, was askew over her curls, and a gaudy necklace was lopsided over her shoulder, as if she had risen hastily from a semireclining posture.

Reluctantly Suzie led us down the dark hall, her feet in their high-heeled boots leaving wet imprints on the parquet floor. Now why, I thought, are her boots wet, if she has been napping?

In the waiting room, which seemed as dusty as she had promised, she turned and glared at Lizzie. "Who are you, miss?" she rudely demanded.

"Miss Alcott's sister," said Lizzie in a trembling voice.

"Don't have no notice to set a chair for you in the circle," Suzie said crossly. "Did you send a card asking to be invited?"

"She did not." I spoke up. "Since Mrs. Percy herself predicted my sister's arrival last week, I did not think she would object to Lizzie's attendance." I was feeling very uncomfortable. Things were not as they should be, and that was saying a lot, since things are never as they should be in a crystal gazer's sitting room.

"Not allowed," Suzie insisted. "No invitation, she can't join the circle. She'll have to wait here." The maid crossed her arms over her chest and glared.

Mr. Barnum and I exchanged glances. Mrs. Percy could not "prepare" for unexpected participants by garnering the gossip—the newspaper announcements of births, deaths, and betrothals, the private household information purchased from upstairs maids and laundresses—that was the lifeblood of her business. So, Lizzie would be excluded.

"I don't mind," said my sister. "Really, I don't, Louisa. There are some finger exercises I want to practice, and I do feel a little queasy after all that cake. I will wait here."

"Haruumph," said Mr. Barnum, his silvery side-whiskers twitching.

Another thought occurred to me. At our first séance, Mrs. Percy had given a similar glare to Amelia Snodgrass and demanded, "There is no one here for you. Why have you come?" Had Miss Snodgrass also arrived uninvited? And if so, why had Suzie allowed her into the séance room?

"Even so," I protested, "please ask your Mrs. Percy if she might let my sister sit with us." I made my voice imperious, imitating Marmee's tone when she had to deal with factory owners who fired a girl for getting in the family way, or a cook who beat the scullery help, for Marmee knew how and when such a tone is useful.

Suzie's glare faltered and she murmured, "Yes, miss."

She returned just moments later, so quickly, in fact, that I wondered if she had really spoken to Mrs. Percy at all, or just pretended to. "Mrs. Percy said no," she grumbled. "Told you she would." Suzie had grown pale as well as rude, and she trembled.

Lizzie would be content, but I felt as queasy as if I had also eaten three pieces of cake, thinking of timid Lizzie alone for an hour in this very strange house.

Some minutes after we arrived, Mr. Phips was shown into the sitting room.

"Aha, Miss Louisa," he greeted me warmly. "We return for more messages from the dear departed. Most amusing, most amusing." He handed his hat and coat to Suzie, who bobbed a curtsy and left us again, after giving me a long glare.

"Nasty weather," said Mr. Phips, striding to the fire that Suzie had reluctantly lit for us in the grate and chafing his hands.

"You should have seen the snow blow over the Scottish moors, sir," said Mr. Barnum in his booming voice. "When I traveled there with Tom Thumb it snowed to beat the band. Almost buried us, the general's carriage being no more than three feet high. I dug him out myself. He was so cold he had rolled up into a snowball."

I understood by then that Mr. Barnum was as much an admirer of fiction as myself, and often "extended" his stories with hyperbole and even a little fantasy.

"I remember newspaper accounts of your travels in Europe," said Mr. Phips, carefully smoothing a crease in his lapel. "Wasn't it Scotland that taxed you four thousand dollars for income even though you didn't live there?"

"They got five hundred, the robbers," Mr. Barnum said. He seemed disinclined to tell more stories after that and paced nervously.

A few minutes later, Mr. and Mrs. Deeds arrived. She was as overdressed as on the first occasion, with diamonds on her ears and wrists and ermine draped over her shoulders. Her husband seemed even meeker, constantly clearing his throat and giving his expansive wife glances that suggested he sought her opinion even before taking a deep breath.

"Mrs. Percy keeps us waiting once again?" asked Mrs. Deeds in her shrill voice.

"She does," answered Mr. Phips. "Promptness does not seem to be one of her virtues." He did not look at us but slowly removed his gloves and put them in his waistcoat pocket.

"Well," said Mrs. Deeds, after Suzie Dear had once again taken away coats and hats. Mrs. Deeds enthroned herself in the only remaining armchair, leaving an uncomfortable-looking ladder-back chair for Mr. Deeds. She arranged her voluminous velvet skirts and retied the lace bow at her throat. She was not wearing the heavy pearl collar she had worn the week before, the one at which Mrs. Percy had pointed and shrieked, "The necklace!" rather like a character from a Poe story . . . or one of my own "blood and thunders." Women shriek often in "blood and thunders." It is a sign of the genre.

"Mrs. Deeds," I greeted her. "Looking so well in that green velvet costume. I had hoped to have another glimpse of that lovely pearl necklace."

Mrs. Deeds compressed her mouth into a very thin line, then forced a gay smile. "It has been returned, for the time being," she said.

From his shadowy corner, Mr. Deeds coughed. "A fortune. A king's ransom, that's what Mrs. Percy was asking. Mrs. Deeds wore it on loan, and it was returned," he spoke up in his thin, high-pitched voice.

The necklace was owned by Mrs. Percy? How had she acquired such an expensive piece?

"We'll discuss it later, dear," his wife said darkly, and then returned to her gay tone. "Miss Snodgrass is not here? Who is this newest member of our circle?" She looked with great interest at Lizzie.

"I am not of the circle." Lizzie spoke up. "I accompany my sister, Miss Alcott, only this far, to the waiting room."

"It is unfair not to include you more fully," said shy Mr. Deeds.

Lizzie studied her boots and did not answer.

"Well," said Mrs. Deeds again, "I do not suppose any of you here attended the Cotton Cotillion last evening?" Indeed, I had not. The cotton factors had too pronounced a sympathy for slavery for me to have attended such an event. But Mrs. Deeds obviously had no such moral dilemma, and proceeded to recount the prior evening—the foods on the buffet table, the flowers, the dances, the clothing, the speeches—in great and misery-causing detail for those of us who would have preferred to sit and wait in silence.

Sylvia took a little book from her pocket and pretended to read. I could not help but notice the title: *Reminiscences of the Summerland: My Journeys Among the Dear Departed*, by Mrs. Agatha Percy. So our crystal gazer was an author, as well? I could not help but think a little more highly of her, though I wished she had been truthful enough to admit to writing romances rather than memoirs.

Half an hour passed. Suzie Dear stuck her head in to inquire whether we needed anything. She plucked nervously at her skirt and gulped. I wouldn't have thought it, but the brassy young woman seemed nervous and even fearful. I thought, at the time, that this change in behavior had been caused by a sharp reprimand from her mistress.

Mrs. Deeds asked for hot tea and sandwiches, but Suzie Dear never brought them. When Mrs. Deeds asked a second time, Suzie answered, "The cook is gone."

"Is she, now?" asked Mr. Phips with interest. "Gone where?"

"Wouldn't know, sir," said Suzie. "Somewhere else, I suppose."

I rose and walked down the dark hall and found the half flight of stairs leading into the kitchen, Suzie dogging my heels in angry protest. "Can't go in there, miss!" she said, trying to block the kitchen door with her own body.

Gently I pushed her aside and entered the kitchen. The cook had indeed gone, in the way that a fair day can be said to be gone when a storm arrives. Drawers had been pulled out and emptied on the floor; the large worktable was littered with chopped carrots, beef bones, and dirty butcher knives; a cold pot sat on a fire that had gone out. The cook had left without finishing the stew. The door that opened into the little room where the cook slept was ajar. It was a breach of privacy, I admit, but I peered inside. The bed had been rested upon, but not slept in. The pegs on the wall were bereft of garments, the drawers bare. There was not a single item to indicate a person had once inhabited this room.

"She were a nervous person," explained Suzie. "I heard her quarreling with Mrs. Percy the day before."

That seemed only half an explanation. Judging from the gleaming pots suspended from the ceiling, the sparkling cleanliness of the windows, and the scrubbed whiteness of the plank floor, the cook had been a tidy woman, proud of her work, yet she had left the kitchen in this state. Why? My uneasiness grew.

"Well, there'll be no tea in the front parlor today," I agreed with Suzie. I returned to the others, certain that other strange events were to follow.

Another half hour passed in desultory fashion. It was growing dark outside, as dark as it can grow on a late-winter afternoon when snow falls in great white sheets. Mrs. Deeds rose from her comfortable chair and began to pace in front of a window that overlooked the street.

"Isn't that Miss Snodgrass?" she exclaimed with some surprise, pausing and drawing the curtain farther back.

It was. Even from my chair she was quite visible over Mrs. Deeds's shoulder, her height, her slenderness, that strange brown costume and extremely old-fashioned bonnet she had worn the week before identifying her. I thought she would come up the sidewalk and ring the bell, but she passed by the house. She kept walking, never once looking over her shoulder. She seemed in a hurry.

How strange. From whence had she appeared?

Fifteen more minutes passed.

"Unacceptable," said Mr. Barnum, rising. He reached for the bell rope next to the hearth. Suzie returned five minutes later, her hair disarranged. She was breathing with difficulty, as if she had been running.

"Tell your mistress we await her," said Mr. Barnum in a clipped, impatient tone of voice.

"Yes, sir," said Suzie, bobbing another curtsy. But she stayed in the doorway.

"Well?" roared Mr. Barnum.

"She ain't feeling well, I suspect is why she's delayed," Suzie said. "Perhaps you all should just go home. She'll send your money back to you, I'm sure."

"How not well?" I asked, standing.

"She didn't eat no dinner. Least, she didn't put the tray back in the hall for me to take away," Suzie said. "It were a good dinner, too, mashy potatoes and beef."

"I will go see her," I said.

"Can't," said Suzie Dear, gulping. "Her door is locked. Bolted, as well."

"Is there a window?" asked Mr. Barnum.

"Yes, but never used and painted shut for all I know," said Suzie.

"Oh! Oh! I sense an evil presence!" shrieked Mrs. Deeds. She swooned to the floor in a heap of purple velvet and black lace.

"Suzie, fetch water and smelling salts," I instructed, much put out with Mrs. Deeds. Swooning is such a dreadful distraction, and I felt a tremendous urgency to see what was inside Mrs. Percy's preparation room. After Mrs. Deeds had been revived and propped up against the red-striped paper of the hall wall, where she fanned herself vigorously and moaned repeatedly, Mr. Barnum, Mr. Phips, and I had a whispered conversation on how to proceed.

Even as we talked, I took note of where everyone was at that moment: Mrs. Deeds sitting on the floor, her husband next to her, Lizzie standing at the end of the hall, watching us, Sylvia standing next to Lizzie, her arm about her. And

Amelia Snodgrass, missing. The hall was dark, illumined only by dim gas lamps turned low, and our shadows played eerily against the red wallpaper.

"Which room is it?" asked Mr. Phips of Suzie, who leaned against a wall, her hand playing nervously with a little ribbon tied around her throat.

"Last down the hall, sir," she said, "the far corner room."

"I will go outside and climb in through the window," said Mr. Phips. "If it does not open, I will break the glass." He held up his hand and explained that the glove was thickly padded. "It will take but a moment."

"Call us as soon as you are inside," I said. "Unshoot the bolt of the door."

Mr. Phips went out the front door and all was quiet for a long while, except for the heavy, snorting breathing of Mrs. Deeds. There was a trellis on the west side, I remembered, where that far corner room and its window would be. Perhaps Mr. Phips had to pull away rose canes. Mrs. Deeds, still fanning herself with great energy despite the swooning fit, tried to rise to her feet but could not. Perhaps, I thought with little sympathy, it was the weight of all those jewels and heavy chains.

Eventually we heard glass shatter and heavy footsteps. The bolt shot back and Mr. Phips opened the door and we beheld Mrs. Percy's red-wallpapered sitting room. It was stuffed with vases of peacock feathers and stands of ferns.

Mr. Phips stood ashen-faced and trembling next to the shattered glass panes of the French door, for in his nervousness he had broken several to find the one opposite the lock.

Behind a bamboo-and-velvet screen we found Mrs. Percy,

prostrate on her chaise longue, her right arm hanging limply over the side so that her hand grazed the patterned carpet. One pillow was bunched up under her head; a second, which proclaimed in bright embroidered letters SCENIC NIAGARA FALLS, had fallen to the floor. Her face was turned away from us, and there was a sickly sweet odor in the room.

"Opium!" exclaimed Mr. Barnum in outrage. For all his showmanship and eccentricity he was, underneath it all, quite a conservative person.

"Opium, indeed," said Mr. Phips. "It smells like one of the Canton dens in here. Evil habit."

I walked to the other side of the chaise longue, so that I might see Mrs. Percy's face. The use of opium was said to cause strange dreams, and I wished to see if those exotic fantasies played on her features.

It was a face I would not soon forget. Her eyes were open, staring at the ceiling, and never had I seen eyes so bloodshot. They were painful to behold. There was a strange set to her thin mouth, as if she wished to speak. But no hint of breath made her chest rise or fall; no sigh or mumble stirred her lips. What she saw was not the plaster molds of roses and painted vines overhead, but a vision of eternity. Mrs. Percy was dead. It is so shocking, mortal reader, to expect an amusing hour with a personage and instead to discover them dead on a chaise longue, the smell of opium heavy in the air—

"Damn, damn, damn!" exclaimed Suzie Dear. I hoped, for the eternal life of Mrs. Percy, that her maid wasn't correct.

"Louy, what is it?" called Lizzie from where she still stood next to Sylvia, in the hall.

"Stay there," I called back. "Do not come in here."

Of course, I had forgotten what it is like to be a younger sister always receiving commands from an elder. Lizzie was in the room before I finished my sentence.

"Oh! What a strange odor!" Then she saw Mrs. Percy. Her long-fingered, artistic hands shot to her face in horror. I feared that she, like Mrs. Deeds, might swoon, but no, Marmee steeled her daughters better, and Lizzie regained her composure. Instead, Sylvia swooned.

"Suzie, more water and smelling salts," I said somewhat impatiently. But Suzie Dear had disappeared.

"Miss Dear!" I shouted, running into the hall. The maid was nowhere to be seen, and the front door, which had just been opened, fell shut with a groan.

CHAPTER FIVE

The Heart Proves Staunch

I DO NOT mean this harshly, understanding reader, but I experienced a kind of exasperation with poor Mrs. Percy, that she had not found the means to resist death. She had become an interesting character study, and now here she was, dead, and only just recently.

"Another one," said young Constable Cobban, bending over to check the wrist of the prone Mrs. Percy for a pulse, which we all knew he would not find. "Corpses tend to accumulate in your immediate vicinity, Miss Alcott."

Constable Cobban of the new Boston Watch and Police, whom we had notified immediately after Suzie Dear's departure, was, as you may have suspected from that above comment, no stranger to me. We had met the winter before, during the investigation of another untimely death.

"People will die," spoke up Sylvia in my defense.

Constable Cobban grinned. He was a young man with orangish red hair, freckles, and a deplorable taste in suits, which tended to be store-made from bolts of large plaid or bold-striped stuff. He tweaked the pillow under Mrs. Percy's head as if trying to awaken her, but she remained unmoving, growing colder each moment. Next he examined an empty bottle of gin, the glass fallen on the floor under her hand.

"What's this?" he said, his voice deepening with curiosity. He had turned to face a little table next to the chaise longue upon which a box of lucifers rested, and next to them a small pot of dark paste.

"Opium," he confirmed, his mouth puckering from the bitterness of the taste, as he had stuck the tip of his little finger into that intriguing pot.

"That seems to complete the explanation of how she came to be dead in a locked room, doesn't it?" I said. "She used the drug too freely."

"Exactly," said Cobban, smiling at me once again. "Opium can be a tricky business, especially if a weak heart is involved. Someday I imagine they will declare its use illegal and protect the citizenry."

"Weak heart?" I asked.

"Look at her lips, her fingernails, the black shadows under her eyes. Our mutual friend, Dr. Roder, would say that not even the changes caused by death would erase the signs of a weak heart in life."

"You have continued a relationship with Dr. Roder?" I asked, interested. The doctor had helped us last winter, when my friend Dot was murdered.

Cobban blushed as only a red-haired man can, turning almost purple with sudden embarrassment. "I visit his dissecting theater and lectures, yes."

"Have you decided to train as a physician?" This young man never ceased to surprise me.

"No. At least, not yet. But I think a knowledge of the body would assist my work in the Boston Watch and Police." He walked once more around the chaise where lay the body of Mrs. Percy, touching this, peering at that.

"It seems a straightforward enough situation," he said after several more minutes. "But where is the pipe? I wonder."

"Pipe?" asked Mr. Phips.

"Mrs. Percy's opium pipe. I don't see it," said Constable Cobban.

"It must be here somewhere," said Mr. Phips. "Shall I look for it?"

"No. I'll have one of my men examine the room. For now, shall we go back to the waiting room, and the others? A few more questions and we can all go home."

Seated once again in Mrs. Percy's waiting room, I watched silently as Mr. Barnum tended to the fire and Lizzie served tea. Mrs. Deeds's teeth were chattering from horror as well as the cold, Mr. Phips had descended into a stony silence, and Mr. Barnum poked at the fire too energetically, sending bursts of sparks into the room and all over Mrs. Percy's new carpet. The door to Mrs. Percy's preparation room had been shut once again.

"Tell me one more time, please, why you were all here waiting?" Cobban demanded, wetting his pencil on his tongue and preparing to write in a little notebook. He was enjoying this; indeed, when I had first admitted I was there to attend a séance, his red eyebrows had shot all the way up his forehead to his hairline. Miss Alcott, sensible, frugal, daughter-of-a-philosopher Miss Alcott. Attending séances!

"You already know," I said patiently.

"Sé-ance," repeated Cobban, writing slowly. His grin widened.

"Obviously you have had no experience with the spiritual world or you would not be quite so lighthearted," muttered Sylvia.

"I know spirits as well as the next fellow. Judging from the smell in there, Mrs. Percy was no stranger to spirits either—at least not the kind that can be poured," said Cobban.

"Oh!" Sylvia stamped her foot. Constable Cobban gave her a long, cool glance and then returned to his notes.

"Young man, I've business to attend to," protested Mr. Phips, rising. "We've told you everything there is to tell."

"Please return to your chair," Cobban said in the same tone of voice with which I have instructed schoolchildren to sit and open their books.

Mr. Phips sat back down.

We had gone over the events of the afternoon several times, each time discovering some minutes later that Cobban wished us to tell them one more time. And each time another detail had been recalled. Cobban, despite that foolish grin and mocking manner, was a young man of fine intelligence and cunning.

"You say that when Miss Amelia Snodgrass walked by, she was wearing the exact same costume as she had worn the week before?" Cobban addressed this question to Mrs. Deeds, who had watched from the window.

"Exact." She sniffed. Mr. Deeds, sitting next to her on the settee, patted her arm.

"Now, the ladies present must inform me, for I am out of my depth here. But do the fair sex like to repeat their wardrobes so exactly?" He addressed this question to Sylvia.

"Usually not, if they can afford variety," said my friend, frowning. "She did seem to wear it more as a kind of livery or uniform, I thought."

Mr. Barnum poked the fire again. "Too much costume," he said. "That's what I think."

"Too much costume?" repeated Cobban, turning his attention to the showman.

"Yes. Mrs. Percy, for instance. Dressed up like a Gypsy, with veils and sequins and heavy bracelets. Totally unnecessary. If you're going to humbug a crowd you don't announce it with a flashy costume. Blend in; that's the key. And that vanished maid of hers, Suzie Dear. Dressed like an opera dancer. Sets the wrong tone for a sober enterprise."

Cobban was writing furiously, his plaid sleeves a throbbing red in the gaslight.

Mr. Phips cleared his throat. "I did notice something else, I just now recalled," he said. "The maid was wearing heavy bracelets, and I would swear they were the same ones her mistress wore last week."

"Theft," said Cobban, frowning. "Theft, and then she skedaddled. I'll have her picked up. Shouldn't be too difficult to find a newly homeless and unemployed working girl down in the stews near the harbor. That's where she'll head."

"How do you know Mrs. Percy didn't give her the bracelets?" I asked. Suzie Dear seemed a young woman in need of guidance, but Mrs. Percy no longer needed the jewelry, and I

disliked the thought of a young woman going to prison for such a frivolous crime. The bracelets were most likely brass, not gold.

"We'll ask a few·questions and find out," Cobban said. "That's it, ladies and gentlemen. Leave me your cards, please, in case there are other questions. And now, go back to your homes and find more sensible pastimes." This last remark did not endear him to Mr. Phips, whose mouth, under his gray mustachios, grew thin with dislike. Dressed now in our heavy coats, we filed out one by one through the front door, back into the winter night. I gave him one of Auntie Bond's calling cards with my name written in under hers.

"Did Walpole suit you?" the constable asked me in a voice low and private, taking the card. "I, for one, am pleased you have returned to Boston. You, as well, Miss Shattuck." He gave Sylvia a little nod of the head, turned on his heel, and strode off down the sidewalk.

Lizzie put her arm through mine and sighed.

"Louy, what a terrible afternoon!" she said.

"It started out with such promise." Mr. Barnum stood beside us, swinging his walking cane to and fro, as if batting at snowflakes. "Ah, well. She has gone to meet her Maker. Let us hope she returns to Him with a clear conscience, though her parlor tricks argue against that event."

"Any sin was as much ours as hers, for we paid for the entertainment and so encouraged it," I said.

"I do feel a fool," said Sylvia. "How will I ever communicate with Father now? Patiently, through prayer and reflection," she whispered.

"What did you say, Sylvia?" I asked.

"Why, I'm not certain! Something about reflection. Do you think the words I just said might have been guidance from poor Mrs. Percy?"

"Sylvia, you need to rest," I told her.

And so my friend returned to her mansion and her mother, probably for another long evening of conversations about marriage and who was betrothed to whom, which heirs were still "on the market." Lizzie and I returned to Auntie Bond's, where my sister practiced her études on the parlor piano and I took a candle up to my attic writing room. Mrs. Percy's face floated before me, pale and round as a moon, with that strange grimace upon it, as if she had just received bad news. This vision entangled itself into my story, now named "Agatha's Confession," and the story became the tale of a woman, once loved, not yet suspecting she has been cast aside in favor of another—her own friend Clara. Character must be accounted for within the plot, and Agatha Percy's character suggested to me a great betrayal. Women happy in their destiny do not turn to crystal gazing. And so I heard her say to me,

I had one friend (or thought I had, may God forgive her the sin and misery she caused me) who possessed all that I lacked: youth, beauty, wealth, and those fresh charms that make a woman lovely in the eyes of men. I had not known her long, but loved and trusted her entirely, grateful that she turned from her gayer friends to sympathize with me. Philip admired her; and I was glad to see it, for thinking his heart all my own, I neither feared nor envied Clara's beauty.

Horror. A knowledge of premature death by another's hand. That was what I had seen in Mrs. Percy's painted face.

The next morning, at breakfast, I had a letter from Father waiting beside my porridge bowl.

Walpole, New Hampshire, December 8

Dear Daughter,

Make no more inquiries about Mr. Phineas Barnum. Your uncle Benjamin says he is on the verge of bankruptcy and no man of business will have dealings with him just now. For the custom of speaking without pay, I've no trouble finding engagements and seek no others just now, being busily occupied with other matters. I have exhausted my supply of writing paper for my diaries; if you might send me more from Mr. Dee's shop. Your mother is well, and is knitting a new shawl for Lizzie for Christmas. We will send it to your rooms, with our love. Remember to control your temper and to read often from Pilgrim's Progress. *Know that I embrace you fondly and am your loving guide.*

Yrs. truly

Father

I put down my teacup and tapped my fingers on the table. Bankrupt? How could that be? Mr. Barnum had made a fortune with his Jenny Lind tour and he had made almost as much money again last year from the sales of his autobiography. I myself had purchased a copy of the book, so good was the promotion, managed by Mr. Barnum himself. The book itself had been . . . well, let's say that it did not aim for high literary quality and it achieved that aim. Bankrupt? I put down the letter and sipped my tea.

"More oatmeal, Miss Louisa?" asked Auntie Bond's maid, Martha.

"I'll have more, please," said Lizzie, who sat opposite me reading her own mail from Mother and Father. Undoubtedly Father had reported to her what I was to receive for Christmas, and now Lizzie and I would have even more secrets from each other. I hummed, thinking about that red leather portfolio in Mr. Crowell's window, and also wished Father had thought to mention the color of Lizzie's new shawl. I could have trimmed a new hat to match from Auntie Bond's scrap bag. But men do not generally think of such things as colors of shawls, and whether that red will clash with that violet.

"Good to see a young woman with appetite," said Martha, scooping a second helping into Lizzie's bowl. "The cold weather is good for digestion, I always say."

"It is not too cold," said Lizzie, looking at me. "Shall we skate today, Louy, and have a holiday? There's ice on Boston Pond."

The thought of a holiday was tempting. I could be out in the air with sweet Lizzie, racing over Boston Pond and enjoying a fine winter day, or sitting indoors and stitching the reverend's shirts by dim candlelight. The choice was obvious; I also hoped a day in the fresh air would help Lizzie recover from yesterday's shock. It is not often, fortunately, that a young girl is turned away from a séance circle only to discover the medium has died of a weak heart that very afternoon.

"Give me two hours," I said. "Then meet me at the pond." While Lizzie finished her second helping of oatmeal, I dressed quickly, brushed my hair to a sheen, and then twisted it into a snood, put on hat and coat, and was out the door.

Boston Public Library, in those days, was still in the old school building on Mason Street, its collections shelved between rows of schoolrooms, so that to approach the periodical reading room I had to tiptoe past a rhetoric class, where young boys loudly and badly disclaimed memorized poetry. Mrs. Simmons was at the desk that day, cotton sticking out of both ears to dim the noise, and she frowned when she saw me, for my requests were often complicated.

"May I have back issues of the New York papers?" I asked her.

"Which ones?"

"All of them, please, for the past month."

Mrs. Simmons heaved a sigh, studied me over her spectacles, then disappeared down a long, dark aisle.

An hour of reading revealed nothing; the showman was known for his manipulation of the presses in his favor, and I began to fear that whatever gossip Uncle Benjamin had about Mr. Barnum's finances was no more than that: gossip.

But then, just minutes before I was to leave to meet Lizzie, I opened the November 28 issue of the *New York Tribune* and found a notice in the legal section. One Edward T. Nichols of Danbury, Connecticut, was being sued by Phineas T. Barnum for failure to pay a $4,000 debt. Furthermore, the notice continued, Mr. Barnum had severed all relationship with Mr. Nichols and would not honor debts or agreements made by that man.

I whistled. I couldn't help myself. Four thousand dollars.

That much would have kept the Alcott family afloat for several years and longer. Mrs. Simmons looked up from her ledger and gave me a stony glance.

So Uncle Benjamin had known of this, somehow. Perhaps he had come into Boston to speak with bankers or some such thing and spent a night at one of his gentlemen's clubs. Oh, how I envied those cigar-smoking, comfortably shod old gentlemen with their private wood-paneled studies and taprooms, where they could sit and talk and exchange news without being interrupted by Nurse Ann from the nursery, or Betty the cook, or the wife and children. How could women ever advance themselves without such institutions?

I swallowed more than a little resentment—we women did, after all, have the *Lily,* our own newspaper and journal, at least, and one so advanced that it advocated the vote for women!—and took writing paper from my reticule.

Boston, December 9

Dear Uncle Benjamin,

A loving hug to you and Cousin Eliza! I miss our walks together and think of you with ever so much fondness, though I am enjoying as well as I might my time here in Boston. Uncle, Father says you know a little something about Mr. Barnum's financial situation.

I paused and chewed the end of the pen. Uncle was exceedingly old-fashioned and did not like to discuss pecuniary matters with females. I must tread carefully.

I have formed a kind of friendship with that personage and humbly ask your advice. Are there subjects of conversation I should avoid to prevent injury of his feelings?

My letter finished, I refolded the newspaper to return it to Mrs. Simmons, who was very specific about the way her papers were to be folded, when on impulse I reopened the paper to the society page. My impulse proved fruitful: There was a notice about Mr. and Mrs. Deeds. She had given a dance the night before, on November 27, and the columnist described in great detail the hothouse roses, the platters of oysters and trays of cream cakes, the six-piece orchestra, the extravagant gowns of the women. "Mrs. Deeds wore a pearl-and-diamond collar recently added to her famed collection of jewels," the reporter had continued. It had to be the same necklace she had worn at the séance, a week later; yet Mr. Deeds had said the price had not been agreed upon, and the necklace was still "on loan." Since she had already boasted, a week before, of owning the necklace, it must have been a great blow to Mrs. Deeds's pride when the purchase was foiled. I thoughtfully refolded the paper.

The letter to Uncle Benjamin was posted on my way to Boston Common, and a little voice nagged inside my head all the way as I walked. Why did I wish such information about Mr. Barnum? The séances were over and I would probably never again see Mr. Barnum; nor had I known him long enough or well enough to form a true bond of caring with him. Yet, I felt I would be holding my breath till I heard from Uncle Benjamin.

This happens in writing a story, as well. You discover a

thread and for no reason other than that it amuses you, you begin to unravel it. And unravel and unravel, till at last, tied at the end of the thread, is the secret you have been working toward without even knowing it was there.

At the Common, the ice was new and slick, the sun poked between clouds, and Lizzie and I raced in circles on the pond, playing tag like children, showing off our spins and backward figure eights till we dropped with exhaustion on one of the benches.

"Oh, I haven't had so much fun since . . . since . . ." But Lizzie couldn't remember the last time we had laughed so long and so hard.

"Your sister should have fun more often; it suits her," a man's voice called to us. "Hot chocolate?" I turned and saw Constable Cobban carefully making his way over the ice toward us, balancing three cups just purchased from a vendor's cart. I knew from the look on his face that the thread I had pulled had a secret at the end.

"Hot chocolate! Perfect!" exclaimed Lizzie, reaching for a cup.

"Lizzie, you remember Constable Cobban of the Boston Watch and Police," I said, somehow not surprised to see him. He nodded, handed a cup of hot chocolate to me as well, and sat beside me on the bench. A girl in a bright red skating outfit glided by and Cobban watched, sipping his chocolate.

"You are not here to skate," I said.

"No. I've come looking for you. Miss Bond said I might find you here."

"It is about Mrs. Percy," I said.

"It is. Her stepbrother came to see me last night. Very angry,

he was." Cobban drank his hot chocolate in one gulp and balanced the white cup on his huge red palm. "Seems a significant quantity of jewelry and money is missing from Mrs. Percy's rooms," he said. "It's not just a matter of bracelets, Miss Louisa. And there's more. He says his sister was in excellent health, no heart trouble at all; her physician will vouch for it. The opium did not kill her. She was not strangled, for there are no marks on her neck. But she probably was suffocated while she slept. Asphyxiation caused the appearance of a weakened heart."

"Oh, dear," I said.

"No, oh, Suzie Dear," he said with an inappropriate attempt at humor. "She must be found and tried for murder."

He rose and returned our emptied cups to the vendor, then gave me a sad glance. His breath steamed in the cold air, and the tip of his nose had turned red and shiny.

"I told you only because you will undoubtedly read all this in the evening paper. I suppose it would be a waste of time if I asked you to forget this occurrence and not entangle yourself," he said. A flash of winter sun caught in his coppery hair, giving him a slightly metallic, ornery appearance.

"Mr. Cobban, I was in the next room to this 'occurrence.' I am already entangled," I said.

"As I thought." He sighed, then grinned. "Good day, ladies. I am sorry if I have injected a somber note. It was pleasant to watch you enjoying yourselves." He walked away, a serious tall, thin man in bright red plaid making his way through the throng of merry skaters. Never before had I noticed the lonely quality of his slightly stooped shoulders.

"Just one thing, Constable," I called after him. "What is the name of Mrs. Percy's stepbrother?"

He answered over his shoulder. "Mr. Nichols," he said. "Edward Nichols."

The name was familiar. I had read about it in connection with Mr. Barnum's difficulties. Mr. Nichols was the man who had cheated him out of his fortune.

CHAPTER SIX

The Locked Room

THE NEXT MORNING, upon awakening, I raised my right hand to the dim light of dawn and inspected my bruised knuckles. Yesterday, after Cobban had left, Lizzie and I had taken one more turn around the rink, and I had fallen. Too bad, I thought, I won't be able to stitch the reverend's shirts today. How will I pass the time?

I already knew, of course. Lizzie was happily ensconced in Auntie Bond's parlor, practicing a thumping march, when I again put on hat and coat, feeling more than a qualm of guilt. How would I purchase Lizzie's Christmas present if I did not finish the reverend's shirts on time? A woman should complete her household duties and maintain order in her little kingdom before pursuing other activities, and when time allows she should study literature, philosophy, and languages. Crime scenes and dead bodies were not a part of this useful system. But, kind reader, I ask your indulgence. If you love a story, where better to find one than where a crime has been committed?

The winter air was mild and the streets more congested. The costumes of the ladies grew much richer as I approached Arlington Street. One woman, attired in scarlet velvet, wore black kid boots buttoned with silver and a large brooch of pearls and peacock feathers. I ached for them the way, as a child, I ached for cake. Someday, I thought, I will earn real money and the Alcott girls will dress in fine things, not hand-me-downs. Our youngest sister especially, May, was particularly pretty and graceful and loved beautiful things, yet was wearing Cousin Eliza's patched country castoffs. Someday, I promised May in my heart as I walked down the street eyeing other women's fashions, I will buy you a dress that will make your heart soar with pleasure. And a necklace, as well, though one of garnets and silver, not pearls and diamonds.

I was not as determined to bring Suzie Dear to justice as was Constable Cobban, understanding full well that girlish desire for new, shiny adornments. If money and expensive jewelry had been stolen, who was to say that another had not taken them? Perhaps even Mrs. Percy's own brother, who even better than a maid might know where such things were hidden, and then in pretended outrage claim them stolen. Perhaps insurance was involved as well.

When I arrived at Mrs. Percy's house, a man stood watch at the door.

"No one is allowed inside, miss," he said stiffly, staring straight ahead. Judging from his posture, he had studied illustrations of the queen's guard at Windsor Castle.

"Is Constable Cobban here?" I asked.

He frowned, not knowing if a good sentry would answer the question. Politeness won out. He was, the man admitted.

"Then tell him Miss Alcott asks a word, if you please."

"But I can't leave the doorway!" The man groaned, now in an agony of indecision.

"Then I will just step inside and tell him myself," I said.

"Very good, miss. He's in the downstairs hall, with the other lady."

Other lady? To my surprise, when I reached the end of the hall, Sylvia was there with Cobban, kneeling on the floor in the dim light and twisting this way and that the knob of the door to Mrs. Percy's sitting room, where she had died.

"Louy!" Sylvia exclaimed with surprise, jumping to her feet. Cobban looked up. Both blushed.

"Good morning, Constable Cobban, Sylvia," I said. "You are up bright and early."

"I could not sleep," Sylvia said, turning even pinker. "I heard Father's voice last night."

"You dreamed it," I suggested.

"No. I did hear his voice, and I was awake," Sylvia insisted. "Even if Mrs. Percy used tricks of some sort I still believe a doorway has been opened. He wanted to tell me about Mrs. Percy. Oh, Louy, she was murdered! Father is quite upset about it. This morning I woke up and a book had fallen open on my night table, and the first words on the page were, 'Believe in this!'"

Sylvia had a habit of reading romances in bed; a familiarity with her favorite authors and titles would easily convince me that any number of books could have fallen to a page with that kind of message, and made an even stronger believer of her.

"And does your father have any idea how this crime was achieved?" I sighed, now in my turn kneeling beside Cobban and trying the door handle. Sometimes, in very old houses, the bolt and lock are so used as to have grown thin and sleek and will unlock themselves if the handle is jiggled enough. But Mrs. Percy had renovated her home; the locks were new.

"Doesn't do it," said Cobban, reading my thoughts. "I've jiggled it till my hand's gone numb, trying to get it open. It holds."

"You see, Louy," persisted Sylvia, "this is what most distresses Father. He thinks another spirit did it, someone still angry with Mrs. Percy but living in the otherworld. How else could she have been killed behind locked doors and windows?" My friend was breathless with excitement.

"Calm yourself," said Constable Cobban, putting a hand on her shoulder.

"I know how it could be done," said another voice from behind us. Mr. Phineas Barnum appeared from the dark at the other end of the hall and came toward us. For a crystal gazer no longer in business, Mrs. Percy seemed to have an inordinate amount of activity in her hall.

"Good morning," said the showman, tipping his hat and leaning his walking cane against the brown flocked wallpaper of the hall.

"And to you, sir," said Cobban coldly.

I offered my hand and we shook, and all the while I studied Mr. Barnum more carefully. But this is a truth of finance: To be bankrupt when you are close to poverty is quite different from becoming bankrupt when you already own a fine home or two, a wardrobe of suits, and several carriages, horse teams, and business ventures. If Mr. Barnum was in financial straits, it did not show in his clothing or in his expression.

The old gentleman's eyes were clear and sparkling. In fact, he seemed in extraordinarily fine spirits. Even, I might have said, relieved of some burden.

"You know how this might be done?" Cobban asked, looking up from the handle.

Mr. Barnum clasped his hands over his chest and rocked back and forth on his heels, just as small boys do when accepting a challenge to turn a cartwheel or steal an apple. "I do," he said. "Magicians have shown me time and again. I need a piece of wire. Now, put the key in the lock on the other side. Of course, you must go on the other side, and bolt yourself in."

"I will assist," offered Sylvia, seeing that Cobban wished to stay on the hall side of the door and watch the experiment.

With a backward glance and a smile that was as much directed to Cobban as to me, Sylvia went through the door and closed it. We heard the key turn in the lock, and the bolt shoot home.

"Ready," she called, her voice muffled by the thickness of the door. "What am I to do now?"

"Leave the key in the lock," Mr. Barnum shouted back. "Now," he said gleefully. From his coat pocket he took an envelope he had ready for posting. It was of good-quality writing paper and quite thick. This he placed on the floor, directly under the lock, so that half the envelope was in the hall and the other half on the other side of the door.

"Now, I need a strong piece of wire," he said. "Ah. Just happen to have this . . ." From his watch pocket he withdrew a coil of gleaming wire. He unwound it, bent it twice to thicken it, and put it into the lock, bouncing it up and down

and sideways for several minutes. We heard a little thud from the other side of the door; Mr. Barnum carefully slid out the envelope from under the door.

"Just so," he said, holding up the key.

"Any schoolboy knows how to do that," said Cobban. "What about the bolt?"

"Part two," said Mr. Barnum, frowning over Cobban's comment about schoolboys. "We must assume that the killer performed part of this trick in advance, and for that purpose I will ask your friend's assistance." He twisted the wire again so that there was a loop at one end of it. "Miss Sylvia, put the loop over the head of the bolt," he called, pushing the wire under the door to her side.

"Done," came Sylvia's voice a moment later. She sounded very far away.

"This is how the bolt was locked from the outside," said Barnum. "The killer hooked the loop around the bolt before leaving the room. He shut the door and locked it. Then, he carefully pulled the wire he had already placed around the bolt, and the bolt slid into place, in effect locking the room from the outside." Mr. Barnum began tugging on the piece of wire. "He carefully . . ." He tugged a little harder. The wire came through the door, unlooped, and the bolt was still open rather than closed.

"He would have brought thicker wire," Mr. Barnum said crossly.

Cobban snorted.

"Try again with the wire, Mr. Barnum," I suggested.

He tried again, a second, third, and fourth time, and each time the bolt stayed stubbornly in place and the wire slipped out again with the loop pulled straight.

"Well, it works in theory," he finally said.

"In theory, the Earth might be flat," Cobban said.

I do not know why men must always outdo one another with an act or a comment. Even noble Father and kind Mr. Emerson, during a discussion of self-reliance or the Oversoul, will get that gleam in their eyes and it will be understood that a challenge has been issued and accepted, and they will argue back and forth till one of them simply runs out of breath.

"May I come back out?" Sylvia asked in a small voice. "I think someone is in here with me."

"Quickly!" I said, frightened for my friend, for if Mrs. Percy's death had been a planned murder, as Mr. Barnum's theory suggested, then this house might still contain secret dangers. "Undo the bolt, Sylvia!"

There was a rattling and a squeak; the door swung open and a very pale, trembling Sylvia rejoined us in the hall. "I think I heard something in there," she whispered, her eyes large as saucers.

Cobban's nightstick was already swinging from his hand. "A person?" he asked. "Did you see him? Where? Behind the curtains?"

"No, actually it was more of a voice," said Sylvia, fanning herself. "Mrs. Percy's voice, I think. She said, 'Peace! I require peace!' At least, I think that's what she was saying. Of course, it could have been 'lease' or 'please.' What do you think it was, Louy?"

An overactive imagination, I thought. "You must have overheard a conversation from the street," I said. Outdoors, the air was thin and light with that transparency that comes at the beginning of a storm, when sound travels well. Undaunted by Sylvia's trembling, I strode into the room and pulled back the curtains, revealing the broken windows.

There, staring back in at me, was a face so pale, so ghastly, that when Sylvia screamed I was half tempted to scream along with her.

"I do beg your pardon," said Miss Amelia Snodgrass.

Constable Cobban crossed the room in three strides and stood next to me, staring out the window. "You would be Miss Snodgrass," he said, recognizing her from the description we had given of her brown coat and hat.

"And you are?" She tilted her head.

"Constable Cobban. Will you come in, Miss Snodgrass? The front door is still open, I believe."

"I cannot. I am in a hurry, you see." She turned, but Cobban reached through the broken glass and grasped her arm.

She gave him a livid look of disdain, but he would not relinquish his hold on her.

"I insist," he said. "Mr. Barnum and Miss Alcott will come round and help you up the stairs. They are icy." For a young man his voice could be quite authoritative. We three did exactly as he said, and a minute later Miss Snodgrass stood with us inside Mrs. Percy's red-papered sitting room. The ferns were wilting from the cold and a lack of water, but the air still smelled sweet and sickly heavy, despite the broken windows.

"I was merely walking past. What right have you to detain me?" Miss Snodgrass exclaimed, lifting her chin high and throwing her shoulders back. Her hair was even lighter in color than Sylvia's, and I couldn't help but think that here before me was the ideal of femininity Father had so often described, blond and of medium rather than tallish stature, with small, fine features. A very handsome woman, indeed, yet dressed like a drudge. "I often walk this way. It is a public street," she said.

"You were standing in the garden outside the room where she was killed," Cobban corrected.

"Killed?" she asked in a shaking voice.

"So it seems," Cobban said. "Moreover, items are missing from her rooms."

"Items?" Miss Snodgrass's hand went to her throat.

"Jewelry. Money."

"You have gone through her rooms?" Miss Snodgrass was now so pale, her voice so weak, that I sighed and rose, knowing I should begin looking for smelling salts. There must be a vial somewhere in the bureau. But Sylvia was one step ahead of me. "Here, Louy," she said, taking salts from her own reticule.

"It distresses you that we have searched Mrs. Percy's personal items?" Cobban asked, though the answer was already plainly visible on Miss Snodgrass's ashen face.

"Did you find . . . letters?" she asked. And then she swooned.

The next half hour was spent fetching glasses of water and a compress from the pantry, no easy chore, since the maid, Suzie Dear, was still missing and Mrs. Percy's housekeeping arrangements had been haphazard at best. The glasses were in a drawer, not a cupboard, and the compress lint was in a basket, not a drawer. Marmee would have set this pantry to rights in a couple of hours, and as she worked I knew what her discussion would be: how a pantry and a kitchen often indicated a woman's state of mind, and the mistress of this pantry was in a very bad state of mind, indeed.

Very bad, Marmee, I told her in my thoughts. She's been robbed and murdered.

"What were you doing in the garden?" Cobban asked Miss Snodgrass as I returned with the glass of water. I could tell from his voice that he had asked this question several times and was growing impatient.

"I . . . I . . . I," Miss Snodgrass stuttered, and did not answer. At least she is not an accomplished liar, I thought. If she does answer, we can accept it as truth.

"I . . . I was hoping to encounter someone. A chance encounter." She blushed, her white face now turning crimson.

Now I understood—both this and her earlier reference to letters. She had been looking for someone who seemed to be avoiding her, someone to whom she had written letters, probably of an indiscreet content, and thought both the letters and the person might be discovered here.

I wondered if Mrs. Percy's stepbrother, Mr. Nichols, was a particularly handsome young man. Mr. Barnum, sitting in a deep armchair in what appeared to be a rapt state of attention, cleared his throat and tapped his fingers disapprovingly on the carved armrest.

Constable Cobban seemed to understand as well. "Go home, Miss Snodgrass." He sighed. "I may have more questions later for you."

"You are certain that Mrs. Percy was murdered?" I asked when the door had shut behind the brown costume of Miss Snodgrass.

"Yes. Her stepbrother's testimony about her health is not

to be denied," said Cobban. "She was of a strong constitution, and her use of the drug was not so abundant as to endanger her health." Cobban sat on the edge of the crystal gazer's settee and studied the carpet. It was a new carpet, a new settee, in an expensive, newly appointed home.

Crystal gazing must offer a good living, I thought. Was that why Mr. Barnum had taken an interest in the subject? Perhaps he had come here looking for a new attraction for the American Museum, only to be very disappointed by that dismal first performance of which even a beginning amateur such as myself could find the methods of the "apparitions" and other parlor tricks. He must have been very disappointed, indeed.

"There's more than the stepbrother's testimony." Cobban looked up.

"The thefts," I said.

"More even than that. Have you seen a dead person—that is, a person who died peacefully more or less in their sleep?"

I had. Making visits with Marmee last winter, I had come across the body of old Mrs. Witherington, asleep in her bed, dead at the age of eighty-three. Surprisingly, at her great age there had been no evidence of disease or damage other than her dowager's hump and her swollen joints. Her face had been peaceful, exactly as the old adage goes; she looked as if she were merely asleep.

Mrs. Percy's face had not been at all peaceful. The mouth had been contorted, the eyes wide with shock or horror.

"Well, I'm down to the harbor to find our Suzie," Cobban said. He stood and put on his wide-brimmed hat, though he was still indoors and etiquette required that he remain bareheaded till he stood directly in front of the door by which he would leave. One of the qualities I admired about the young constable was his almost total disregard of etiquette.

"May we come with you?" I asked.

"Miss Louisa!" Mr. Barnum protested, his spiky black eyebrows moving up and down with disapproval. "The docks are no place for a lady!" For a man who had stitched together the top half of a stuffed monkey and the bottom of a fish and called it a mermaid, he could be, I thought, very obstructionist.

"If you find Suzie, I think it would be well to have a woman with you," I said to Cobban. "She looks the hysterical kind, I think. And I don't understand why Suzie, if she had murdered her employer, let us sit in that waiting room for so long instead of just telling us to go home. Wouldn't she have tried to remove us if she knew her employer was dead?"

"She wasn't thinking clearly," insisted Cobban.

"I'll come, too," spoke up Sylvia. She gave the young constable another sideways glance.

For the third time we quit Mrs. Percy's waiting room.

"I'd like to see the cook's room again," I said.

"Female curiosity?" asked Cobban, with a knowing smile.

"Perhaps something more," I said, but did not specify. I wondered how Mrs. Percy had treated her cook, and the room itself would tell me much of that relationship.

We found the bedroom just off the kitchen, a large corner room with several curtained windows, a rug on the wood floor, and a tile stove with a large bucket of coal next to it. It was a fine room, comfortable and convenient. From it, I would have guessed that relations between cook and employer were amiable. Appearances, however, can be deceiving.

"Satisfied?" asked Cobban, revealing a masculine indifference to what lace curtains and a thick carpet can say about the management of a household.

"Yes." I said. We returned to the front hall and went back out that front door, leaving behind the dim and dreary aspect of a house too expensively furnished and too poorly lighted, leaving behind the nuances of emptiness behind all those heavily closed doors. It was a very, very big house for a woman and a single servant and a brother who visited occasionally, and a sense of Mrs. Percy's isolation and loneliness pierced me like an arrow: to die alone like that, behind a locked door, and perhaps violently.

We went into the bright afternoon winter, the white-and-silver streets and the bustle of humanity on those streets, and as we passed through Mrs. Percy's white wicket gate I had a strong sense of leaving behind the true Slough of Despond, of which Mr. Bunyan wrote: . . . *for still as the sinner is awakened about his lost condition, there ariseth in his soul many fears and doubts, and discouraging apprehensions, which all of them get together, and settle in this place. And this is the reason of the badness of this ground.*

Thank you, Father, I thought, for reminding me to read *Pilgrim's Progress.* Where else could I have found such an apt description of the confused souls who seek their dead and lost ones in hired parlors, and of the woman who lived so well off those fears and doubts?

At the corner, Mr. Barnum tipped his top hat and went off in the opposite direction. "I will write to your father, if I may," he promised jovially. "I still await Mr. Alcott's response."

Cobban's silence was so pointed that Sylvia felt compelled to explain. "He has offered to hire Mr. Alcott for speaking engagements," she said.

"Father will not agree, of course," I added.

But young Constable Cobban's mouth went very tight as he repressed a smile, obviously enjoying the same bizarre vision that I'd had of Father onstage seated between a magician and a contortionist.

Cobban and Sylvia locked eyes and then looked furtively away from each other.

"One other thing," Cobban said. "We still haven't found the pipe she used. Searched all over that room. Seems strange, don't it?"

"Many things about this affair seem strange," I said. We three walked in companionable silence then, concentrating on keeping our footing on the slick sidewalks and thinking our own thoughts.

The docks were busy that afternoon. There was some ice in the harbor, and the commercial vessels had weighed anchor farther out, so that an entire fleet of smaller boats rowed back and forth, loading and unloading. The sailors and dockworkers rushed to and fro, and the women who gathered in places where the laborers sought amusement had themselves gathered in taprooms and coffee shops for gossip and talk of the town.

I did not like to think of Suzie Dear in such a place as the Sailors' Arms. She was young. She still had choices ahead of her that could lead to a happier and healthier life.

"She lay low yesterday," Cobban said. "But she'll be hungry by now, and feeling less worried about it all. She'll be out and about and probably wearing some of Mrs. Percy's jewelry on herself, if I've got this right."

He had it right. We found Suzie in the fourth taproom, sitting at a little table, surrounded by other women at various ages and stages of their lives. Two looked as young and pretty as Suzie, with smooth faces, thick hair, and slender arms. Three were middle-aged and already thickened and wrinkled; a sixth woman was in her fifties, white-haired, slack-jawed, dressed in little more than rags. They could have served as a Currier illustration of the downfall of woman.

Suzie Dear giggled when she looked up and saw us. "Some tea, ladies and gentlemen?" she asked, and then almost fell off her chair, so hard did she laugh. Her hair had come undone and fell over her eyes and shoulders in riotous black curls. Her companions fell into similar bundles of mirth. There were several empty gin bottles on the crumb-strewn table.

"None today, thank you," I said, though I knew she was laughing at me and all those she deemed respectable, predictable, fussy, and boring. It did hurt my feelings a little, but I remembered the times that I and my sisters had secretly laughed at some very pompous matron or a tut-tutting gentleman.

"Miss Dear," I said gently, "could we speak in private for a moment?"

Constable Cobban had no such niceties in mind. "Stand up," he ordered. "Put your coat on."

Suzie fell into another fit of the giggles and did not stop laughing until Cobban pulled her from her chair. Standing now, she struggled into a much-worn woolen coat with a ragged fur collar, her heavy gold and silver bracelets clattering and clinking. I recognized those bracelets. Mrs. Percy had worn them.

The collar of Suzie's coat rolled under, and Cobban reached up to straighten it.

"Here, now!" shrieked one of Suzie's companions, and the others began to shout and push in protest. For a moment I feared there might be a riot, but the publican, seeing what was up, shouted, "Drinks on the house!" and Suzie's friends fled her to seize their free glasses at the bar.

"Am I under arrest, then?" asked Suzie Dear in a small voice. She sucked her bottom lip.

"You are," Cobban said.

CHAPTER SEVEN

The Thieving Maid Speaks

"SHE GAVE ME the bracelets," Suzie insisted. "They was gifts." She lifted her hands before her face and rattled the gold and silver bangles on her wrists.

Suzie had sobered up fairly quickly once she was placed behind bars in the Boston jailhouse. This was a gloomy place of which I had more than a passing acquaintance, but I won't go into those details now, patient reader. Suffice to say that I already knew that in Suzie's cell the walls were unadorned except of graffiti, the floors bare except for stains I chose not to speculate about, and that the only window was so high up on the wall that even on tiptoe Suzie would not obtain a view of the streets below. Moreover, even that very high window was barred, so wherever light entered the room—from the gas lamp in the hall, or the sunset outside the window—it entered in thin, guilty strips. A more doleful place I'd yet to find, except for the city morgue, several floors beneath our feet. Mrs.

Percy, downstairs, would probably happily change places with Suzie, if she had a choice. She didn't.

"Not according to Mrs. Percy's brother, Mr. Nichols, they weren't gifts," Cobban said. He sat next to me in a straight-backed chair, looking in at Suzie through the bars.

"Mr. Nichols? Pggh." Suzie screwed up her mouth and spit onto the floor. "That's what I thinks of him."

"You should use the cuspidor," said Sylvia, pointing to a bucket in the corner. Suzie ignored her.

"The feeling is probably mutual, since you murdered his sister and absconded with her cash and jewels," Cobban said.

"I didn't murder no one, and didn't ab . . . absco . . . make off with the goods. Not I. I learned my lesson last year."

When Constable Cobban had half pulled, half pushed Suzie Dear into the building, another constable, sitting at a desk and reading the afternoon newspaper, had looked up and winked at her.

"Suzie, is that you? I thought they rode you out of town on a rail. How have you been?" he asked jovially.

"Go bugger yourself," the girl had told him.

"Get her for soliciting?" the man had asked Cobban.

"No. Theft and murder." Cobban was standing awkwardly, bent at strange angles in various places since Suzie, in her wooden-heeled boots, was trying to stomp on his feet.

"Whew!" The other man let out a long whistle. "You're in for it, Suzie."

"They was gifts!" she insisted a few minutes later, staring forlornly at us from behind the bars.

"You are bleeding," I said to Cobban, gingerly touching

the long scratch Suzie had left on his face. "Perhaps you should go look to it." He made a noise very much like a horse snorting with exhaustion at the finish line, and stood.

"I'll go with you," offered Sylvia. "Men are useless at that kind of thing."

When Suzie and I were alone, I gave her a look I had learned from Marmee, and Suzie cowered.

"Tell me the truth," I said sternly. "I will help you only if you tell the truth."

"I am," she whined.

"They will search your room," I said. "Will they find more money and jewelry?"

"A little, yes, ma'am." The whine had grown higher and shriller, and I could see she was ready to begin bawling. She coughed and sneezed and choked and wiped her nose with her ragged dress sleeve.

"Pay attention," I said, "and tell me this. Did you kill Mrs. Percy?"

"No! I never!"

"Then who do you think did? For murdered she was."

"I'd speak with that brother of hers, Mr. Nichols." Suzie gave me a long glance and hiccuped.

"You appear very guilty, Miss Dear."

"I didn't steal all of it. Some of it really was gifts, Miss Alcott, really. Gifts." Suzie Dear pouted, looking like a child accused of stealing cookies, not gold bracelets.

"You mean bribes. To help with the séances," I said.

" 'Twere my job," she protested. "And a hard one, it was! I had to learn by heart ever so many signals and such, and then run up and down the stairs, back and forth, knocking on the floor here, switching off gas lamps there. I did what Mrs. Percy told me to do. I didn't do nothing wrong."

Cobban and Sylvia returned, a plaster sticking to his forehead and another one to his hand, where Suzie's grimy nails had left other marks. Sylvia looked very pleased with herself.

"Let's leave Suzie to think about the situation," Cobban said, extending a hand to help me from the chair. His choice of moments to practice gentlemanly behavior always left me a little confused. He was a most unpredictable young man. But he was also an officer of the law and I had no official status, so I rose from my chair.

"Do I get my supper?" Suzie called after us when we turned down the dark corridor. Our heels clicked against the bare floor, and somewhere in that cold and sinister building, in yet another locked room, a man yelled and pounded his fists against the wall.

"Theft, yes," I commented when we had reached the stairwell. In addition to being unpredictable, Constable Cobban jumped too quickly to conclusions. "But coveting baubles does not indicate a violent nature. If so, far too many maids and manservants would be on trial for murder, and in fact it is a rarity."

"I'll vouch for that," said Sylvia, who as an extraordinarily wealthy heiress had known her share of domestic disturbances and searches in the maids' rooms.

"Moreover," I continued, "I believe that at least some of the jewelry was given to her freely, by Mrs. Percy."

"Some, but not all. Is that your opinion?" Cobban asked. He spoke slowly and thoughtfully. We had descended the staircase and he had me by the elbow, as men do when they are herding women, and he was herding me toward the front door of the building.

"Did you not think yet of this, Miss Alcott? Suzie wore the stolen jewelry the same day, when you and the others arrived for the séance. She did not fear being seen in it. That would indicate she knew her mistress was already dead. And how would she have known that if she had not been herself involved in the murder?"

An excellent point. But there had to be a second answer. My woman's instinct said that Suzie was a silly, greedy child of questionable morality but not a murderer.

"Where does this stepbrother, Mr. Nichols, reside?" I asked.

"Go back to your home and leave this matter to me," Cobban said, hooking his thumbs in his suspenders with an air of male authority.

"His address will be in tonight's paper, in Mrs. Percy's obituary," I said with, I admit it, a hint of impatience in my voice. "Are you coming, Sylvia?"

"Of course, Louy." But she gave Cobban such a long glance over her shoulder that my heart sank. She waved good-bye to him with her fingertips, as little girls do.

"Sylvia," I said gently, hooking my arm through hers, "you have been giving Constable Cobban strange looks. Can you explain why?"

"Is he not a pleasing young man?" said my friend. "His eyes are particularly fine, I think."

"Your mother would not find him so pleasing," I pointed out. "He has neither fortune nor family."

"You know, Louy, I think Father would find him very agreeable. The son he never had, hardworking and intelligent. Ambitious. Father was not born with a fortune, you know. Nor did Mother have one when they married; she was rather in Amelia Snodgrass's position, with lots of family history and connections but holes in her boots, if you see what I mean. No, Father earned his wealth. And Cobban will, too, I think." Sylvia grew dreamy eyed.

Outdoors, in the fresh air again, I inhaled deeply, trying to clear my lungs of the foul airs that accumulate in large public buildings where people are housed in less than sanitary conditions. It was midafternoon, and my stomach was hollow with hunger. I wondered how Lizzie had amused herself after returning home from skating.

"Sylvia," I said, "you need a new diversion to occupy your thoughts. Would you like to study music with Lizzie? Or read the new volume of Dickens? The Boston Ladies' Lyceum is offering a series of lectures on phrenology that might interest you."

"But I have a new interest, Louy," she protested. "Every night I light candles and wait to speak with Father. I am learning spirit writing, so that he might write to me, as well."

"Did you learn nothing from the events at Mrs. Percy's?"

"I did. There are frauds out there, Louy. I will be much more careful in my next selection of a spiritualist. I will inquire more deeply into her reputation."

"That is a lesson, at least," I said, though I had hoped she had given up séances completely. Sylvia, though, wasn't quite through with this phase, it seemed. "We might inquire more deeply into Mrs. Percy's reputation to discover who and what she really was," I thought aloud. "Woman who are exactly as they appear to be rarely fall into such difficulties as being found murdered in their rooms."

LIZZIE, WHO HAD returned home from the skating pond earlier in the day, greeted me at the door with a cup of hot tea, my house slippers, and a shawl. Just like Marmee.

"Was it exciting, Louy?" she asked. "Apprehending a murderer? Tell me all about it."

"I would, dearest, except I don't think we did apprehend a murderer. Come sit by the fire with me." Oh, the dear parlor! How pleased I was to be home, to sit in the gentle glow of the hearth. Yet I could not stop thinking about the crystal gazer.

"Oh, Louy." Lizzie sighed. "You are involved again. I can tell by the face you are making, and how you have jammed your hands into your pockets. Soon you will begin to whistle and worry. You always whistle a little when you are worried."

"Do I? Then I shall try to break that habit."

"You have a letter, Louy. It arrived this afternoon."

The paper was expensive, more costly than the Alcotts could afford, and the writing had a laborious quality to it, often the sign of a person who has lived abroad and must learn to write in a manner to suit foreign eyes not accustomed to the loops and curlicues of script. The letter, when opened, revealed the sender as Mr. William Phips.

My dear young woman, he had written. *May I call you friend? My dear friend Miss Alcott, if you have not yet read the evening papers (my dear wife always read her correspondence before the papers; I hope you also have that prudent habit), I implore you to set aside today's editions, for they contain horrible news, news unworthy of troubling the imagination of a fine young woman. I will tell you in brief: Mrs. Percy's obituary has been placed in the evening edition. You are too young, my dear friend, to contemplate death and obituaries. May I call on you some afternoon? Mr. Alcott, I understand, is out of state, and I would be pleased to offer my protection.*

"It is from Mr. Phips," I said to Lizzie, who had been rocking quietly in her chair by the fire. "He would like to call upon us, for we are without a father's protection."

"How quaint," said Lizzie.

"I suppose I must invite him over for tea." I sighed. I disliked those long hours of weak tea and small talk that courtesy required, but a gesture of friendship should not be refused.

Auntie Bond, who had been in the kitchen giving instructions for our supper, came into the parlor and sat with us. How cozy we were, three women on their own, glad for a warm fire and companionship, a busy day behind us and a long winter evening before us. Auntie Bond crocheted lace doilies, Lizzie practiced finger exercises, and I stitched at the reverend's shirts with a distinct lack of enthusiasm, disliking the work but knowing that each stitch brought me closer to the purchase of Lizzie's music portfolio and that lottery drawing for the lessons with Signor Massimo.

I stitched and occasionally rested my eyes from the close work by staring into the flames of the hearth, thinking, and resisting the impulse to whistle. The evening paper was on the floor at my feet, folded to the page with the death notices. Mrs. Percy's obituary occupied a full quarter of the page because she had been a woman "of singular interest," as the journalist had described. I had read it, of course, despite Mr. Phips's concerns for my emotional well-being.

The journalist had used far too many words to describe her gifts as a medium and a crystal gazer, and revealed that she was originally born in New York City. She had been a vocalist for some years, touring in the United States and England, but had been forced into early retirement by an inflammation of the throat. She had married Mr. Percy, a Chicago banker, upon her retirement, but Mr. Percy had, for a weakness of the lungs, relocated to Havana.

In other words, I thought, her husband had wearied of her, abandoned her, and resettled in a tropical clime. No doubt he had moved the family finances with him.

There was, the death notice said, some confusion over the manner of death and a suggestion that it might not have been natural. Ah. Hence Mr. Phips's concern that I not read the article. Young women, in his philosophy, should know nothing of murder and the darker deeds of the world.

Mrs. Percy, the reporter continued, was survived only by a stepbrother, Mr. Edward T. Nichols of Cleveland, who was visiting his sister in Boston. Mr. Nichols was also a cousin of Phineas T. Barnum, and involved with him in several business ventures.

What strange connections were revealing themselves!

Something Mr. Ralph Waldo Emerson once said to me chimed through my thoughts as I sat before the fire that evening. He had been explaining his theory of the universal mind, of which he said, "Every man is an inlet to the same and to all of the same. History, Louisa. Just imagine, you might have the exact same thought that Plato once thought."

"Or Sappho," I had added, and Father had harrumphed, for he had no great fondness for lady poets, ancient or otherwise.

And then Mr. Emerson had said, "Of the universal mind each individual man is one more incarnation. All its properties consist in him. Each new fact in his private experience flashes a light on what great bodies of men have done, and the crises of his life refer to national crises."

As you have guessed, reader, I jotted his words in my journal and memorized them, even though at the time I was young enough that I had no fine understanding of them. I knew someday I would.

That evening Mr. Emerson's words returned to me, and I saw that they were so true that their opposite would also be true: What emotion the killer of Mrs. Percy had experienced, I too might experience, and the facts, however strange, that had led to her death were still there, had in fact now become part of history, and thus were available for discovery. Each fact would flash a light on what base, death-dealing men have done. Moreover, whatever crisis had led to Mrs. Percy's death was part of a larger crisis, a failure of moral behavior not just at the individual level but at the national level.

I felt exhilarated.

But would I ever have the courage to reveal to Mr. Emerson that I had used his Transcendental philosophy to begin to untangle a murder?

My latest run of thread had come to an end. I bit it with my teeth, carefully placed the needle in its case for the night, and smoothed the sleeve I had been seaming. The fabric seemed different, I realized. Much too light for a winter shirt.

Your imagination, I told myself. You are daydreaming too much, finding mystery in everything.

THERE WAS A letter from Uncle Benjamin in the morning mail. Lizzie and I had been sitting in the back parlor working on the reverend's shirts, and she had just voiced a desire to purchase one of Mr. Singer's new sewing machines to make the sewing go faster.

"It is such drudgery," she said, sucking a finger that had just been pinpricked, for though she was a nimble little needlewoman, Lizzie sometimes was bored and careless when faced with hours and hours of seams to sew.

"If we could afford a Singer machine we wouldn't need to take in sewing," I pointed out. "But if it will make you feel better, I'll confess to writing a new story that I may sell, and if Mr. Leslie purchases it, I'll get you a new packet of needles."

Lizzie made a face.

"And a new dress," I added hastily, already sorry for having teased her.

"I'd rather have more sheet music, dear, if you don't mind," said my musical younger sister.

Auntie Bond poked her head in through the doorway and held out the little silver tray on which mail was placed.

"All from Walpole," she said.

"Hurray!" shouted Lizzie, throwing down her sewing. "Marmee and Father and Abby. Do you think she is still painting the mountains of New Hampshire, or has she decided on a different subject for her canvases, Louy?"

"Still the mountains," I guessed. Whereas Anna, the eldest, had a talent for acting and singing, and Lizzie was musical, Abby was an artist, and in her time second only to the great Turner himself, or at least that was the family's opinion of her landscapes.

"I have a letter from the darlings, and one from Uncle Benjamin as well. Let us take a break and read them as we walk in the garden," I suggested. "The air will do us good."

"It's snowing, Louy!"

"Even better," I insisted.

Dressed in coat, hat, gloves, and galoshes, I paced back and forth in front of Auntie Bond's row of holly bushes, the only patches of green left in the snow-covered garden. Uncle's letter did not reassure.

Walpole, December 11

Dear Louisa,

Why this interest in Mr. Barnum? He is an upstart, you know, a snake-oil peddler who, for the moment, lives in a mansion in Bridgeport and travels the world at the expense of the poor fools he humbugs with his trickery. By the by, I've misplaced my cane again. Things seem to walk away on their own; have you noticed? And Mr. Tupper asks if you would like some jars of his rhubarb preserves sent down to you, since they are difficult to find at this time of year. But you asked about Phineas Barnum. Well, talk at the club is that he and his cousin, Eddie Nichols, have had a very serious falling-out. You will remember that Eddie is the same young scoundrel who speculated in tickets during the Jenny Lind tour. Or perhaps you don't remember. That is what comes of letting the females in the house read Greek philosophy. Their thoughts go highfalutin and they skip the newspapers.

Eddie so upset Barnum during the Lind tour that the boy moved to Cleveland and set up his own theater and speculated in real estate. I believe he was also involved in several lotteries. All in all, not the kind of boy you bring home to meet the family. The missing cane, by the way, is the one with the bust of Hathor on top, your favorite. I hope I find it soon; I'm lost without it.

Your father is still eating carrots for dinner and supper. I have encouraged him to have a glass of port with me after that mess of vegetables, to strengthen his blood. Well, it seems that Barnum himself loaned much of the money Eddie needed for his new start, and sent drafts through the mail. My solicitor, who is a friend of a solicitor who has rooms next to Mr. Barnum's solicitor, says that Eddie hoodwinked his cousin Phineas out of many thousands of dollars by also forging his signature to drafts not sent, this act being necessary since the money Phineas had sent had all been used to pay old and new gambling debts. As I say, Eddie is not a man to bring home to Sunday dinner.

I'm certain you're not understanding a word of this, so I will explain in terms a female can comprehend: Eddie Nichols robbed his cousin, Phineas Barnum, of many thousands of dollars (as much as forty thousand altogether, my solicitor speculates), and now Mr. Barnum is taking the scoundrel to the courts. Not much good that will do. The money is gone and Barnum is ruined. He'll have to go back to keeping a shop. The most Barnum can hope for is revenge.

Your cousin Eliza sends her warmest regards. The children are down with catarrh and sleep much of the day, so she is putting her feet up and reading. Do you know Mr. Leslie's magazine, Lou-

*isa? There is some fine fiction in it, fantastical stuff with lots of
adventure and wayward females. I send my affection. If you can
think where the cane might be, let me know.*

> *Yrs. truly*
> *Uncle Benjamin*

Three words leaped off the page and into my speculations. The first was *magazine*, and with a thrill of excitement I wondered if it was some of my own stories, published anonymously, that Uncle and Cousin were reading. The thought gave me goose bumps of delight. There is nothing a writer enjoys more than learning her stories are being read, even if she cannot, at the time, acknowledge them as her own work because of the "fantastical stuff" and "wayward females" in those stories. I must, I thought, get back to my desk and finish "Agatha's Confession." First, though, I must ponder the other words in Uncle's letter that had caught my attention, words having to do with Phineas Barnum.

Forgery was the second word. I remembered Mrs. Percy, Eddie's stepsister, at her séance table, her bracelets clanking as she forged written messages from the dearly departed.

The third word that repeated and repeated in my thoughts that evening was *revenge*.

CHAPTER EIGHT

The Showman

IT IS HARSH to have to think of a new acquaintance, and an acquaintance for whom one is beginning to feel a certain affection at that, as a homicidal maniac.

But Mr. Emerson's theory of the universal mind argues against much coincidence, and I knew what he would think if I relayed to him that a man had been cheated of a great fortune by a scoundrel of a cousin who was also related to a forger, and that the forger had then turned up dead.

Still, I found it difficult to reconcile homicidal tendencies with the playful twinkle in Mr. Barnum's fine gray eyes. Maniacs are many things, but rarely playful, and murderers, at least the few I have met, have dreadfully blank stares rather than twinkles. I decided to put the letter aside and think about it later. I also knew what Mr. Emerson would say about that: "Procrastination, Louisa, is an enemy of both self-reliance and self-preservation."

A quick glance out the window revealed that the bright

evergreen leaves of Auntie Bond's rhododendrons were flat and relaxed rather than curled up at the sides; it would be a mild winter day.

"Lizzie, would you enjoy another morning off from stitching shirts?" I asked my sister, who was sipping her tea.

"I could almost dread these hours away from the sewing room," said she with a little smile. "Such strange things occur. But yes, who would not desire more time at the piano and less time seaming? But where are you off to, Louy?"

"To pay a condolence visit," I said, "to Mr. Edward Nichols."

"Have I met this gentleman?" asked Auntie Bond, frowning and looking vague.

"I hope not," I said, "since he seems to be a ne'er-do-well of the worst order. But his stepsister has passed away."

"Well," said the sweet lady, "even miscreants deserve the occasional word of kindness. But do keep your feet dry, Louy." Do you see, gentle reader, why the Alcotts loved Miss Bond so well that we included her in our greatly extended family?

It was still early, so I spent the next hour outside the pantry door, trying to perfect the trick Mr. Barnum had described, of looping wire around a bolt so that the door might be bolted from the outside. I chose this location in case the trick actually worked: If the door locked, I could enter from the porch and undo the bolt. Once, it almost worked. I held my breath as the wire-captured bolt squeaked half an inch behind the door, but the wire stuck and the bolt would move no farther. It would need to be greased. Why hadn't I checked Mrs. Percy's door to see if the bolt had recently been greased?

"Louisa," said a startled Auntie Bond, who had just come up behind me, "why are you kneeling before the pantry?"

"I dropped something," I told her, unwilling to reveal that I was practicing a trick of locking and unlocking doors.

Sylvia accompanied me on my errand that morning, arriving ten minutes early at our prearranged meeting spot in Boston Common, and dressed very austerely, for Sylvia at least, in a plain brown frock and overcoat, and a hat without a single silk flower on it.

"Has Miss Snodgrass's plain style of costume become a fashion?" I asked her after giving her a kiss in greeting.

"I am engaging in a simpler plan of trimming," she said. "One more befitting a woman of modest means."

"But, Sylvia," I protested, "you are dizzyingly wealthy."

"I may not always be so. I may, in fact, marry a man of modest rather than excessive income. I may need to learn economy, at least until his fortune has been made."

"Well," I admitted, "Father would approve, but I am not certain I do. You looked lovely in silk and cashmere, and you enjoyed it so. That kind of luxury seemed a small vice, and small vices often save us from larger ones."

"You worry that I am falling into vice, Louy?"

I was worried that she was falling in love, but that I chose not to reveal.

Mr. Nichols, according to the paper, was spending a brief residency in Boston in Mrs. Klegg's Boardinghouse on Chandler Lane, an alley in a very unfashionable part of town near the harbor, far from the stately old homes of Beacon Hill or the smart new mansions of Commonwealth Avenue. If Nichols had profited from his association with Mr. Barnum, it would appear he had already exhausted those profits. Nor did his relations with his stepsister seem to have been particularly close, if he slept in a boardinghouse instead of her home.

"Should we be walking here unescorted? I fear that women of modest means must pay much more attention to propriety than those of dizzying wealth," Sylvia complained when we had progressed from broad avenue to narrow street to cramped lane. Cats and dogs prowled through piles of refuse in the gutters, and a group of thin children clambered around our knees, begging for pennies. I had given them all I had in my reticule, and Sylvia did likewise, yet they followed, pulling at our coats and gloved hands.

"It seems we are escorted," I said. Stopping in the midst of them, I gave a handkerchief to one, a bent copper brooch to another, my wool sash to a third, and to a fourth girl with enormous eyes who was as tall as my shoulder I gave my gloves. They were large, but she would soon fit into them. I could keep my hands in my pockets.

"Louy," said Sylvia, "you cannot pay a sympathy call without gloves!"

"What of your simpler plan for trimming and economy of wardrobe?" I said.

Mrs. Klegg's Boardinghouse badly needed a coat of paint and curtains at the windows. Nor was there a bell or knocker, so I pounded on the door with my fist. A woman with reddened eyes, colorless thinning hair, and the shapeless figure of one who dines too frequently on potatoes, only potatoes, opened the door after several minutes.

"What d'ya want?" she asked with great irritation.

"Is Mr. Nichols at home?" I asked.

"He'd better be," she said with great gloom. "He ain't given me the week's rent."

"We would like to pay him a call," I said.

"Suit yourself. Top of the second stairs, last door on the left."

"Is there not a parlor where we may sit?" protested Sylvia.

"Parlor's rented out to Mr. Legrand. He pays on time, and tips as well," said the landlady with even greater gloom.

"We will go up to Mr. Nichols's room," I said.

We did, with Sylvia protesting about propriety and pulling at my hand all the way up the two flights of dark, windowless stairs. Only when I knocked upon the door did she desist and grow quiet.

The door opened quickly enough, and I realized that Mr. Nichols had been expecting someone. His face fell when he saw us standing before him. It was a handsome face, with a strong jaw, blue eyes, well-trimmed brown beard, and curling brown hair falling over the broad brow. A hero's face, I thought. But it had been ruined by a puffiness about the mouth, a pinkness in the eye, that suggested dissolution. His shirt was open at the throat; the unattached collar lay forgotten on the floor like a wounded white bird. His hands trembled as he attempted to push studs through his shirt cuffs.

"You'll have to come back next week," said Mr. Nichols, turning in a kind of little circle so that he could avoid looking directly at us. "The draft from my cousin has not arrived."

"Mr. Nichols, we have come to offer our condolences for the passing away of your stepsister, Mrs. Percy," I said gently.

"Mrs. Percy," repeated Sylvia, for he now looked confused.

"Oh, yes!" he exclaimed with a little too much glee. "I thought you were bill collectors! They get deuced tricky, these tradesmen, sending all sorts to collect for them. I thought you were collectors!"

"May we come in?" I asked, for he stood in the doorway blocking us, a tall and powerfully built man, though of the type that soon turns to fat, Father would have said of him.

"I am . . . I am rather busy at the moment. Could you come back later?"

I decided to take a large leap and risk a dreadful error. "If you are waiting for Suzie Dear, I'm afraid she is not coming," I told him. "Now, may we come in?"

It was not a dreadful error, but rather terribly accurate, judging from his reaction. He turned white, then red. His hands trembled even more and he gave up entirely the effort to close his sleeve cuffs. Sylvia and I entered.

The air was unpleasantly thick with cigar smoke, and there was little furniture in the room, no more than a bed, roiling with unmade linen and yesterday's clothing, a single wobbly chair, a dresser badly in need of dusting and polishing, a wardrobe with a cracked glass door, and a small hearth with a wooden mantelpiece. On the mantelpiece were the assorted cuff links, loose change, pipe cleaners, and other paraphernalia that accumulate in men's rooms. I also spied a small brass locket, half a locket really, the kind that lovers give each other, with halves that fit into a whole.

Sylvia and I stood side by side, our backs to the unmade bed for modesty's sake.

"Where is Suzie, the little traitor? She was supposed to be here an hour ago," he mumbled. "Never count on a woman."

"You yourself cast suspicion on her when you told Constable Cobban that money and jewels were missing from your stepsister's home, and now Miss Dear is arrested," I said. "And yet you castigate womanhood? It is not only unfair, but also illogical."

"Don't money and jewels always go missing when someone dies?" muttered Mr. Nichols. "How was I to know they would take Suzie for it?"

"The jewels were insured, were they not?"

"Of course they were," he said. Again he turned in that strange little circle to avoid looking directly at me. He had set in place a scheme, I realized, one of the most common, to insure a relative's possessions for more than they were worth, and usually against that relative's knowledge, for just such a day as Mrs. Percy had encountered, when heirs and survivors could step forth and claim their booty. It seemed to me a motive for murder, if the insurance were large enough, and the man destitute enough.

Yet, Suzie Dear was in jail for wearing too much jewelry. Be truthful, I told myself. She is no innocent.

"Suzie was your accomplice," I told Mr. Nichols.

"Say, I thought you were here to offer condolences."

"My sympathy," said Sylvia. "But I suspect you won't be getting any from your cousin, Mr. Barnum." Sylvia had taken a great liking to Mr. Barnum, and when I had explained earlier how this man had cheated him of a great deal of money, she had spluttered with anger.

"None of those charges has been proven," said Eddie Nichols. He sat on the bed and eyed the window, looking for escape, but he was three floors from the street. If he made a

run for it, he would need to go past us to the door. Taking Sylvia by the arm, I moved to the side to avoid being trampled in that event.

"Mrs. Percy was also your accomplice," I said.

"This visit is over," he said. "Will you leave, ladies, or must I push you out?"

We left.

"Some good has come of this visit," I said to Sylvia when we were once again in the little lane and taking somewhat large strides to remove ourselves to a more accommodating section of Boston. "I am certain that he is a man of sleepless nights. A guilty man. But how far does his guilt extend? Is he merely a thief and conspirator, or is he also a murderer?"

"If a murderer, why would he kill his accomplice, Mrs. Percy, if that is what you are suggesting, though I still believe that Mrs. Percy is entirely a victim in all this." Sylvia was panting, trying to match her pace to my own. "Louy, there was a nuance in your statement that makes me uncomfortable. If only some good has been done, you are suggesting some bad has been done as well, are you not?"

Sylvia's perspicacity surprised me sometimes. "I fear we may have frightened Mr. Nichols, and he seems the type to leave town hurriedly," I replied. "Perhaps till this matter of Mrs. Percy's death is satisfactorily cleared up, a watch should be put on him."

"It would be wise if I informed Constable Cobban of this," Sylvia announced solemnly. "I will go there immediately."

And so we parted ways, I to pay another visit to Mrs. Percy's house, and she to have a conversation with Constable

Cobban. I only hoped that among the many matters she obviously wished to discuss with him she would remember to tell him that Mr. Nichols should be monitored, if there were volunteers or paid watchmen Cobban could set in front of Mrs. Klegg's Boardinghouse.

Oh, how I wanted to jam my cold hands in my pockets and whistle! Ever since Lizzie had pointed out that I whistle when worried, I had wanted to do nothing but whistle. I passed a vendor's stall selling papers and tobacco, and that man was whistling. A little boy running past me with his skates over his shoulder was whistling. Unfair to be denied that solace simply because of one's gender. So as I walked, I put my hands in my pockets to hide them from the newly falling snow, and I whistled softly. I felt much better.

The snow was falling heavily in flakes as large as a baby's fist by the time I reached Mrs. Percy's house. It was a most beautiful afternoon, all white with gay flashes of color from the scarlet or blue coats of women walkers returning home from shopping or going to pay calls, a snow-globe kind of afternoon where the world feels safe and lovely. Except I was going to a home where a murder had been committed. I was convinced of it now, after that visit to Mr. Nichols.

According to Mr. Emerson's theory of the universal mind, all history can be discovered in the hours of an individual life, and each life can be read as fable. If so, then the history and fable most visible in Mrs. Percy's life was that of Orpheus, who played such lovely music that all who heard him followed, and when his bride, Eurydice, died, Orpheus followed into the underworld and spoke with her.

Orpheus came to a bad end, dear reader, a violent end.

Not content to speak with his beloved, he turned to look at her, and thereupon she disappeared forever and Orpheus wandered the world, playing his mad music, till he enraged a group of women who murdered him. Mrs. Percy had been a vocalist, married and then lost a wandering spouse, had turned to speaking with the spirits, and now was dead. Moreover, one need only consider her close associations to see that a violent end was almost unavoidable: Her maid was a known thief and streetwalker, her stepbrother a schemer and forger, and she had, I suspected, enraged a very powerful man, Mr. Phineas T. Barnum, by forging the documents that had led to his financial downfall.

But of all the associations that she had made, the one that most confused me was her relationship to Miss Amelia Snodgrass, that woman dressed all in brown like a shadow at midday. What was their connection?

When I arrived at Mrs. Percy's house, there were footsteps in the new snow leading up the sidewalk and onto her porch. This was a complication I had not anticipated. How could I practice my recently acquired door-opening skills with an observer present? I confess that in my pocket I had placed a skeleton key for the front door, and a thick, sturdy wire for the interior door.

For the front door no key was needed. It swung freely open.

"Shocking," said a voice from deep inside the dark hall.

"Mr. Phips?" I asked, and my voice echoed in that darkness in a most disconcerting manner.

"Yes, dear girl. Isn't it shocking? The constabulary left the door open for any who might wander in."

He stepped closer to the door, into the light, and I could see that I had frightened him as much as he had frightened me. The old man was trembling.

"I did not expect anyone else to be here," I said, stepping half out the door again so that I might brush the heavy snow from my coat without dripping on Mrs. Percy's carpet.

"Permit me, dear girl," Mr. Phips said, stepping closer and brushing some snow off the back of my hat, where I could not reach. "This feather will never be the same, I fear."

"Then I will pull it out and use it as a quill," I jested. "Why are you here, Mr. Phips?"

"Ah. I was afraid you would ask." He sighed mightily, then grinned the way boys do when they confess they have a frog in their pocket. As a teacher of small children, I have some experience with those circumstances. "I wanted to see the scene of the crime again. This is the most thrilling event I have encountered in years, and when I describe it at my club I want to get the details correctly. Would you say that is a Queen Anne chair?" He pointed to a much-abused chair standing in the hall. "Is that a Currier print, do you think? The door was open, so I came in. Please do not tell anyone, dear girl, most embarrassing, you see. Breaking and entering? Is that what it is called?"

"Well, you certainly did not break," I said, hoping to defer the question I knew was to follow.

"Why are you here, Miss Alcott?" His boyish glee, always so appealing in an older gentleman, turned to confusion.

"To test a theory. I have been trying, you see, to open a bolted door using the trick Mr. Barnum showed us."

"And have you succeeded?"

"Not yet. But I have bought a thicker wire to try upon Mrs. Percy's door."

His pale blue eyes opened wide, his white eyebrows quivered. "But then . . . how were you to enter the front door if it had been locked?"

My silence caused him to frown, and then he realized.

"Dear girl!" he exclaimed with delight. "What spirit! If I were thirty years younger . . ."

"Shall we go examine the bolt together?" I asked hastily, interrupting him.

Mrs. Percy's hall, without even the dim gas lamps she had used to illuminate it, was pitch dark, and we made our way down it slowly, bumping into furniture and occasionally each other, the latter event always causing Mr. Phips to chuckle with embarrassment.

The crystal gazer had renovated much of the house, including the hall, and I couldn't help but wonder why she had purposely left the hall in such complete darkness, with no glazing on either side of the front door to admit daylight, and no sliding doors from adjacent rooms to admit light from other areas. Probably the hall was meant to be included in some parts of the performance; perhaps it, like the séance room, had a false ceiling from which descended trumpets and swags of gauze and other accruements of the trade.

When we paused before what we believed was the correct door, it being difficult to discern in such darkness, I asked Mr. Phips if he had a lucifer upon him. I had thought to bring a candle stub in case the gas had been shut off, but the matches in my pocket were soaked from the snow and in no lightable condition.

"I do," he whispered with some excitement, reaching into his waistcoat pocket.

I opened the door, which had been unlocked and unbolted since the discovery of Mrs. Percy's body, and with Mr. Phips close behind me entered once again the scene of the crime, as Mr. Phips had described it. There was considerable light in this room from the windows and the gauze curtain; it would seem that Mrs. Percy, when she was not speaking with the dead, had preferred a bright environment. Her preparation room was just as it had been last time I had seen it, with the Niagara Falls souvenir pillow on the floor and that lingering odor of poppy in the air, except now, of course, there was no body on the chaise.

"It looks mundane enough, doesn't it?" Mr. Phips whispered. "The sofa, the curtains, the rug. Is it Aubusson, do you think?"

"Imitation Aubusson," I answered. "The room does indeed appear quite ordinary, except for the broken windows where you acquired entrance that day." The little points of glass were still on the floor under the window, and were now covered with a light layer of snow that had drifted in. "The floor will be ruined," I said. There are moments, dear reader, when Marmee seems to speak through me.

I turned back to the door to examine the bolt from this side.

"Perhaps Mr. Barnum is right," I said, as much to myself as to Mr. Phips. "I shall try. Mr. Phips, in a moment bolt the door behind me, will you?" I looped my thick wire around the bolt head, held it firmly in my grasp, and stepped back into the hall. After Mr. Phips shut the door, I tugged gently on the wire. It moved, slowly and with difficulty, but it moved. Judging from the wire, the bolt was halfway home. Then it stopped, somehow stuck, at the same point at which the trick always seemed to fail. I tugged a little bit harder, trying to slide the bolt without undoing the loop. It began to move again, in minuscule jerks, and then would move no farther.

"It is bolted!" exclaimed Mr. Phips with great wonder. "My dear girl! You've done it! Will you allow me to give a tea some afternoon? You will, of course, bring the chaperon of your choice."

He seemed so eager it pained me to disappoint him, but, "I am so very busy just now, Mr. Phips," I told him.

His brow clouded with displeasure. He was, I saw then, a man used to getting his own way.

"Life requires boldness, Miss Alcott," he said. "A young woman should not only think of duty, but once in a while of entertainment as well." He strode off, his shoulders back and his chin high.

"YOU SHOULD NOT have gone to see Mr. Nichols without me," said Constable Cobban, plainly irritated. He sat in Auntie Bond's best parlor with a teacup and saucer balanced on his knee, and a cake plate in his left hand. I had sent him a note explaining my visit to Mrs. Percy's stepbrother.

"More poppy-seed biscuit?" asked Sylvia, holding the silver cake tongs poised over the cake stand. She sat close beside him on the settee, and he looked at her as if she were a misbehaving puppy that had climbed onto the furniture without permission.

"I realize that now," I said quietly. "I do ask your pardon, but I'm certain you have set all to rights. I have no doubt that any little disturbance we caused was quickly remedied by your competence."

Faced with such feminine meekness he was at a loss, which had been my intention, of course. The best way to disarm a man's wrath is to allow him to feel the false superiority underlying the temper tantrum, and then to flatter him.

"Not all of my day's work was bungled," I continued, and then described my visit to Mrs. Percy's, and running into Mr. Phips there.

"The door was open? I'll have to have a word with my men," Cobban said. His red-and-black-checked suit contrasted very badly with Auntie Bond's blue-and-gray floral carpet, and he had forgotten to remove his hat. "Very bad procedure," he continued, frowning. "They should know better. Taints the entire robbery investigation, knowing the door was open. What was stolen before the murder, and what was stolen after?" How such a bright and freckled face could look stormy is a mystery in itself, but he looked stormy with fresh anger.

"The orange cake is delightful," said Sylvia.

"Do stop going on about the cake," said Cobban and I together.

"I have irritated you." She put the tongs down and leaned back into the settee. "Thank heavens for stopping me. I don't know what got into me there for a moment. Do you think it was Father, encouraging me to be a good hostess?"

Cobban looked at her in wonder, and his expression softened.

"The robbery investigation is secondary to the murder, isn't it?" I asked, returning to the main subject. "Besides, if you depend on Mr. Nichols to provide the quality and quantity of the goods removed from his stepsister's home, that investigation is already severely tainted."

"You've got a point there," Cobban agreed. "I wouldn't trust him with a penny of mine."

"And Mr. Barnum trusted him with many thousands of dollars," I said. "But the point is that I tried the wire trick that Mr. Barnum taught me to bolt a door from the other side, and it worked. We know now how we came to find a murdered person inside a bolted room. Of course, we've only the stepbrother's say that it was murder. Perhaps he lied about that as well. Perhaps Mrs. Percy did have a weak heart. Oh, my." I put my teacup down so quickly and so hard on the table that it rattled.

A new thought had just occurred to me. What if Mrs. Percy had died of natural causes, and Mr. Nichols merely wished us to think she had been murdered? Why would he? Because Mr. Barnum would be a suspect; Mr. Barnum, to whom he owed an honest lifetime's wages; Mr. Barnum, who was taking him to the courts in a lawsuit. Is there no end to perfidy? How much greed can a society allow, and still survive?

"But it *was* murder," Cobban said. "I saw Dr. Roder this morning, and took him to see Mrs. Percy at the morgue."

"Is he to do a postmortem?" Sylvia asked cautiously.

The last time she had sat at a postmortem she had almost fainted.

"No need." Cobban put down his teacup and saucer as well, and looked greatly relieved when he had been freed of those fragile objects. "He could tell from her eyes. That blood-shot pinkness was cerebral hemorrhaging, he said. She'd been suffocated."

"The pillow on the floor," I said. "The souvenir pillow from Niagara Falls."

"Well, I won't be going there on my honeymoon," decided Sylvia.

"Are you engaged, Miss Shattuck?" asked Constable Cobban, and both his voice and expression were those I would imagine sheep would use (if they could understand and speak in our language) on the day the farmer prodded them into the slaughterhouse. Sylvia did not answer, but once again passed the cake plate.

"So it is murder. Again." I could not restrain a sigh. Marmee would not be pleased to hear this. She had reasonable objections to having her second-eldest daughter involved in squalid and dangerous affairs. I knew the neighbors would talk about us again, for one thing.

"That Alcott girl!" they would say. "Always tripping over dead bodies! Makes one wonder, don't it?"

"Yes," another would say. "I hear she even whistles in public!"

"Why are you smiling, Louy?" Sylvia broke my train of thought.

"I am sorry. That is highly inappropriate and disrespect-

ful to poor Mrs. Percy," I said. "So, it is murder. That means, of course, there is a murderer, no doubt about it."

"Yes. And we have her locked up," said Cobban, mumbling through a mouthful of seed cake.

"You have been wrong before," I reminded him. "First suspicions are not necessarily correct. I have an instinct about Suzie Dear. . . ."

"And your instincts have often been incorrect," Cobban retorted, reaching for another piece of cake.

"Dear Constable Cobban," I said somewhat primly, "consider the evidence you have. Suzie was wearing some of the crystal gazer's jewelry when she fled the house. She maintains that the jewelry was given to her as a gift, meaning a bribe, of course, to assist with the séances and to keep quiet about the tricks. As for fleeing the house, she fled because she knew the constabulary would jump to the exact conclusion to which you have jumped."

"But how did she know the medium was dead," Cobban said, "if she didn't kill her?"

"Instinct," I said. "Mrs. Percy was very late that morning, and not responding to knocks upon the door."

"We searched her rooms. We found a diamond ring and a bag of money. About two hundred dollars, I'd say. Explain that, Miss Louisa. Do you really think Mrs. Percy was that generous?"

Oh, Suzie! So much greed leads to dire consequences!

"A thief," I said. "Perhaps Suzie is a thief because too much temptation was put in her path. But not a murderess."

"I don't share your opinion." He brushed crumbs from his boldly checkered trousers and rose to leave.

"I haven't finished," I said. "Please stay another ten minutes and hear about the rest of my afternoon."

"You bolted the door from outside," Cobban said patiently. "My congratulations on learning to emulate the behavior of the lower classes. What else happened?"

Sometimes I wanted to thwack Cobban on the head, he could get so smug. "After Mr. Phips left, I saw Miss Snodgrass again. She was standing in the side garden, looking at an upstairs window."

CHAPTER NINE

The Cook Sleeps In

I NOW HAD the young constable's full attention. "All in brown again?"

"Yes. And when she saw me looking at her, she almost turned and fled, then decided to stand her ground."

"I don't like the look of this," Cobban said.

"Nor do I. Her behavior is suggestive, but what it is suggesting I cannot yet identify."

Cobban reached for a third piece of cake, changed his mind, and jammed his hands in his jacket pockets, which were stretched and rounded from this repeated gesture, making his suit look even shabbier. A good-looking young man, I thought, but with little regard for appearances. Maybe Lizzie is right: I shouldn't put my hands in my pockets and whistle.

"Did you speak with her?"

"Yes. She came into the house when she saw the front door was open. We exchanged 'good days' and such and she said she had been drawn to the house by a morbid curiosity about Mrs. Percy's death."

"Sounds innocent enough," said Cobban. "The citizenry often show up to peer at crime scenes."

"Miss Snodgrass never asked how Mr. Phips and I came to be at the house, and it seemed she had been standing and watching us for some time. It would appear her morbid curiosity is somewhat limited," I said.

"She was preoccupied." Sylvia spoke up. Cobban and I both turned to look at her. She was sweeping crumbs off the tray. "Women in love are forever preoccupied, and she has just become engaged, remember."

"True," admitted Cobban.

"The afternoon was not yet over," I continued. "Mrs. Deeds also arrived. She was coming up the path just as we were going out the front door. She seemed most surprised and unhappy to see us there."

"Did she explain her visit?" Cobban asked. "More morbid curiosity about the crime scene?"

"Quite the contrary. She was hoping that Mrs. Percy's cook had returned to the house, so that she might employ her in her own kitchen. 'She is out of work now,' she had said. 'Why should I not have her?'"

"Vultures." Cobban snorted. "You don't think Mrs. Deeds would resort to murder to obtain a cook, do you? I do wonder where the cook has gone, and why she fled. Makes her look guilty, don't you think? But why would a cook murder her employer?"

"It has happened," said Sylvia darkly. "When I was a child and old Mr. Paterson hadn't given his cook her Christmas envelope, he got terribly ill the next week, and the family all claimed he'd been fed rat poison from the larder."

"Sylvia, there are weeks still before Christmas," I pointed out. "And Mrs. Percy seems to have been a generous rather than a miserly employer. Cook had a large room with windows and a good mattress, as I recall. No, the Chinese woman would have no cause to murder her employer. She fled for some other reason."

"Well, I must continue my rounds," said Constable Cobban, rising. Sylvia rose also and went to get his hat and coat.

We had walked to Auntie Bond's hall by then, and Sylvia stood there, smiling, holding the constable's coat. "Do stay warm," she told him. "It is snowing again. Here, wrap this." She reached up and twisted a brightly colored muffler around his neck.

"What's this?" he asked, frowning.

"I knitted it," said Sylvia.

"Did you, then! Thank you, Miss Shattuck. Well, congratulations on your engagement, and I wouldn't let my comment about Niagara Falls spoil your honeymoon plans."

When the door was closed, I turned to my friend. "You purposely let him think you are affianced," I accused.

"I did," she admitted with a little smile. "There's more tea cake in the parlor. Shall we finish it?"

THAT NIGHT I stayed up late writing, sitting before smoky candle stubs in my attic room so that Lizzie could sleep undisturbed in our bedroom. Progress on "Agatha's Confession" had slowed, because my thoughts more and more settled on

the mysterious fate of Mrs. Agatha Percy rather than her namesake. I realized that my story was tied to the investigation, that to know what was to happen to my Agatha meant knowing what happened to the real Agatha. Tomorrow, I decided, questions must be answered. And then, out of nowhere, came a paragraph for the story, about Agatha, deeply in love with Philip but seeing her lover conversing with her friend Clara:

> *They stood together, both beautiful and gay in the flood of light that shone down from the shaded lamps. Dark and plain and sad, I sat apart in the twilight shadows, struggling silently to find some outlet from the maze of doubts and fears that filled my heart and brain.*
>
> *I wanted to be generous and just, to forget self and think of Philip's happiness alone. But my great love rose up so importunate and strong, I could only listen to its pleading and cling fast to the old hope and faith, though both were broken reeds, I knew.*
>
> *I watched and waited many days, trying to seem unchanged. But the veil had fallen from my eyes, and the blessed calm was gone that for a little while had brooded over me. Ah, what a little while it seemed! I saw the cloud coming nearer and nearer which should overshadow me and leave them in the sunshine I had lost.*

Jealousy. That was why Sylvia had suggested to Cobban that she was engaged: to make him notice her, to awaken his own feelings, if there were any. And now my poor Agatha, plain and poor, must suffer this most terrible of feelings. I sat chewing the end of my pen for some moments; more than Sylvia's little ploy had begun this train of thought, but I could not yet identify the source of my musings. That is one of the defects of the universal mind, I thought. We may all step into the same stream, but that does not mean we see the source!

Who was jealous of whom? And what did it have to do with Mrs. Percy, murdered in her preparation room? Shadows leaped about the dark attic as my candle stubs flickered; a sudden gust from the ill-fitting window snuffed them both, and I sat in the dark with snowflakes landing on my face and hands like the cold touch of an invisible presence. I shivered with more than cold and quickly relit the candles. What a strange time we live in, I thought, when grown people sit in the dark and frighten one another with ghost stories. As if there weren't enough in reality to make us cower: slavery and bank failures, the homeless. How lucky I was to have my health, the means of earning a living, and my family. This year, though I was parted from them, we would have gifts for one another.

I chewed my pen again, this time daydreaming about several winters before, when Father had been traveling and the Alcott brood and Marmee had spent a long winter night before the fire, talking about the Christmas to come.

"Christmas won't be Christmas without any presents," I had grumbled, for we were even poorer than usual then, and Anna and Lizzie and Abby had complained as well, until Marmee came home, wet and cold and exhausted but beaming with joy because she had a letter from Father in her pocket.

"Our burdens are here, our road is before us, and the longing for goodness and happiness is the guide that leads us through many troubles," Marmee had said.

Sighing, I put away my paper and capped the inkwell,

then made my way down the narrow attic stars. I kissed Lizzie on the forehead and went to sleep.

Morning came early for me, well before dawn, for I had several errands to do that day, and had determined to finish at least one more of the reverend's shirts before stepping out of the house.

"Louy? Up so early?" said Lizzie, rubbing her eyes and stepping into the sewing room. "What time is it?" She had wrapped a blanket about her shoulders and looked very young.

"Not yet six," I said. "Go back to bed and sleep some more, two more hours at least."

"Ummm," she murmured. No one but Lizzie murmurs in the notes of a Chopin étude, I thought, smiling and threading my needle with grim determination. By nine o'clock I had finished the shirt and my bowl of porridge, and was ready for the first errand of the day. Mrs. Dahlia O'Connor, a friend of Mother's, would still be drowsy, but she was a sharp creature and I would be at a slight advantage if I caught her off guard.

She lived on the other side of Beacon Hill, where clusters of somewhat desperate-looking ramshackle houses provided shelter for Boston's free blacks, the day servants and laundry-women, and the increasing numbers of Irish immigrants. On this side of the hill, slop buckets were emptied in the street, not in private privies in the back, and simply walking could be a hazardous business if one did not check the placement of each step. Unemployed young men loitered on corners, and streetwalking women finally done with the night's work made their exhausted way to the single, often shared room they called home. Just on the other side of the hill were the old mansions and old names and old blood of Boston; the contrast always seemed a parable to me, that nothing but a mound of soil separated the classes, the newcomers from the old comers, in life as in death. How fragile, secure reader, is estate and esteem!

"Mrs. O'Connor be abed," said the girl who opened the door at number seventy-two. She eyed me in an unfriendly manner. "Did that Mrs. Wilkinson send you?"

"No. I'll go straight up," I said. "We're old friends." This was only half-true. Marmee had found work for Mrs. O'Connor on several occasions, and I hoped that Marmee's good actions would assure me at least a wary welcome.

"Miss Louisa! Something wrong with your mama?" was the first thing Mrs. O'Connor said, sitting up in bed, her eyes wide with alarm, when I opened her door at the top of three flights of stairs and went in.

"No, she is well," I said. "But I am in great need of a favor. Will you help me?"

Mrs. O'Connor put on a ragged bed jacket and straightened her sleeping cap over her unnaturally red hair. She pulled a fraying rope at the side of the bed, and I heard a bell chime somewhere in the depths of the boardinghouse.

"Can't do no cooking for you," she said. "Mrs. Wilkinson is giving a ball and has hired everyone this side of the Great Divide. I'm making the breads and cakes." Mrs. O'Connor looked pleased with herself. "I can be a few more minutes late, though. I'll just stick the yeast dough closer to the fire to make it rise faster, so we can have a nice chat. What ails you that Mother O'Connor can help with?" Her brogue was thick and warm and her smile, when she gave it, huge, but Mrs. O'Connor was nobody's fool, and I knew I must tread lightly, for once offended she never forgave.

"I have some questions about Mrs. Agatha Percy," I said, pulling a chair over to the side of her bed, since she showed little inclination to rise. I couldn't blame her. There was no fire in the room, and crystals of ice shone inside the curtainless windows; I kept my coat on, and my muffler.

Mrs. O'Connor let out a laugh that was more like a snort, and snapped her fingers. "That biddy!" she exclaimed with great disgust. "Louisa, my girl, don't waste your dimes on that old girl. She's a fraud through and through."

"That is a harsh judgment," I said.

Mrs. O'Connor snorted again like a horse that has a pebble wedged between shoe and sensitive foot. "Did she use a crystal ball? Yes? That proves it. No self-respecting ghost would show up in a ball. They die to be free, not to be captured in a body once again. You see, Louisa, only frauds— and newcomer frauds at that—use the ball. Your Mrs. Percy learned her 'art' [another snort, dear reader] at the theater in one of those plays, perhaps 'The Ghost of Windham Falls.' That was making the rounds again a couple of years ago, I think, and wherever it plays a whole stew of crystal gazers rises up like weeds in the pumpkin patch. No, the only spirits Mrs. Percy talks with come from a bottle."

That had been Constable Cobban's assessment as well, but I did not mention that to Mrs. O'Connor, who had no great fondness for the law.

There was a loud rap at the door, and a disheveled girl came in carrying a tray. "Tea," she said. "I'll leave it here. I don't come in no further." She put the tray on the floor, caught the penny that Mrs. O'Connor tossed her, and slammed the door shut again.

"Shall I pour?" I asked.

"Do, sweetie," said Mrs. O'Connor. "And tell me more about Mrs. Percy."

I poured tea and picked black specks out of the sugar jar before sweetening our cups. "She wrote messages from the spirits," I said. "And a trumpet came down from the ceiling."

"One of the messages was from a dead father," Mrs. O'Connor said. "There's always a message from a dead father in such rooms and circumstances."

"This was a little more specific," I said. "The message was from my friend's dead father, and the message was that she should marry."

"This is serious, then. Your Mrs. Percy may be a fraud, but she is no amateur. She is a prep artist. Pass a bit of that bread over, Louisa, with jam, please. Help yourself, dear. Plenty for two." But there wasn't plenty, so I spread thin yellow preserves on the stale crust and gave it to Mrs. O'Connor.

"What is a prep artist?" I asked.

"She would have paid off a servant in your friend's household to discover what the private conversations were, and the gossip—what woman is in the family way, what husband is cheating. All the sordid details." Mrs. O'Connor smacked her lips with pleasure. "And she would have paid someone else to scour the cemeteries. You paid more than a dime, Louisa.

Such creatures charge more to cover their expenses. Unlike women like me, who have no such expenses."

Reader, have I not mentioned that Mrs. O'Connor spoke with the dead? In fact, it was her preferred occupation, except that when the spirits spoke through Mrs. O'Connor they spoke in somewhat foul language and without any discretion, and so her clientele was ephemeral at best. The strange thing about Mrs. O'Connor was that her "spirits" were almost always correct. Once, Mrs. O'Connor channeled Marmee's mother, who told her where a lost brooch could be found, and there it was, wedged between the stone wall and the pickle jar in Uncle Benjamin's cellar, just as the spirit had said.

"You said she would scour the cemeteries?" I asked.

"Tombstones. Best source of information. Most common trick." Mrs. O'Connor pulled a long face and deepened her normally shrill voice. "I see a woman, elderly, seventy-eight years old, looking down at you and worrying. She is speaking. I can just hear her . . . oh, she's saying, 'The way is narrow but the reward is great to he who perseveres.' Then the target—that's the customer, my dear—the target jumps up in joy and shouts, 'Mother! Mother! That's what you always used to say to us!' And all that, Louisa, my girl, is just from one tombstone, no gossip added."

"I see. More tea?"

"No, thanks. My day must begin, though this visit has been lovely. Are you going back to see this Mrs. Percy creature?"

"I can't, Mrs. O'Connor. She has passed over."

"Dead?" asked Mrs. O'Connor with perhaps more glee than was suitable. "Can you give me the names of your circle, Louisa? I'll send them my card."

Why not? I thought, and wrote down on a scrap of paper the names: Miss Amelia Snodgrass, Mr. Phineas T. Barnum, Mr. and Mrs. Ezra Deeds, Mr. William Phips. I omitted Sylvia's name. She'd already received too many messages from the dead.

"Mr. Barnum? Himself? Oh, happy day," said Mrs. O'Connor when I handed her the piece of paper. "I see me now in the American Museum, greeting my clientele in a room with red curtains and gas lamps! Sometimes I see the future, you know." Mrs. O'Connor clapped her hands with joy. "Did I ever tell you how I saw Mesmer hypnotize the queen of France? He himself had to disappear first."

Since Mesmer had died some years before, I assumed Mrs. O'Connor was describing one of her "dreams" or "visits" in which the dead revealed things to her. "You'll have to tell me some other day," I said. "I have one last question, if you don't mind, and I'll let you get about your day's business. What can you tell me of Amelia Snodgrass?" As a cook for the finer houses in Boston, Mrs. O'Connor had access to more information and gossip than a hundred constables could obtain, perhaps more than Pinkerton himself.

She had a most flexible face, capable of dozens of expressions, the kind of face that would have done well for her onstage. Now Mrs. O'Connor's bright eyes grew narrow and her mouth twisted; she looked sly. "That one," she purred. "How I'd like to get her in my séance room. I'd tell her a thing or two. Her and her airs, and everyone belowstairs knows about those carryings-on."

Impatient reader! Before she could speak a further word, the door exploded open and a maidservant stood there, wet with snow and pink in the face with rage! She was from a good house; I could tell from her clothes and the thickness of her boots.

"Missus says you are to come now," muttered the girl. "I left my own biscuits browning in the oven, and if they burn because of your laziness I'll . . . I'll . . . I'll pull out your dyed hair, I will. I'll put ground glass in your damn raisin cakes! You and that new Chinee cook, between the two of you I'll lose my mind!"

It's rare for a woman of Mrs. O'Connor's girth to move with such alacrity, but in less than three seconds she had risen from bed, pulled a day dress over her chemise, and begun to button boots over the stockings in which she had slept.

"Got to move, dear girl," she said. "As for that Amelia creature, I'll give you one warning: Things are never as they appear, but especially with women like her! Ask about the necklace and what really happened. Ask about the friend what aren't no gentleman."

Tucking Mrs. O'Connor's words and advice into a corner of my thoughts for later consideration, I turned to the glowering, red-faced woman who loomed in the doorway, waiting. "Did you say there is a new Chinese cook?" I asked.

"There is," she muttered. "Can't fold a napkin decently, but at least she don't sit in bed till noon swilling gin!" That last was directed at Mrs. O'Connor.

"It were tea, my fine woman, and if you abuse me further

I'll quit, I will, and then what will your mistress do for the buns and scones?" Mrs. O'Connor answered.

"I will accompany you," I said. Mrs. Wilkinson's maid did not look pleased, but neither did she protest.

The Wilkinson home was one of the new mansions on Commonwealth Avenue, built in the newly revived Greek style with tall pillars, whitewashed, and with enough rooms for an army of people, not simply a family. But then, Mrs. Wilkinson was one of those matrons who desire a spacious, luxurious home and a maid for every room. Entry to this fashionable home presented a difficulty, since Mrs. O'Connor would be required to use the side entrance and I the front. Yet I did not wish to offend that good lady who had proven so helpful, so I broke yet another rule and went in by the servants' entrance, arm in arm with Mrs. O'Connor.

There was a row in the back rooms when we entered. The lady of the house, Mrs. Wilkinson herself, was shouting at a frightened young girl. "On the left!" Mrs. Wilkinson screeched. "Serve from the left, take from the right. Cannot you keep it straight? How can you serve at the buffet if you can't even handle a simple breakfast table?"

I cleared my throat.

"Are you the florist's assistant?" she asked, turning and looking me up and down. The maid fled.

"I am not, Mrs. Wilkinson. I am Miss Louisa Alcott."

She looked at me askance and then, remembering her manners, uttered some niceties about my father, with whom she had a superficial acquaintanceship. The year before, Mr. Wilkinson had had Father give several "conversations" in their best parlor, and since then the Wilkinsons had called themselves "Friends of the Philosopher" and made much show of giving yearly donations to certain charities.

"But you have come in through the servants' entrance!" declared Mrs. Wilkinson, confused.

To her apparent disapproval, I asked if I might speak with her new Chinese cook.

"To what purpose, Miss Alcott?" she asked, now worried that I planned to steal her employee.

Having witnessed the display of temper with which this woman treated a minor discrepancy of table service, I decided against mentioning that her new cook might be needed for inquiries into a murder investigation. I told a very small lie.

"I think I may have met her before and wish to determine if so," I said. "She made a wonderful salad of noodles and I would like the recipe."

"I know the salad! She is preparing it for me. Well, I think that is not a difficulty. This way, Miss Alcott. I will show you to the kitchen myself." I followed behind Mrs. Wilkinson's wide, swaying green skirts, through a narrow tunnel downstairs, and then into a kitchen the size of the entire ground floor of our little cottage in Walpole.

"We are busy, as you see," said haughty Mrs. Wilkinson. "Dances are so much effort, but they must be given, I suppose; else how will good society continue?"

Busy indeed. A dozen people worked at various chores, basting meats, chopping vegetables, whipping cream for cakes, piling meringues for baking. The noise was deafening, for the cooks shouted back and forth at one another as they worked, and so did not notice our approach.

In the far corner, kneading a large ball of dough, was a small woman I believed was the cook I had seen so very briefly at Mrs. Percy's house. She was in a brown plaid woolsey dress, not a blue tunic and trousers, yet her face with its large upturned dark eyes was familiar.

She must have felt my eyes on her. She looked up, her serene expression turning to horror.

CHAPTER TEN

A Thief Is Captured

SHE REMEMBERS ME from Mrs. Percy's house, I thought. Too late, I noticed the door, immediately at her back.

"What is her name?" I asked Mrs. Wilkinson.

"I can't remember. Some outlandish thing, Meh-ki, I think. Why? I assure you, Miss Alcott—"

"Meh-ki!" I called. "Please. I just want to speak with you." I forced my way past the salad cook, past a woman balling melon (melon! in the middle of winter!), the pastry chef who was twisting dough into swans' necks, the meat roaster who was larding chickens, toward that back corner, toward Mrs. Percy's former cook. Meh-ki watched me, knife now in hand, noodle paste forgotten, the terror in her eyes increasing every second.

"Meh-ki!" I called again. Next to me a pan clattered to the ground; I had bumped into a wooden dish rack. There were groans, curses, white-aproned bodies throwing themselves in my way as they scurried to pick up pans and pots.

Meh-ki gave me one last look, then was out the door.

I followed, but she ran down the lane next to the house and out into the busy, congested street, freeing herself of apron and kitchen cap as she ran; now she was just one of many women dressed in winter brown, rushing off to somewhere else because there was a hint of snow in the air. Except that Meh-ki hurried for other reasons. I lost sight of her.

Where would she go?

Mrs. Wilkinson was furious, so furious she actually stamped her foot. The other workers in the kitchen, already restored to order, looked down or giggled into their sleeves when I returned to offer an apology and a very limited explanation that I wished to ask Meh-ki a question or two about an earlier employer.

"The noodle salad was to be the centerpiece of the buffet! What am I to do now? What if she doesn't return?" Mrs. Wilkinson roared, her only concern the impression her midnight feast might make.

"Put the melon balls in the center," I suggested. "Father always says fruit is the masterpiece of a meal."

"Does he? Does he?" Mrs. Wilkinson grew thoughtful and clapped her hands together beneath her chin. Father's name carried the weight of authority in this household. "It is unusual, fruit in the center. Perhaps, perhaps."

I left Mrs. Wilkinson's after Mrs. O'Connor promised that she would send me a note when, and if, she saw Meh-ki again.

That afternoon I again visited Suzie Dear in jail, accompanied by Sylvia. Guilt tensed my shoulders, for I was making little progress with Reverend Ezra's shirts, and he had

wished them done before Christmas; certainly if he knew the circumstances—a woman murdered, a killer loose in Boston—he would understand? Even if he did not, this mystery seemed much more important to me than his wardrobe. What was not less important to me, though, were the presents I had to purchase for my family in Walpole, Christmas presents that could not be purchased if I did not receive payment from the reverend. Lizzie's portfolio sat in Mr. Crowell's window, waiting.

"You are muttering to yourself, Louy," said Sylvia, following behind me up the darkened stairway of the city jail. "Whatever is the matter?"

"The reverend's shirts," I said. "However will I get them finished, with mediums being murdered and jewelry stolen and cooks fleeing before me?"

"I do feel guilty." Sylvia sighed. "If I hadn't insisted you come to the séance with me . . . But then, it wasn't all my doing. I didn't know Mrs. Percy would get herself killed. Oh, dear," she said. "I felt better looking at your back. You should see your face, Louy."

"Suzie," I called when we were upstairs, and standing outside the barred door of her prison cell. She was curled up on a little cot, a dirty blanket drawn up under her chin.

"Miss Alcott?" She sat up and peered at us through sleepy eyes. Her hair tumbled about her face, and her nose was red from weeping. "Oh, you have to get me out of here, Miss Alcott! I can't stand it, I can't! There's a madman next door, rants all night, and the food is something awful. And I'm so lonely!"

"For Mr. Nichols?" I asked.

"How did you know about that?" She pouted.

"I went to see him," I said. "He was disappointed that you missed your rendezvous that morning. Suzie, you must tell us everything that happened the day that Mrs. Percy was murdered."

"Missed me, did he?"

"Sorely," I exaggerated.

Sylvia brought us two ladder-back chairs from the far end of the hall, and we sat facing the prisoner.

"Well, it's like this," Suzie began, combing her hair back with her fingers. "Mrs. Percy weren't only a medium. She had other business interests."

"Such as?" I prompted.

"Mr. Nichols, her stepbrother, would find jewelry, nice pieces, and since he don't have a shop of his own, Mrs. Percy would sell them for him."

"It's called fencing," I corrected. "And by find, might I assume you mean steal?"

"Not always," said Suzie, plainly hurt. "This he bought fair and square, I know. I was with him." She produced from under the collar of her much-rumpled dress a little locket. Half a locket, actually, half a heart.

"Mrs. Percy had other interests," I said. "Tell me what happened that day."

Suzie tucked her locket back into the stained lace of her dress and sat upright like a schoolgirl about to recite a lesson.

"Well, the night before I didn't sleep well. I thought I heard voices downstairs. A man and a woman, Mrs. Percy being the woman. They were quarreling. Very angry, they were. So I put a pillow over my head and tried to go back to sleep."

"You were accustomed to hearing voices downstairs at night," I guessed.

"Mrs. Percy were a great one for company of the gentlemanly sort," Suzie agreed.

"Was it by any chance her stepbrother, Mr. Nichols?" asked Sylvia, who had been listening intently.

"No. Eddie's voice I would know. This one I wasn't certain of. It sounded familiar but I couldn't place it. Maybe one of her clients, the one with the curly black hair. It were a deep voice."

Mr. Barnum, I thought. "Could you hear what they were saying?" I asked.

"Something about misdeeds, about it costing too much, from the gentleman. Mrs. Percy laughed and said he was to leave her alone, or pay."

"And then what?"

"It got quiet. I figured they were making up. I heard the sound that Mrs. Percy's brandy cabinet makes when it's opened. The door squeaks. Then I heard the cook, the Chinese woman, moving around downstairs. Her bedroom is right under mine. Sometimes she gets up early to bake yeast bread, and I didn't think nothing of it. I went back to sleep. Needed my beauty rest, you know." She grinned. She'd had an appointment with Eddie the next day, she explained.

"Well," she continued, "when I got up the next morning, the cook was gone and Mrs. Percy was locked into her preparation room, where she'd been sitting the night before. She fell asleep in there. Least, I thought she was asleep." Suzie yawned. "Don't sleep well here. Wish I had some of those sleeping powders of hers. Or maybe not," she corrected.

"Continue with the events, please."

"In the morning I run down, quick, to the kitchen, to get the breakfast tray for Mrs. Percy, and lordy, was that kitchen a mess! Broken plates everywhere, things spilled, and that cook up and gone. Nowhere to be found. I looked in her room, and she had taken her valise and hairbrush and left. Left me in a bad spot, she did!"

"Time's up," shouted a man's voice up the stairs.

"Ten more minutes, please!" I shouted back. There was a deep muttering, a clanging of keys, but the footsteps retreated and I was allowed more time. Being Mr. Bronson Alcott's daughter carried some weight.

"Quick, Suzie," I said. "What more can you tell me about the cook?"

"Mrs. Percy hired her a year ago. Our other cook had just quit to get married and move to Worcester. Mrs. Percy found her in a poorhouse. Mrs. Percy goes—went—to poorhouses sometimes, just to get gossip for her séances. Kicked-out servant girls will talk on and on about their employers, you know. Reveal all sorts of things."

"And what had Meh-ki revealed?"

"Nothing that I know, but Mrs. Percy kept saying how lucky she was, that first week that Meh-ki was there. I thought she just liked the cooking. Meh-ki did tell me once that she'd been working in New York, but her employer died and she came north, hearing there was work in Boston. She seemed afraid, though, and would never say why. Almost never left the house, 'cept to go to market. Said once she was going to go back to New York as soon as she could get the money."

"Did she have any visitors?"

"None that I knew of."

Heavy footsteps came down the darkened hall. Keys jangled. A man with a shock of black hair falling into his eyes glared at us. "Time's up," he repeated. "You were to have fifteen minutes with the prisoner; that's all. Don't know what females are doing in a jail, anyway. Not fitting."

"Hey! Ain't I a lady?" Suzie protested, tossing back her dirty, uncombed hair.

"Yeah. And I'm the king of France." He snorted.

Outside, in front of the courthouse we encountered Constable Cobban, who was returning from some errand or investigation. He tipped his cap and stopped to speak, which delighted Sylvia and pained me, for I must now tell him I had again interfered and perhaps caused some difficulty. I would have told him eventually, reader, but I had hoped for a moment of peace to gather my thoughts. Fate willed otherwise.

"Afternoon, ladies. Having a little visit with your Suzie?" He grinned at me and nodded politely at Sylvia, lifting his head up and back in an exaggerated gesture to show that he wore the muffler she had knitted for him.

"She needs a bath," said Sylvia. "Are there facilities?"

Cobban blushed. "I'll bring in my mother and have her attend to it, Miss Sylvia."

"How is your mother?" I asked, delaying. I had never met this undoubtedly long-suffering woman, but I imagined her as a feminine form of her son, tall and lanky, carrot-haired and freckled.

"You are withholding," he said. "I know that look in your eyes. They turn hazel instead of green."

"Now that you mention it, I should report that I found

Mrs. Percy's cook," I said, using one booted foot to wipe snow off the other so that I would not have to meet his gaze.

"Splendid. Where might I find her?"

"Well, that is the difficulty. She saw me, and fled."

Cobban took off his cap and slapped it in his palm; he turned in a little circle, shaking his head and muttering, probably cursing, under his breath. Temper often accompanies hair of that hue.

"That beats all," he said. "You couldn't have sent word to me first, before sending another suspect into hiding?"

"She was already in hiding, and there was no time to send for you," I said firmly.

Sylvia reached up and tied more tightly the muffler about his throat. Reader, I have mentioned before that young Cobban blushed frequently, but at this touch from Sylvia he turned livid purple and then whiter than snow. Sylvia smiled at him and he began to tremble.

"All is not lost," I said.

"Indeed it is not," said he, looking at Sylvia.

"I refer to the matter of Mrs. Percy's cook." I sighed and stamped my feet, which were growing cold.

"Of course," said Cobban, shaking himself as does a person awaking from a dream. "Explain yourself, Miss Louisa. Please."

"We might make inquiries of Mr. Deeds."

"Deeds?" said Sylvia and Cobban in unison.

"I learned the cook's name today. It is Meh-ki. And Agatha Percy delivered a message to Mr. Deeds from Mickey, or we heard it as Mickey. I believe she meant Meh-ki."

"How could she?" asked Sylvia. "Meh-ki is very much alive if you just saw her this morning."

"As is my sister, whose arrival she announced," I reminded my friend. "I begin to suspect that Mrs. Percy's messages had more in them than met the eye . . . rather, the ear, of course."

"We'll pay him a little visit. Let me just go inside for a moment and tell them I'll be away a bit longer," said Cobban, rushing up the courthouse steps. He turned back to wave at Sylvia, as if they would be parted for years, not moments, and stumbled in the snow.

"Oh, Sylvia." I sighed in irritation.

"I know. Isn't it wonderful? He wore the muffler," she whispered in delight. "I think Father will be pleased."

"VERY, VERY INCONVENIENT," Mrs. Deeds fumed at us over her maid's shoulder when Sylvia, Cobban, and I arrived at her doorstep half an hour later. "I am most busy, and wish to forget this sordid business with Mrs. Percy. She was a great disappointment." Mrs. Deeds was dressed plainly in blue wool and a white cap with no necklaces, no bracelets, no jeweled rings, quite unlike my memory of her from the séance. Why this lack of adornment from a woman who prided herself on her jewels? I wondered.

"It is important," insisted Cobban.

She glared, then ushered us in.

Mr. and Mrs. Ezra Deeds resided at 6 Newbury Street in a large, cluttered house filled with acquisitions: cuckoo clocks from the Black Forest, rows and rows of glass vases and paperweights from Venice, painted fans from the Japans, tapestries of peacock feathers from India, huge bouquets of silk flowers. Her home felt like the interior of a shop, the type that sells mementos and gifts and never a truly needed item. The windows were hung with four layers of lace and draperies; each table—and there were many, all located where more sensible people might wish to circulate—was covered with three cloths each, one atop the other.

"I trust this will be brief?" she said when we were seated in her back parlor, where the furnishings were less fussy and had a slightly worn quality that better suited me. "I am expecting guests."

I hazarded a guess then as to why she was dressed so plainly. She was not expecting guests, at least not guests of the usual variety. At last, my luck had changed, but I could not inform Cobban until we had a more private moment.

"We'll need to speak with Mr. Deeds as well," said the young constable.

She glared, knit her brows, decided a veneer of politeness would work well in the situation. "Very well. I'll go bring him in. He is working on his insect collection. He discovered a strange moth in his wardrobe last evening." Her smile was forced.

"Yes?" asked the beleaguered husband a few minutes later. He stood in the doorway of the parlor, his stooped posture and genuine surprise indicating he rarely was summoned from his collection to the parlor, even the back parlor.

"Please be seated," said Cobban. "I have some questions for you about Meh-ki."

"Who?" asked Mr. Deeds, scratching his head, ruffling the thin gray hair that fringed out from a bald circle like a monk's tonsure.

"Mrs. Percy's cook," I said.

"Oh, that woman!" Mrs. Deeds exclaimed. "Bad enough that her séances were a bore, and then she died and upset my schedule for a week, for I had counted on her to come and do a private séance for a party I was giving." Mrs. Deeds seemed very put out that her crystal gazer had had the bad taste to die before fulfilling her social engagements.

"Mrs. Percy's cook's name is Meh-ki, and I believe that Mrs. Percy gave you a message regarding her," Cobban said to Mr. Deeds, who had begun wringing his hands.

Mrs. Deeds glared at the clock on the mantelpiece.

"Couldn't have," said Mr. Deeds. "I don't know her."

"The message was from Michaela," said Mrs. Deeds, still staring at the clock.

"So we thought. Actually, I believe Mrs. Percy said Meh-ki," I said. "The exact message was . . ." I took out my notebook, in which I had recorded the séance the evening I returned home, the better to have the details should I wish them for one of my "blood and thunder" stories. ". . . was that Meh-ki was afraid of something, that she had a secret, and there was a cost. Ring any bells, Mr. Deeds?"

"No," he insisted, looking genuinely perplexed. "How could she have a message for me, if we have never met?"

Cobban, who had taken out his own notebook, slapped it shut and rubbed his fingers over its worn leather cover. Mrs. Deeds cleared her throat and made a show of looking at the timepiece pinned to her dress. She cleared her throat. "I am somewhat pressed for time," she said again. Mr. Deeds shrugged and looked confused.

We rose. Cobban shook Mr. Deeds's hand in a way that seemed to indicate sympathy, I thought.

Outside, the snow fell heavily, a beautiful snow that made me joyous with one breath and anxious with the next, for it reminded me of Christmas, and the presents I wished to buy for my family, and the shirts that must be stitched before such presents could be purchased.

"I think we should wait a bit across the street, behind that shelter for the omnibus," I said, for I had formed a speculation about why Mrs. Deeds had forsworn all jewels that afternoon.

"It's cold, Louy!" complained Sylvia.

"It will be worth the wait, if I am correct. Button your coat, Sylvia, and pull the collar tighter."

Cobban undid the muffler from about his neck and put it around Sylvia's. She gazed at him with adoring eyes.

We stood in silence for ten minutes, shifting our weight back and forth from foot to foot and wrapping our arms about ourselves for greater warmth. Because I had given away my gloves my fingers were numb, and I longed for the warmth of Auntie Bond's hearth. But I was correct; the wait in the cold was worthwhile.

At exactly three o'clock, a closed carriage pulled up in front of Mrs. Deeds's home; a man in a high-collared coat and low-brimmed hat descended from the carriage. He looked furtively about before climbing the steps to Mrs. Deeds's door.

"It is Eddie Nichols," I said, "come to sell her some jewelry. That's why she was wearing none. When you are to bargain for a good price, it is better not to wear your wealth about your neck."

Cobban let out a low whistle. "Ladies, return to your homes. I'll take care of this."

"LOUY, I HAVE never seen you stitch with such determination," Lizzie said to me later that evening. I was finally warm, with dry stockings and house slippers, a thick shawl over my shoulders, and a cup of hot chocolate on the table at my side. When I had returned home Auntie Bond's house smelled of cloves and oranges, for she had been baking her famous fruit-cake, and the scent of that seasonal delight drove me to a frenzy to finish the reverend's shirt order—or at least diminish it, so that I might move closer to the reward, the promised payment.

"I am far behind," I told her. "There. Two shirts done. I shall finish the third this evening, I think."

"Nine more to go. And the cuffs need double-stitching, and there should be a touch of embroidery on the button placket. I shall do that."

"It doesn't seem fair, Lizzie," I confessed. "I am sewing shirts to purchase a Christmas present for you, yet you are doing the work as well!"

"Oh, Louy." She came and knelt by me and put her blond head on my knees. "Don't you know it is gift enough to have this time with my sister? I have you, and letters from Father and Marmee, and a piano, and a hearth. What else could I need?"

A red leather portfolio of Liszt, I thought. And to help read the music, a series of lessons with Signor Massimo, who teaches only the best of the best and has agreed to work with the winner of Mr. Crowell's lottery.

"Speaking of letters, there is a note just arrived for you, Louisa," said Auntie Bond, coming in to join us. She handed me an envelope and sat down in her favorite chair, a soft chenille one near the hearth.

"From Constable Cobban," I said, recognizing the writing on the envelope. I tore it open. "Mr. Edward Nichols has been detained for questioning about certain thefts and the distribution of jewelry of questionable provenance."

"Justice is done," said Auntie Bond, who had been following my adventures in the aftermath of Mrs. Percy's death.

I had half expected Constable Cobban to write me that there had been a fond reunion, albeit brief, between Suzie Dear and Eddie Nichols, but it had not fallen out quite that way.

He called her a snitch and several other less pleasant names, and when he passed by her cell she reached out and pulled at his hair. She took a good chunk of it. He was dazed by her violence, but then the name-calling grew very nasty and loud. I was relieved that Miss Sylvia was not there to hear that language.

Poor Suzie, I thought. She had thought herself in love, I suspected. And poor Mr. Cobban. Did he realize yet what was in store for him?

CHAPTER ELEVEN

The Bride's Tale

I SAT UP stitching long past the moment when Lizzie, sighing, stretched and yawned and went up to her bed; long past Auntie Bond's cheerful, "Good night, Louisa, sleep tight," till the last embers in the hearth had turned gray and cold, till my fingertips were numb, picking pieces of white linen from the basket and matching sleeve to shoulder, front seam to side seam, doggedly stitching what are known as French seams, twice-stitched first on the right side then outside in so that the stitches don't show and there are no unfinished edges. It is, in the correct frame of mind, satisfying work, almost meditative, though I doubt Father and Mr. Emerson have so meditated despite their passion for Transcendence.

One thought ran through my mind over and over: If the message about Meh-ki wasn't for Mr. Deeds, as I strongly suspected it was not, since he seemed incapable of guile, then for whom was it meant? And why had Mrs. Percy taken such a roundabout path to deliver the message?

I put down the shirtsleeve and took my notebook out of my pocket.

Mrs. Percy had first asked Meh-ki with whom she wished to speak. Meh-ki's spirit or presence, or whatever Mrs. Percy pretended it was, did not answer. She had then asked Meh-ki if she had a secret, and there had been two taps. Yes. And then the only other part of that "message" had been from Mrs. Percy herself: "When the soul's ether is so unwilling to make itself known, it desires only continued secrecy. There is a cost. Am I understood?"

There is a cost. Am I understood? Was Mrs. Percy threatening someone in the room? Asking for payment? Who?

Immediately after had come the "message" for Sylvia: "Marry," and then that strange garbled deep voice that had issued from Mrs. Percy saying, "Marry in haste, repent, repent; marry out of your station, woe, woe. But marry well, and prosper after. None will know."

None will know. There is a cost. Am I understood? None will know. The secret message had been hidden in the others. I flipped two pages back, to the message to Mr. Barnum: "Forgiveness rather than vengeance. Women are easily led astray and abused by those with power."

Tomorrow, I decided, I would pay a visit to Miss Amelia Snodgrass, and then to Mr. Barnum. I looked at the pile of unstitched linen shirts next to my chair and sighed. I was making such little progress! Nine more to go before the full order could be delivered to the reverend and payment made. Nine more shirts before I could purchase Lizzie's sheet music and lessons with Signor Massimo; how long would Mr. Crowell be willing to hold them for me? Mrs. Percy, I complained to her in my thoughts, why couldn't you have waited till after Christmas?

She answered immediately. At least, the voice that was revealing the story of "Agatha's Confession" answered:

> *At last, feeling that concealment was ungenerous and unwise, I went to Philip, saying calmly, though my heart was nearly broken by the sacrifice I tried to make: "Philip, if I have lost your affection, give me at least your confidence. If you love Clara, do not hide it from me, and I will break the tie that has become an irksome fetter, and henceforth try to find my happiness in making yours."*
>
> *This touched him deeply, as I knew it would. He drew me fondly to him, saying half gaily and half sorrowfully while his frank eyes looked down into mine:*
>
> *"I am but fascinated by her beauty, little friend. But tell her to be less lovely and less kind; it will be better for us both. Indeed, I do not love her; so forget your fears."*

For this is the truth of human nature, kind but imperfect reader. We speak in half-truths and know not even our own selves; we mistake fear for virtue and are foolishly surprised when passion turns to violence.

Another hour later, exhausted by the long day but with four more pages added to my story, finally I joined Lizzie in our shared bedroom and slept deeply, dreamlessly.

THE NEXT AFTERNOON Sylvia joined me for the visit to Miss Snodgrass. During the walk there we did not speak of Constable Cobban, but she did speak of her father, whom she insisted again was visiting her in dreams and speaking to her.

"Father sees my loneliness," Sylvia said quietly, putting her arm through mine.

"Are you so lonely?" I asked.

"I have not mentioned this before," said my friend, "but when I see the joy on your face as you think of the Christmas gifts you wish to purchase for your family, then I think, 'And what gifts will I present, and to whom?' Mother has everything. Who has need of a gift from me? Other than you, of course. Poor Louy, your hands are blue from the cold. You should not have given away your gloves."

"Gloves are easier to replace than a heart that has been given," I said gently.

"He is a good man. Kind and honest," Sylvia said. "As for those plaid suits, I will see to it that they are replaced. Ah. This is the house, isn't it?" We climbed the steps of the porch and knocked.

Miss Snodgrass's maid, an ancient, hobbling creature who muttered constantly, opened the door of the old Beacon Hill home and took our coats. She admitted us to a back parlor, where Miss Snodgrass sat before her tapestry frame, working a pretty scene of woodlands and pheasants. Miss Snodgrass wore bright green and purple; in her own home, it would seem, she abandoned that strange taste for nondescript brown garments. In fact, she looked quite festive compared to her parlor furnishings, which were ancient and mismatched, of excellent quality but in need of new upholstery. The stenciled walls were faded, the leaded windows dull and distorted with great age.

"How kind of you to visit," said Amelia Snodgrass with evident lack of sincerity. She paused in her stitching, her right hand holding needle and crimson thread poised over the frame. The rules of calling would be rigorously followed, I assumed. For ten minutes we would have to make small talk and drink tea before I could announce the purpose of the visit.

The tea tray was brought in. Miss Amelia Snodgrass poured tea in a way I could only dream about. Not a drop missed its mark. When she passed me the cup and saucer, there was no rattle of china on china. Her aim was sharp, her hand absolutely steady. For the required ten minutes we spoke of the weather, which was nasty, and the Christmas decorations in the store windows, which were lovely.

Of course, the tea was appallingly weak, more dirty water than orange pekoe, but I had come to expect that in houses where the family tree had more items in it than the family bank account.

"You have heard of the circumstances of Mrs. Percy's death?" I asked finally, sipping the weak tea.

"The death notice indicated some questions of cause," she said. "Some seed cake, Miss Alcott?"

"Murder, probably," said Sylvia.

"Oh, dear." Miss Snodgrass put her cup and saucer on the table and folded her hands in her lap. "How dreadful."

"Forgive me, Miss Snodgrass, but I would not have thought you the type to frequent séance parlors," I said. "How did you choose Mrs. Percy?"

"Now you will learn of my indiscretion," said Miss Snodgrass, sighing. "I have a curiosity about such things and heard from a friend that Mrs. Percy could provide an amusing afternoon."

"No more than curiosity drew you there? Yes, I will have a piece of seed cake, thank you."

"Well, perhaps a little more. Will this piece do? I had lost a necklace and thought she might be able to tell me its whereabouts. Silly, I know, but I've heard such things happen."

"A valuable necklace?" I asked.

"Oh, it's quite hideous, really. But a family piece. I was at a house party, and it disappeared. Isn't it a classic! Mother warned, 'Dear, don't take the real thing with you to a country house full of strangers; take the glass pearls.' But one is young and, yes, vain, and one takes the real thing. And it disappears. Mother was right. As usual."

"I know exactly what you mean," Sylvia exclaimed. "I lost a garnet bracelet at an ice-skating party last winter, and thought I would never hear the end of it from Mother. I think I do know who took it, though. Warren offered to clean it for me after I fell into a drift and then I became all distracted because Annabelle would attempt a spin and fall and injure her ankle, and by then I had forgotten the bracelet. Two months later I saw it on a housemaid at Warren's birthday party. She was very pretty, that maid." Sylvia's voice trailed off. I had kicked her, very gently of course, under the table.

Miss Snodgrass sipped her tea.

"How terrible for you!" I exclaimed to Miss Snodgrass, when Sylvia had lapsed into silence. "And was the thief caught?"

"I did not say it was stolen," said Miss Snodgrass. "I am quite certain it fell into the well when I leaned over it. Mother never forgave me." Miss Snodgrass smiled, as if we discussed a lost pin, not a family heirloom. She was determined to make light of it, which suggested to me the loss was very serious.

"And was that the meaning of Mrs. Percy's message, do you think, when she yelled, 'The necklace!'?"

"My dear Miss Alcott," she said. "That was a message for Mrs. Deeds, was it not? It had nothing to do with me."

"How shockingly bad my memory is," I agreed. "Is that a portrait of your mother?" I looked at the wall behind the settee, where a group of disagreeable-looking paintings had been circled around a wreath of silk flowers. There were four men with beards of varying length to distinguish them, and one woman who looked, I imagined, as Amelia herself would look in another twenty-five years, and I understood why so many women feel the need to marry sooner rather than later.

"That is Mama," she said coldly. "She died six months ago. I must wait the full year of mourning before I can marry, of course."

"And is that the necklace that fell into the well?" I asked, for the woman in the portrait wore a collar of pearls and diamond drops.

"Yes. I was to have been married in it. Family tradition, you know," she answered coldly. Her little finger crooked over the teapot. "More tea? I don't know what I'll say to Wilmot; he is so looking forward to seeing the necklace. He had a bracelet specially made to match, and earrings as well. They are to be my Christmas present." Her lack of enthusiasm for the gift was apparent.

"The necklace looks strangely like the one Mrs. Deeds wore to the séance," I said.

"What a coincidence," agreed Amelia Snodgrass.

"I understand Mrs. Deeds returned her necklace to Mrs. Percy. It was only on loan."

"Really? It was returned?" Miss Snodgrass lifted an eyebrow, which was, for her, a gesture of great passion.

"Does your fiancé not know of the theft of the necklace? I mean the loss, of course. Down the well. It wasn't in the papers?" I asked.

"Of course it wasn't in the papers, Miss Alcott. Whatever are you thinking, a name like Snodgrass bandied about on the same page as items of horse theft and pickpocketing. And I have not yet found the appropriate time to inform Wilmot. . . ."

I was beginning to suspect there might be a considerable list of missing items about which the fiancé did not know—the better pieces of silver now represented by empty spaces on the sideboard, the bright patches of unfaded wallpaper where oil paintings had once hung, the paste necklace at Miss Amelia's throat, cheap jewelry worn now not to protect the "real stuff" but to replace it entirely.

"Who was at the country house, Miss Snodgrass?" I asked, leaning forward.

"You are full of questions," she said, and her tone let me know that my curiosity was now bordering on a lapse of manners. "You are friends with that awful Constable Cobban, are you not?"

Sylvia, sitting next to me on the settee, stiffened.

"Such a strange acquaintance for a young woman of a good family," Miss Snodgrass sniffed. "Mrs. Percy was there, among others. It was how we first met."

I rose from my chair and moved closer to the portrait of her mother for a better examination. How the woman frowned! If I were to pay an artist and sit before him for many hours, I would at least smile a bit.

"Very lovely," I said, touching a chipped porcelain rose-bud that rested on a crowded shelf beneath the portrait.

"Limoges," said Amelia Snodgrass. "A wedding present from my grandfather to my grandmother."

"I'm sure she was pleased with the gift," I said. "Was Mrs. Percy's brother there, as well? Mr. Edward Nichols? At this house party?"

Amelia poured us more tea. "Let me think." She sighed. "Yes, I believe so. Was that his name? I forget. Nichols, you say?" As she put down the teapot she splashed tea over an album of photos that sat squarely on the table. I am sure, do-mestic reader, you know the type of album I indicate: It is invariably trimmed with lace and hand-marbled paper and is exceedingly heavy and so cannot be moved quickly out of the way of unexpected tides of tea or lemonade or hot chocolate. The liquid always lands on such albums, always leaves a large stain, and many a family has suffered days, weeks of tan-trums over such events.

"Oh, dear," said Amelia Snodgrass calmly. "I do hope Papa's portrait hasn't been wetted." But she made no move to clean the spill or examine the damage. Instead, she rose with a graceful smoothing of her skirt, indicating that the visit was now over. She had said very little, and revealed much.

"That wedding will be an awful affair," Sylvia said when we were outside again in the chill winter air. "I know the kind. I think I will elope. Won't that be exciting, Louy, an elopement? No one will approve, of course, at least not for a while."

"I think Amelia might have preferred an elopement herself." I took Sylvia's arm, for the sidewalk was icy and my boots very thin from wear.

"Elope with Wilmot Green? He is very wealthy, but I don't think he's quite bright enough to know how to lean a ladder against a wall," Sylvia said, pulling her fur muffler tighter about her neck. My friend was acquainted with most of Boston society, thanks to her persistent mother's attempts to marry her off.

"I wasn't referring to Mr. Green, but to Miss Snodgrass. I think she is very eager for this wedding to occur before . . ."

"Before what, Louy?"

"Before Mr. Green discovers the loss of the necklace and the extent of Miss Snodgrass's impoverishment, and before he discovers . . . Oh, I really shouldn't say. It is cruel to gossip in this way, when a woman's reputation is at stake."

"Now, Louy, I insist you tell all! I will not repeat a word of it, and how can I assist you if you withhold information?" She stamped her foot.

"You sound like Constable Cobban," I said. "But let that pass for now. The gossip is this, and you are never to repeat it. I suspect Miss Snodgrass was involved with Eddie Nichols."

"Suzie Dear *and* Miss Snodgrass? Oh! The cad!"

"He is a man of some charm, when not in jail, and she is a complex woman. They were at a house party together. Her necklace might have been taken in a moment of intimacy. That's why she never reported the theft. That's why she never tried to have Eddie Nichols arrested for it. He would be able to give information of a very secretive nature and claim she had given the piece to him. And I think that's why she was at the séance: to beg for her necklace back from his associate, Mrs. Percy. Perhaps to try to buy it back at a fraction of its real cost, so that she might wear it at her wedding."

"Oh, Louy, I would be furious!" Sylvia said.

"As was Miss Snodgrass, I'm certain. Furious. 'Hell hath no fury like a woman scorned.' Bad poem but often a correct sentiment. I wonder exactly how furious Miss Snodgrass can become? Because of course Mrs. Percy, being a woman of business and not a woman of conscience, would not have returned the necklace or sold it back for less than full value, since she knew full well that Miss Snodgrass could do nothing about the theft without ruining her own reputation."

By habit we turned in the direction of Boston Common for our walk in the bracing air. There was just enough snow on the ground to roll a good snowman, should a child be so inclined. I picked up a handful, made a ball, and threw it at a tree.

"Good aim," said Sylvia. She tried the same experiment, but her snowball went amiss from the tree and instead knocked the top hat off a gentleman who was also out strolling a few yards ahead of us.

A group of young boys went scurrying and laughing in the other direction, certain they were to be blamed rather than the ladies. "Here now, stop that!" the gentleman shouted angrily, turning around.

It was Mr. Phips! I hastened to fetch his hat and brush it off, while Sylvia apologized profusely.

"No harm, no harm," he insisted in a kinder tone after our

apologies. "Young girls are frightful throwers." He chuckled and packed a handful of snow. His ball hit mine, square in the center of the tree trunk.

"Well-done!" I said. "You throw like a champion!"

"I played at sports as a student," he said, stroking the lapels of his greatcoat and rocking back and forth on his heels. "Are you young ladies headed anywhere in particular? May I escort you?" He made a gallant little bow.

"I am buying Uncle Benjamin a new pipe for Christmas. Will you come with me to the tobacconist and help me select one?" I asked. Understanding reader, as concerned as I was with the purchase of Lizzie's present, Marmee and I had agreed that Uncle's present must be purchased first, and packed off through the post in plenty of time for Christmas, to thank him properly for all the hospitality he had shown the Alcott family during a difficult time. Marmee and Father and Abby were still residing rent-free in his Walpole house, and sincere gratitude was in order. I did worry, though, that every quarter spent elsewhere pushed me further from the purchase of Lizzie's music portfolio.

"My dear, it shall delight me," said Mr. Phips. "Take my word, nothing pleases an old man like a new pipe, and I hear there are some excellent meerschaums just in for the holiday season."

"Tell me, Mr. Phips, what do you think of this business with Mrs. Percy?" I asked as we three fell into step together, our feet leaving prints in the freshly fallen snow as we headed in the same direction, toward the little row of shops on the other side of the park.

"That the death was unnatural? Hogwash. She died of a

bad heart. The new Boston police are just trying to prove they earn their keep by inventing crimes. I don't trust that Cobban fellow."

Next to me, I felt Sylvia stiffen again.

"Dr. Roder said she did not die of a diseased heart," I answered.

"Well, if it was a murder, I can't say that I am all that surprised or shocked. Mrs. Percy was a woman of questionable morality. Who else would go into such a business as hers? I would say her past caught up to her."

"You believe no longer in spiritualists and mediums?" asked Sylvia.

"I do not, young lady. Let the dead rest in peace. Poor Emily would have been shocked by such doings. She would have said, 'William, dearest, you should know better!' And I think women should stay at home, where they belong, and certainly not receive strangers in their parlors. I would never have permitted my wife such questionable associations."

"Did you know of Mrs. Percy's association with Eddie Nichols?" I asked, ignoring his last two comments. Men rarely admit how much work can take place at home, in the very parlor they uphold as a bastion of indolence. I thought of the pile of sewing awaiting me in Auntie Bond's parlor.

"Nichols? The fellow who's making so much trouble for poor Barnum? There was talk at the club. It was all hearsay, of course. You know, I think I was pickpocketed during that séance! When I returned to my rooms, my pocket watch was missing, and I would have sworn that when we were sitting in the dark, holding hands, I felt someone standing quite close behind me."

That would have been Suzie Dear, I thought. Richer by another watch.

"How did you meet your wife?" Sylvia asked, being in a romantic frame of mind. I was wondering again about the composition of the circle that Mrs. Percy had formed, with Mr. Phips, the Deedses, Amelia Snodgrass, Mr. Barnum, myself, and Sylvia.

"That is a story both romantic and sad," said Mr. Phips. "I was friends with her fiancé, August Pincher. Yes, she was engaged to him before we had met. August and I served to-gether in China, where he spoke often about Emily Grayling and showed me her portrait. He carried it in his pocket. You wouldn't know it to look at me now, hobbling along with bad knees and gout in the toe, but I was man of action in younger days. I lived boldly."

"And you were a hero in China," I said, repeating what Mr. Barnum had told me. "You saved many lives during the siege of Canton."

"Messy business. Downright ugly," he said. "Too many civilians involved. Battles should be between men who know what they are about, and why. Men trained for the fight and willing." He shook his head with disapproval.

" 'To lead an uninstructed people to war is to throw them away,' " Sylvia quoted. Both Mr. Phips and I turned to look at her. "Well, I did study Confucius for many months," she said with a little smile. Sylvia could be most astonishing.

"War, as terrible as it is, brought me to my beloved wife, may she rest in peace," said Mr. Phips. "August made me prom-ise that if anything happened to him, I would return that little portrait to her, with his eternal love. I kept that promise."

Mr. Phips reached into his coat and brought forth a very old-fashioned, finely painted enamel portrait of a woman's head and shoulders. She was a brunette, with great, sad dark eyes and a long, regal nose.

"Oh!" Sylvia gasped. "How very romantic!"

"And Emily Grayling became Mrs. William Phips," I guessed. "That you have the locket still in your possession would indicate she wished you to keep it. And since the locket is obviously a love token, then it seems you were able to heal her grief."

"I was greatly honored," agreed Mr. Phips, "to earn the trust of such a devoted and loving woman. For ten years she made me the happiest man on earth."

"What a fine story! And how many children have you, Mr. Phips?" asked Sylvia.

His face clouded. "Joy is limited. We were not blessed."

We were at the tobacconist's by then, and I thought it wise to steer the conversation into less private realms. I pointed at various pipes in the shop window and asked Mr. Phips's opinions, but he was fussy about such matters and we could not agree.

Inside, the store smelled pleasingly of tobacco and wool, masculine scents associated with reading rooms and home studies. I found a small display of pipes in a dark corner. How fanciful they were, long and carved of ivory and wood, with all manner of embellishment.

"Will this do?" I asked Mr. Phips, holding out one I found particularly handsome.

The shopkeeper coughed into his hands and cleared his throat.

"No, no, Miss Louisa!" protested Mr. Phips. "That is for smoking opium! It is a fine specimen, though, I admit. I collect opium pipes—just for show, of course, a sentimental habit left over from my service in China. We'll put this one back on the rack. Consider this pipe, my dear. Any uncle would be most pleased to have it as a Christmas present."

He handed me a rather mundane-looking item, assuring me that the cherry wood would add a pleasant nuance to any tobacco, that the handle was well formed and the pipe a very good one. I purchased it, and was now one dollar and twenty-five cents poorer, and further away than ever from purchasing Lizzie's present. But there was a quarter left over that I could put on my account at the music store.

"I have one more errand to run. Will you both excuse me?" I said when we were again outdoors.

Mr. Phips and Sylvia, chatting merrily about true love and other matters, headed back toward Commonwealth Avenue. I went into the music store. Six of the twelve Liszt portfolios had been sold, and my heart sank.

When I returned home, there was further cause for dismay: a piece of paper, folded and sealed, had been pushed through the mail slot in Auntie Bond's door, addressed to me. The writing seemed masculine, with thick, heavy lines, and in some places the pen had been pressed so deeply it had almost perforated the paper. Its message was simple and direct:

Mind your own affairs. Stay away.

CHAPTER TWELVE

A Misadventure

I HAD THREE jobs before me: to finish the reverend's shirts so that I might purchase the Christmas presents for my family; to complete my story "Agatha's Confession" so that I might send it out and hope for a publication; and to discover the secret of the fate of Mrs. Agatha Percy, the crystal gazer, for of course I would not stay away, or mind my own affairs. Crime is the concern of each citizen. We have an obligation to aid in the restoration of morality, not turn our back on vice.

It would seem obvious that bringing a murderer to justice would require priority over the linens, perhaps even over writing, for if one woman has been murdered there is always the possibility that others might follow, habit and inclination seeming an indication of the murderer's state of soul. This was part of the sickness of our times, that evil could so easily be repeated, Mr. Emerson had once told me. A single act of evil is the crack in the dam; a flood will follow.

Therefore, other people were in danger. Suzie was in jail

and most likely safe there, for the time being, as long as I could find the true murderer and protect Suzie from hanging. The missing cook was either the murderer or another possible victim, since the timing of her departure would suggest she knew much of the strange goings-on in that household. Perhaps she had threatened to turn Mrs. Percy and her stepbrother in to the Boston police. Or perhaps she had murdered and robbed Mrs. Percy herself before fleeing. It is not true that there is honor among thieves.

Miss Snodgrass, another suspect, might be in danger because of her association with Eddie Nichols and her moral lassitude. Eddie had stolen a pearl-and-diamond necklace from her when she had been most vulnerable, and he was also in an excellent position to blackmail her, if she had been silly enough to write love letters to him. Did she still have so-called tender feelings for Mr. Nichols? More important, had she killed Mrs. Percy to get back her stolen necklace? That had been particularly cruel of Mrs. Percy to give the necklace on loan to Mrs. Deeds, and have her wear it to that first séance, where Amelia could not help but see it.

Mrs. Deeds was incomprehensible to me, and just as unamiable because of her habit of knowingly purchasing jewels that had been illegally obtained. Yet like Miss Snodgrass, Mrs. Deeds's own moral lassitude might be placing her in danger. She knew evil things about shady people, and she was talkative if caught off guard. On the other hand, shady people knew evil things about her; could our matron, Mrs. Deeds, have murdered Mrs. Percy to keep her silent?

Was Sylvia in danger? Logic and my heart said no. Sylvia

had been invited to the circle because she was wealthy and easily gulled, but Sylvia had not been a part of the darker deeds of that circle. And Mr. Phips, likewise, had been invited because of his wealth, his desire to speak with his dead wife, and his willingness to pay for that conversation.

Oh, how foolish is humanity!

But Mr. Barnum worried me. I liked the gentleman, yet of all people in that circle, he had excellent reason to wish Mrs. Percy dead, if it were true that she had assisted Eddie Nichols with the forgeries that had brought Barnum to the brink of bankruptcy.

So it was that on the morning after my visit with Miss Snodgrass and my walk on Boston Common with Sylvia and Mr. Phips, it was with some dread that I discovered a letter from Uncle Benjamin next to my place at the breakfast table.

"It just arrived," said Lizzie, pouring coffee into my cup. She had dark circles under her eyes, as if she had been straining her vision and getting inadequate sleep.

"Lizzie, did you practice the piano all of yesterday?" I asked with concern.

She sat heavily in her chair, and a tiny crease appeared between her fair eyebrows. "Yes. I am having such difficulty with a passage from Chopin. I can't get the fingering correctly, and I don't know what to do. I think that today instead of the piano I'll attend to the reverend's shirts."

"We must be close to finished," I said, giving a somewhat hostile glance at the sewing basket in the corner of the room.

"Nowhere near," said Lizzie, pouring herself a cup of coffee.

"Impossible." I stood confused before the open basket, a shirt in each hand. "I finished three shirts, and now there are only two."

Lizzie frowned and bit her bottom lip, as she did when worried.

"One, two," I said, holding them in the air. "Everything else in the basket is piecework waiting to be sewn. Maybe Auntie Bond took the other shirt to be washed and pressed."

"What other shirt, Louisa?" Auntie Bond asked, having just come into the room, still stretching and tucking strands of gray hair back into her bun.

"The reverend's third shirt. Have you taken it for the laundry?"

"I would not touch your sewing basket, Louisa!" protested that kindly lady, somewhat offended. "You have misplaced it."

"Yes," I agreed, crestfallen. Though I knew I had not. They had all been together in the basket. And now, somehow, I was even later than I had thought for finishing the order, for payment, for purchasing Lizzie's portfolio and music lessons. There was porridge with a spoonful of strawberry preserves in the middle for sweetness, and bacon and bread with butter, but I could taste nothing.

"What does Uncle Benjamin say?" Lizzie picked up the envelope that I had not yet opened.

I slit the top with a knife and took out the thick, crisp paper that was Uncle's stationery and read with little interest, still distracted by the missing shirt. Or was I so distracted by Mrs. Percy that I could not even account for my labor?

"Marmee and Father are well," I reported, preoccupied.

"They have had a foot of snow and went sledding, and next week they are to put up a Christmas tree."

"Will we, Louy? Will we put up a Christmas tree?" Lizzie asked with excitement.

"I don't see why not," said Auntie Bond. "I'll take the little table out of the parlor corner, and we can put the tree right there. We'll make a garland, and I have a box of German glass tops and balls, and little silver candleholders for the branches. Oh, how lovely!" Auntie Bond clapped her hands at the wonderful vision she had created.

"We can place our presents under the tree," said Lizzie shyly.

"Marmee says that Uncle Benjamin is sending presents," I said. "A boxful, due to arrive next week. I guess I'd better wrap mine and get them ready for the post."

"What else does Uncle Benjamin say?" asked Lizzie, buttering a piece of bread.

"Not much. Mostly bits and pieces of rumor about Mr. Barnum."

"I like Mr. Barnum very much," Lizzie said.

"You think kindly of everybody." I kissed her on the forehead and went to pace in the garden, to think. For this is what Uncle Benjamin had written:

It's known Barnum has a temper almost as great as his pride, and this situation with Eddie Nichols has been his undoing. He's now in debt to the tune of $40,000, I've heard, all from those bad notes that Nichols forged to pay his gambling debts. Barnum calls his cousin a serpent and a libertine and has pledged to get satisfaction. I've heard a woman was involved as well. There will be a court case, it *is certain, and it will be a blow to his pride. What's worse, he genuinely liked the boy, treated him like a son, and this betrayal has embittered him. They are already making jokes about it at the club. "What did P. T. Barnum say to General Tom Thumb? 'Why, you're as short as my bank account!'" Poor Barnum.*

You asked to know the color of the shawl your mother was knitting for Lizzie. It is blue, kind of lightish rather than deep. Summer-day blue rather than stormy-weather blue.

Love from all here. Your fond uncle embraces you.

If Mr. Barnum was so angry with Eddie Nichols, would he brutally attack Mrs. Percy? Perhaps. The two were conspirators, after all. Mr. Barnum would be returning home to Bridgeport soon. First I needed to speak with him.

"Louy, light the fire in the downstairs sitting room before you go, will you?" called down Auntie Bond, who was rummaging through her sewing room to find the boxes of Christmas ornaments. "And take some caramel toffees with you! I just made the first holiday batch. They're on the hall table."

So distracted was I, the box of lucifer matches ended up in my pocket with the toffees, instead of back on the mantelpiece. Small gestures, even accidental ones, can make such a difference.

Outside of the yarn shop, I saw Constable Cobban coming around the corner toward me. Sylvia was with him, and they were walking arm in arm. They broke apart like guilty children when they saw me. I pretended that I hadn't observed them until Sylvia tucked her hands into her fur muff and we all stood shyly, looking anywhere except at one another's faces, for the embarrassment was great.

"Miss Louisa." Cobban blushed and tipped his hat, and picked a piece of lint off his bright plaid coat sleeve.

"Beautiful day, isn't it!" I said, studying my boots. "Have you come to purchase yarn?"

"I have. I'm knitting socks. The pattern is ever so interesting," said my dearest friend in the world next to my sisters.

"I bumped into Miss Sylvia on the way to see you, Miss Louisa," Cobban explained. "I have news."

"Judging from your expression, it is not good news." I rocked back and forth on my heels and chafed my hands, wishing I had time to knit myself a new pair of gloves.

"Eddie Nichols has posted bail. Seems he had a bit of savings put away. We can't hold him, though he must stand trial, based on what Suzie has said about the stolen goods."

"But what if he was involved in the murder of Mrs. Percy? He will flee!"

"There is nothing to point that way. He insists he was at the theater that night, and he can provide witnesses. Dancers." Cobban grinned. "I checked the alibi. Of course, they would say about anything for a dollar."

"So he is free." I sighed. Poor Suzie. He had used her badly, and now she was in jail, and he was not.

"Well, not quite." Cobban grinned again. "We can't keep him, but Pinkerton men from Cleveland arrived this morning with their own warrant, in pursuit of Mr. Barnum's case against him there. Nichols will be arrested again before he has time for a good shave and bath. Probably already in custody. He'll stand trial in Ohio, for thievery and forgery if nothing else, and if Mr. Barnum is telling the truth."

"At least Nichols will answer for some of his crimes." But

would he answer for all of them? Oh, if only the dead really could speak! Mrs. Percy, I thought, show me the face of your murderer! Tell me his name!

"Mr. Barnum will be pleased by the news, though it won't get him his fortune back." Constable Cobban ended our conversation with a little nod of the head, rather than taking his cap off again. The day was becoming very cold, with a stern wind coming in from the northeast that promised bad weather ahead. Tiny flakes of snow danced around us, the kind of snow that appears when it will soon be too cold for any snow at all. A hard freeze would curl the rhododendron leaves in Auntie Bond's garden and freeze overnight the water in our washbasins. I realized that by thinking about the weather, I was avoiding thinking about Mr. Barnum. Lizzie liked him. So did I.

Before parting, Constable Cobban told me, upon my request, that Mr. Barnum had taken rooms, during his Boston visit, at a boardinghouse on Arlington Street. Why hadn't I noticed this before? He was just seven houses away from Mrs. Agatha D. Percy's home! I must not have been paying close attention when Constable Cobban took our names and addresses. Of course, having just discovered a body, I was reasonably distracted, but this proximity of his address to the victim's surely was of significance. How easily he could have slipped from his rooms, attacked Mrs. Percy, and returned home without even as much as a half hour passing. And wasn't it Mr. Barnum who had showed us how to lock a door from the inside, even though one was standing outside the door? Had he been boasting of his deed?

I dreaded the visit with him. To delay it, I stopped in

front of Mrs. Percy's house. Had the front door finally been locked? I walked up the unswept steps and tried it. It was. I walked around back to the kitchen door, passing the windows that Mr. Phips had broken to gain admittance to Mrs. Percy's preparation room. It had been boarded with planks, but not well enough to keep the snow from seeping in. Again, I thought of that beautiful parquet floor being ruined. There were old footprints in the snow by the back door, old enough that they had melted into a larger shape than the original and then filled in again with new drifting snow, so that I couldn't tell if they had been large or small, man's or woman's. The kitchen door had been forced open by someone else and swung easily in my hand, and there on the floor, where it had been hastily removed and accidentally dropped, lay a solitary man's glove. I picked it up.

I paused there on the doorstep, a sudden thrill of fear making me hesitate. What if someone were inside? The murderer? My chest felt hollowed out; my head was light. Yet I knew I would go in.

The kitchen was dark, because all the curtains had been pulled. Remembering the lucifers in my pocket, I lit a candle I found on a side table. There were wet footsteps on the wooden floor, steps leading to the doorway that connected the kitchen with the pantry, which led into the hallway, which was as dark as night, since Mrs. Percy, for her activities as a medium, had shut out as much light as possible by removing or covering windows.

As I walked, slowly as possible to avoid creaking boards and bumping into furniture, I thought of who might be in the house, and why. Constable Cobban or one of his policemen would have lit a lamp for their work. This person preferred darkness.

Barely breathing, I made my way through the hall, bending low so that the candle might illuminate the floor and I could follow those wet footprints. They led to the circular staircase, and there they stopped, for the staircase had been carpeted.

The house seemed very still. The air was so cold my breath frosted before me. No fires had been lit here since Mrs. Percy's murder. Who was there to light them? Suzie was in jail, the cook had fled and was in hiding, and Mrs. Percy's stepbrother, Eddie Nichols, was being escorted back to Ohio for trial.

Or was he? Had Eddie Nichols avoided a second capture, and was now upstairs, going through his stepsister's possessions, taking anything of value he could discover? Mrs. Percy would have had hiding places, of course, for her good jewels. All women did. Perhaps he knew those places.

A noise, something between a cough and a curse, sounded beneath my feet from under the floorboards of the hall. A cellar. I held my breath for a long while, aware of him below. I did not wish him to be aware of me. When I moved, it was as slowly as in a dream. Candle wax dripped on my hand and I pressed my lips closed against the pain.

There was a door behind the stairs. It was slightly ajar and I could see a gleam of lamplight underneath it.

Moving even more slowly than before, I made my way down the stairs one step at a time. The sixth step squeaked as soon as I put my foot on it.

Quiet was no longer necessary. We were aware of each

other. I moved quickly down the stairs, wishing I had thought to bring a fire iron with me, or even a large pot from the kitchen, for I realized I was completely defenseless and moving toward a person who might be a murderer.

Or it's just a thief, or even one of Mrs. Percy's clients come out of curiosity, I reassured myself. Just a thief, I thought. A thief would be interested in this place, for at the bottom of the stairs I saw that Mrs. Percy's cellar was a bare dirt floor with several impressions in the dirt, as if things had been buried, and the walls were dry stone without mortar, easily removed and replaced. A single rustic wooden door separated two parts of the cellar; the other section, I supposed, was for coal.

Before I could see more, the cellar went dark. The lamp the other person carried had been extinguished and I was alone in the dim circle of light provided by my single candle. Not alone. I heard someone breathing behind me. Pain, a sensation of falling a great distance. And for a great while, nothing.

WHEN I CAME to, I was in complete and total darkness without even my candle to comfort me. I sat up and stretched my arms before me. There was a wall just two feet away. I turned and stretched the other way. Another wall, this time perhaps three feet away. And so I turned in a circle, my panic growing as I realized I was locked into a space that was only five feet long by four feet wide. The ceiling grazed my head, and scratchy cobwebs fell onto my face.

Where was my candle? Wherever I had been felled, still

on the ground, I supposed, for it was quite clear by smears of stiffened mud on my clothing and the ache in my wrists that I had been dragged to this place.

The door was at my right side; I found the latch, pulled and twisted it. The latch moved freely, but the door did not budge. I kicked the door. It held steady. I flung myself at it. It did not even shake on its hinges.

Slowly, I ordered myself. Breathe slowly. Think of sweet-grass blowing in the breeze. Think of my special hiding place when I was a child, an ancient wagon wheel half buried in a Concord meadow that I could lean my back against and stare up into the huge blue sky, as curious free-flying birds swooped overhead. Space is infinite, and a silly wooden door could not cut me off from the world that easily.

But reader, I was terrified! I knew cellars of this kind, so thick-walled that I could scream and shout for weeks without a passerby hearing. And I knew doors of this sort, old and ancient but cut from hardwood thicker than a man's wrist, a door meant to last for generations. No one would think to come looking for me here, since no one knew I had come.

Think. What are your resources? I quizzed myself. Lucifers. The matches were still in my pocket. You may light one. Just one. Conserve them.

I lit the match. The room was even smaller than I had thought; my measurements had been optimistic. I could take no more than two strides in either direction. The ceiling beams were thick, the stone walls completely intact. Panic made me dizzy. The match burned my fingertips and then went out.

My head ached. There was a bump growing under my hair where I had been hit in the attack. What had he hit me with? That does not matter, I told myself. All that matters is to find a way out.

But I knew there was none.

CHAPTER THIRTEEN

The Showman Confesses

How many hours passed? Strange that without light one can still feel the passing of time, the day's tingling shift from afternoon to evening, that lugubrious march into the dusky hour that a French tutor once described as "the hour between dog and wolf."

Strange that one can be overwhelmed by the worst panic imaginable, and still remember that there is such a thing as time.

Repeatedly I reached out in the dark and touched those dank walls, willing them to move away from me, though they did not. Repeatedly I put my hand to my breast and willed my heart to cease racing, and it did not. Repeatedly I forced my imagination, my inner eyes, to "see" the huge horizon over Boston Harbor, to feel the largeness of that place and the freedom of the birds in the sky following the fishing fleet, but I could not. The large, open skies of my childhood in Concord had instilled in me a dislike of closed spaces; now that dislike had turned to fear. My breath came only with difficulty, as if I had run a great distance, and I grew light-headed.

By the hour of the wolf I had consumed the half dozen toffees from my pocket, not because I was hungry but because the activity of unwrapping paper and chewing distracted me for a few seconds. By the hour of the wolf I had hoarsened my throat from shouting, and bloodied my fists by banging against that stubborn, relentless wooden door. And I was no closer to freedom.

I forced myself to whistle for comfort, knowing that Lizzie would not mind that my promise to her had been broken for this purpose. Lizzie. How I longed to see her, and Auntie Bond, and Sylvia. Even Cobban. His freckles had started to become endearing, though I did wish he could be weaned from that passion for bold plaids. Maybe Sylvia could convince him to venture into the more visually pleasing lands of gray flannel or blue wool stripes. The thought of Sylvia's romance lightened me, but a moment later I felt the walls move closer once again.

My stomach rattled; my head ached. My eyes would tear, even though I sternly warned myself that self-pity would be more useful when I was out of the mess, not while I was still in it. I needed my wits about me.

To do what? the child in me yelled back. I can't break down the door. I can't make myself heard to a passerby. What exactly can those fine wits accomplish? I wanted Marmee's strong, comforting arms about me. I realized I might never see her again, and the thought made me shout with anger and disbelief!

"Hello?"

The voice was thin, distant. Had I really heard it?

I shouted again. This time I was rewarded with the sound of a board creaking overhead.

"Down here!" I shouted, hoping to be heard through the thick, tightly fitted floorboards. More footsteps overhead, then silence.

Tears started again. Had I not been heard? Was I abandoned?

No! Minutes later I heard shouting again, much closer. A man's voice, in the cellar. "Hello!" it called. "Where are you?"

"Behind the door!" I yelled back, pressing my mouth close to the grimy door, the better to be heard.

"Hold tight! I'm coming!"

Oh, bless Constable Cobban and his plaids and freckles, for by then I had recognized his voice! A minute more, the sound of something heavy being dragged across the floor, the latch lifting, the door groaning open, and a flood of light from Cobban's lamp.

"Miss Louisa!" he said, distress plain on his open face. "What has happened? What are you doing here?"

"Help me upstairs, and I will explain," I said, for at that moment more than anything I wanted fresh air, openness, a view of the sky, or at least of the stars in the sky if it was even later than I thought.

"You were locked in? The door must have fallen shut behind you," he said. "Terrible coincidence, terrible. The slamming of the door must have loosened that rafter." He pointed out a thick beam, the wood that had barred my door so effectively that he had had to drag it away to free me.

Coincidence? I did not think so. Leaning heavily on the

young man's shoulders, almost swooning I am afraid I must admit, I made my way out of that dark and damp place with him, back upstairs, to the front porch, to air and light.

It was not yet dark. I had been imprisoned only an hour or two, though I had thought it was many hours. A setting sun cast slanting beams against white snow-covered trees, passing black carriages, the red scarf of a little boy dashing home, and the spotted fur of the dog that ran loyally beside him. The world glittered as I inhaled so deeply my shoulders lifted and my chin tucked; how wonderful to breathe fresh air! How beautiful the late-winter afternoon was!

"I am a little afraid of close spaces," I said to Cobban. "And that space was very close," I answered in response to his question of whether I was quite ill or not.

"How did you come to be there?" He tenderly brushed cellar dust from my sleeve. I began to see what Sylvia saw when she looked at him, or at least to appreciate his friendly freckles a little more than I had.

"Curiosity," I confessed, taking another deep breath, letting the cold, fresh air do a better job of revivifying me than smelling salts could. "How did you come to be here?"

"Mr. Barnum sent an errand boy to find me. Said he had been coming home and passed Mrs. Percy's house, and heard strange noises. Said we should investigate before the neighbors started to claim the place was haunted."

"Mr. Barnum?"

"None other. You look strange again, Miss Louisa. I think I should get you home. Shall I send for Sylvia—I mean Miss Shattuck—to sit with you?" Constable Cobban was fussing, brushing snow off my shoulders, chafing my wrists, shifting his weight back and forth on his large feet as boys do when they are trying to be polite but wish to run off. His pale blue eyes shone with anxiety.

"I am fine," I insisted. "I'll walk home myself and you can get about your business. First, though, you might do another check of Mrs. Percy's house and see if anything has been disrupted or disappeared, since I am certain someone else was there before me." Someone who had lured me downstairs and then locked me in a very small space, I did not say. Why? Obviously I was searching where one of Mrs. Percy's acquaintances, perhaps her murderer, did not wish me to search.

I had been warned. But who had sent that warning: the same man who arranged my freedom, Mr. Barnum? Could he wish me harm? If he were guilty of a crime, he could, my imagination answered back.

"Before we leave, Mr. Cobban, would you do me a favor?" I asked. "Go back downstairs to that cellar, and yell at the top of your voice."

He sighed as men do when they think women are being flighty and moody, but did as I wished. Five minutes later he was standing beside me again on the porch, in the snow, breathing loudly from exertion.

"I didn't hear a sound," I told him. Nor, then, had Mr. Barnum heard me shouting.

MY ADVENTURE LEFT me exhausted and contented with an evening in front of the hearth at Auntie Bond's. I took up my sewing once again, too preoccupied to worry further about the missing shirt and the lightweight quality of the fabric. I was pleased, for the time, to listen to Lizzie in the next room, playing her scales and études and practicing the old and beloved Christmas carols: "Christians Awake," "The First Noel," and "Angels We Have Heard on High," for Auntie Bond had decided we would have a caroling party after the tree was up. How sweetly Lizzie played! How she made my foot tap with eagerness for the holidays to come. And how my breast ached to be finished with my sewing, collect my fee, and purchase one of the remaining portfolios in Mr. Crowell's Music Store.

Shadows danced about the room. The fire crackled and blazed. Lizzie played on and on as snow fell outside the window, covering the houses and street with shining fairy dust. I refused to think of Mr. Barnum. Tomorrow would be time enough. And because I put one mystery out of my thoughts, another seeped in. I knew what had to be the crime in "Agatha's Confession," for where there is confession there must have been a crime, and Agatha's great sin would be inspired by the afternoon's misadventure and one of my own deepest, darkest fears. What is claustrophobia but a fear of premature burial?

In my story, Agatha has realized that her heart's delight, Philip, has fallen in love with her beautiful best friend, Clara. Philip denies it; Clara is not kind, will not give him up or even cease working her charms on him, since he has proven vulnerable to her type of fickle nature and cruel beauty. Twice Clara, beautiful but frail, comes close to death, and twice Agatha helps her back to the land of the living. But when Clara continues to come between Agatha and Philip, Agatha proves she can be crueler than any simple coquette. I remembered the close darkness, reaching out my fingertips to feel the walls pressing against me.

Abandoning the sewing once again, I took my candle up to my writing room, lifted the cap from the inkwell, flattened a sheet of paper before me, and began to write what that storyteller's voice in my head dictated.

Clara now lies dead in her coffin, victim to a family illness of premature disease. Agatha bends over the coffin to give her rival a final kiss.

> *As I spoke, I bent to put away a lock of hair that had fallen on her cheek. In doing so, my hand touched her forehead, and a strange, quick thrill shot through me, for it was damp.*
>
> *I put my hand to her heart. Her pulse and lips were still. I touched her brow again, but my hand had wiped the slight dew from it and it felt cold as ice.*
>
> *I stood white and still as herself for a few moments while the old struggle raged in my breast fiercer than before.*
>
> *Fear whispered that she was not dead—pity pleaded for her lying helplessly before me—and conscience sternly bade me do the right thing, forgetful of all else. But I would not listen, for Love cried out passionately:*
>
> *"Philip is my own again. She shall not separate us anymore and rob me of the one blessing of my life."*
>
> *I listened to the evil demon that possessed me.*

Agatha, for revenge, allows Clara to be buried alive so that Philip might once again be hers alone.

Sitting in the attic, penning my story, I shivered with fear and delight and wrote page after page. Once my hand was wearied and stiff and the words of the story no longer came to me, I capped the inkwell once again, rose from my desk, and went down the stairs to my bed, whistling "Silent Night" quietly to myself.

Of course, I slept not at all that night. I had been locked in and then written a cruel story, one I could never show Marmee for fear of her reaction, and my punishment for being both victim and criminal was to sit up most of the night, listening to Lizzie's innocent, regular breathing and anticipating my meeting with Mr. Barnum, for meet with him I must.

Too much of this business with Mrs. Percy had to do with him, and he of all people seemed to have most reason to wish her harm, for what is simple greed compared to the desire for revenge? Agatha, for revenge and to get her own way, allows a friend to be buried alive; what would Mr. Barnum do for revenge and to get his way? Holding a pillow over the forger's face till she ceased struggling was certainly one way to end the forgeries and to obtain revenge at the same time.

Sylvia joined me for breakfast that morning.

"You look as if you haven't slept a wink," she said brightly, helping herself to a large portion of hash potatoes from the platter.

"I haven't. Save me some hash, will you?"

"Grumpy, aren't we?" said she, spreading a second helping of butter onto her toast. "I believe Mr. Cobban prefers his women filled out, so I am attempting to put on some weight. Have I succeeded, do you think?"

I studied Sylvia and tried to remain calm. Lizzie came in just then and sat in her accustomed dining chair in front of

the window so that she was lit from behind by the most en-
chanting pale winter morning light. That calmed me.

"I heard, Sylvia," said my sister. "You look fine to me, and
Marmee always says that weight gained too quickly stresses
the digestion."

"Well, I always pay attention to Mrs. Alcott's directives.
Thank heavens. I dislike potato hash." She pushed the potatoes to one side to make room for bacon, which was more to
her liking. "I have something for you, Louy. A note from my
young man." She grinned. I could not help but smile back. It
was the first time she had referred to Cobban in that intimate
manner.

"Is he now?" I asked. "Yours? And does that please you?"

"Very much."

"You are not being precipitous, Sylvia?"

She blushed prettily. "I think Father likes him. We've had
some very pleasant conversations about young Cobban. The
other day I was practicing my spirit writing, and the words
on the page were quite clear when I opened my eyes again:
'Fine boy. Fine. Future.'"

"Well, from what I know of your long-departed father, he
was as decisive as you. Didn't he pass over the exact day his
doctors said he would? Louisa, there is a message for you."
This latter comment was from Auntie Bond, who had come
downstairs in her white nightcap and blue flannel housedress
and robe to join us at the breakfast table.

"Did you know Father, Miss Bond?" Sylvia asked.

"Not well, I admit. Oh, dear. We seem to be running
short of hash. Lizzie, dear, go to the kitchen and ask Cook for
more, will you, dear? What was I saying? Oh, yes. Not well.

But we played cards together on occasion. He was brilliant at the card table. Very decisive. Much like you, my dear."

Sylvia beamed. I suppose if one has never known one's father, one must be pleased to learn there is a strong connection despite that early loss.

"You said something about a message for me?" I reminded my aunt.

"Ah, yes. Here it is." She took the paper from her pocket. It was from Cobban. *I hope you are feeling better,* he had written. *I took your advice and searched Mrs. Percy's house again and found a wall safe we hadn't noticed before. It was opened, and empty. You might also want to know that Mr. Nichols managed to evade the Pinkerton men sent to bring him back to Cleveland.*

"Eddie Nichols is not in custody," I said. Reader, the news delighted me! It provided hope that Mr. Barnum had not been the one who had locked me in the cellar the day before. Perhaps it had been Mr. Nichols. Without thinking, I pursed my mouth and whistled. Lizzie, just returned from the kitchen with a fresh plate of potato hash, made a face.

"Sorry, Lizzie," I said. "Sylvia, eat quickly, if you don't mind. We have an errand to attend to."

Ten minutes later, we were out the door and on our way. We had to pass Mrs. Percy's house to arrive at Mr. Barnum's rooms. I shivered, remembering that small, locked cellar room of the day before.

PERHAPS MR. BARNUM was there, his landlady said after I had given her one of my cards. Would we wait in the second parlor, and she would discover if he were at home, and if so, ask if he would receive us? That suited us splendidly, we said, and thanked her.

Tea was not sent in. That suggested several things. First, that Mr. Barnum had instructed his landlady that his visitors were to be treated casually and with a noticeable lack of warmth unless and until he stated otherwise. That, of course, meant that he had anticipated many unpleasant and unexpected meetings while in Boston, probably from creditors. Word gets about quickly when a rich man suffers financial embarrassment. Jackals, was how I had heard Uncle Ben refer to debt collectors, though that seemed harsh to me, since tradesmen have families to feed as well.

Mr. Barnum kept us waiting for twenty minutes. When he arrived in the parlor, hemming and hawing and apologizing for his "preoccupation," he was dressed again in the suit he had worn for Mrs. Percy's first séance, that bold and bright fabric that suggested a man well-off and at ease in the world. His face was not at ease. His heavy eyebrows met over his nose in a stormy manner; his thick, curly hair stuck out over his ears in unruly style, and his red cravat was poorly tied. Preoccupied, indeed.

"Mrs. Barnum has been ill again," he said, holding up a letter he had obviously recently received and read. "My financial difficulties have made her headaches return. Oh, for vengeance on those who have ruined me." Then he seemed to recollect himself, and gave us a half smile.

"Mrs. Moony, these are friends of mine. Will you bring us tea?" he said to his landlady. Mrs. Moony grimaced in a continuing unfriendly manner.

"You find me much reduced in circumstance," said Mr.

Barnum, when the parlor door had been shut. "I prefer hotels to boardinghouses, but the wallet is thin these days." He smiled, but the smile did not reach those fine, piercing eyes of his.

"That is what I am here to discuss," I admitted.

"Ah! Progressive education! I approve, I approve." He nodded his large, shaggy head vigorously. "Young women these days!"

"Not your finances," I explained hastily. "Rather, the purpose of your visit to Boston."

He sat heavily in a chair opposite me and crossed his legs, folding his hands over his knees and nervously revolving his thumbs back and forth.

"Did you ever see Madam Josephine Clofullia, my celebrated 'Swiss Bearded Lady'?" he asked. Our expressions indicated we had not; moreover we were not familiar with the name. "Poor woman. Face as hairy as a man's. The beard came all the way down to her waist. But you know, audiences wouldn't pay a nickel to see the poor unfortunate until I myself spread the rumor that she was a man posing as a woman. I prevaricated, much wounding the lady's feelings, but you see, the crowd doesn't want the truth. It wants fantasy."

"I have heard of your mermaid," offered Sylvia.

"The Fiji Mermaid. Half stuffed monkey, half stuffed fish." He sighed again. "Stank something awful. But when people looked at it they believed, wanted to believe, that they were seeing a real mermaid. It was good old Yankee tomfoolery." His thumbs revolved even faster, then ceased. "What I'm trying to explain to you, my dears, is that I have done things of which I am not exactly proud. I chose a hard business—the business of entertaining the masses—and for that I often quarreled with my own conscience. Why, right down the hall from my exhibit of wax figures I kept a private office where the gullible public might meet with fortune-tellers and clairvoyants. Madame Rockwell even claimed she could see the future by staring at a rock. I grew rich off such humbug. But I am a God-fearing man. A God-fearing man. And I wished to set some things right again between my God and myself. I wanted to find a woman of true spirituality who might offer something genuine to the American Museum."

"And so you came to see Mrs. Agatha Percy, the crystal gazer?" I asked in amazement.

Mr. Barnum shook his great, sad head in a bovine manner, as if looking for the next patch of grass to graze.

"Not Mrs. Percy," he said. "There is a Miss Adelaide Lynch here in Boston. You've not heard of her? You see, she doesn't bill herself in the papers or promote herself to a crowd. But I had heard she was the real thing. She could really speak with the dead and carry messages back and forth between people and angels. I came to meet her. I came to find something true and good and spiritual." He sighed and leaned back in his chair, looking up at the ceiling.

"You did not find it to be so," I guessed.

"She is a sweet child, not a calculating woman. However, her older sister controls her and uses her. Imagine the scene: trumpets fall from the ceiling, 'apparitions' appear out of nowhere."

"Like at Mrs. Percy's."

"Very much like at Mrs. Percy's. And that is why I return to Bridgeport in a day or two. My business here is concluded."

"Mr. Barnum, all of us at Mrs. Percy's séance were there by invitation. I must ask: Why were you there? Did Mrs. Percy ask to see you, or did you ask to see her? Did it have something to do with Mr. Edward Nichols, your cousin?"

Mrs. Moony returned with the tea tray, muttering all the while under her breath, and Mr. Barnum waited until she had again left before responding. He rose from his chair and stood in front of me, looking earnestly into my face. His large belly sloped, his shoulders were rounded with defeat, but his eyes had the candor of a child's. My heart went out to him, but my reasoning faculties did not.

"You have already guessed, Miss Louisa. I am certain you know of my financial difficulties, and that they are largely caused by that relation of mine, Eddie Nichols, who has been stealing tremendous quantities from my bank accounts by writing checks. Forging checks. Yes. A second purpose brought me to Boston."

"Mr. Nichols had the assistance of Mrs. Percy, who seemed adept at imitating other people's handwriting," I continued. "And who is now dead."

"Yes. Eddie let it slip out last year that he knew an excellent imitator of handwriting. He even gave me her name, as if he were boasting of it! I went to meet Mrs. Percy, to plead with her to give evidence against him, in exchange for which I would pledge my word that she herself would not be prosecuted."

"She laughed," spoke up Sylvia. "In your face." Then Sylvia laughed—"Ha, ha, ha!"—a hoarse, rude sound very unlike herself.

I turned and looked at my friend. When the terrible

laughter ceased, her face was pale and radiant as a candle flame, her eyes larger than usual and glistening.

"I hear her voice," Sylvia said. "What is that? An apology? Oh, Mr. Barnum, she is ever so sorry!" Sylvia burst into tears.

"Drink this," I said, handing Sylvia a cup of tea. "Steady yourself." I put my arms around my sobbing friend.

"She did laugh!" Mr. Barnum said, amazed. "And then she gave me the invitation to the circle and said if I came I would hear interesting things."

Sylvia twisted and turned, sat back on the settee, and put her hand to her face.

"Why, I'm weeping! What is happening, Louy?"

"I have no idea," I said, "but you seem to have had some sort of fit."

"I give you my word, I did not harm Mrs. Percy," Mr. Barnum pleaded.

"He did not," said Sylvia, her voice growing strange again.

"Oh, no more of this!" I cried to Sylvia in exasperation.

"My word of honor," said the showman. "And now we must end this interview. I have some last visits to make before my departure. May I accompany you somewhere, ladies?"

We rose in unison and went back into the hall, where Mrs. Moony handed us our coats and hats, evidently much pleased that we were leaving and she could restore her parlor to its clean and unused condition.

"My gloves, Mrs. Moony," said Mr. Barnum, putting on his top hat and searching his coat pockets. "I've only one glove. Where has the other got to?"

"Is this it?" I pulled from my own pocket the glove I had discovered yesterday on the floor at Mrs. Percy's house.

His stormy expression returned. "Give me that!" he said, grabbing it.

"Why were you at Mrs. Percy's house yesterday?"

The front door was open and an icy wind blew at us, rustling the peacock feathers in the vases of Mrs. Moony's hall.

"Curiosity, Miss Alcott. It is how I made my first fortune," he said angrily.

"You were looking for something. Did you find it?"

Mr. Barnum's gray eyes glared; his eyebrows moved up and down as he considered his reponse. "I did not," he said after a long pause. "I wanted to find an example of Mrs. Percy's forgery, a letter or check, to help prove my case against Eddie. I found the safe, but it was already opened and completely empty."

"That is how you heard me shouting from the cellar," I said. "You were upstairs, not in the street. Why did you not tell this to Constable Cobban?"

"Breaking and entering, Miss Alcott. A man about to go to the courts for bankruptcy cannot afford even minor transgressions of the law."

Oh, how I wanted to believe him.

Outside, snow crunched underfoot, a soothing, familiar sound, and there was a smell of roasting chestnuts in the air and of wood fires from the thousand hearths of Boston. It was a day meant to reassure that all was as it should be. But it was not.

CHAPTER FOURTEEN

Mrs. Agatha Percy
Speaks—Again

READER, I ADMIT feeling great discomfort over both discoveries: that Eddie Nichols was still free and that Mr. Barnum had dropped that glove discovered at Mrs. Percy's house. I hoped with all my heart that Mr. Nichols was my enemy and not Mr. Barnum, for I had developed an affection for the showman. Undoubtedly one had locked me into the cellar, and the only comfort was that my adventure had been meant as a warning, since if either had wished to harm me it would have been easy enough to arrange for the beam to fall on my head rather than across the door.

That was small enough comfort, however. I was being told in a very indiscreet way to mind my own affairs.

"Are you well, Louy?" Lizzie asked me that evening, as I sat sewing before the hearth. "You are making the most awful face."

"I have been thinking of the séance at Mrs. Percy's house."

"An awful business. I cannot help feeling sorry for Mrs. ·

Percy, though." Lizzie picked up the sleeve and resumed her stitching. Have I mentioned how fine her stitches were? I watched in wonder as she placed fifteen stitches to the inch, each as even as the one before. I watched, and thought.

A log crumbled and burst into sparks in the hearth, and that little explosion seemed an expression of this situation: There had been violence, and then little sparks of momentary illumination, and then . . . nothing. I was at a standstill, and though I spent another hour going through my notes about the séance, I found no pattern pointing to a solution, only two names that appeared over and over—Nichols and Barnum.

But what of Mr. and Mrs. Deeds? Mrs. Deeds had wished to buy the pearl collar, but Mrs. Percy had asked too high a price. It seemed obvious to me that Mrs. Deeds had earlier business with Mrs Percy. "I recognize that diamond brooch," Mrs. Percy had said at the séance; perhaps it was another stolen item Mrs. Deeds had purchased after a quarrel over the price; perhaps years of enmity had built up?

In my heart I hoped time would prove her guilty of the crime. Such greed, such lust for luxury when so many others went hungry and poorly clothed in the dead of winter, such rapaciousness surely were excellent motives for murder.

And what of the disappeared cook, Meh-ki? Was it guilt or fear that had made her go into hiding? It certainly wasn't uncommon for servants to wish their employers dead, especially when a safe and theft are also involved, but the two very brief glimpses I'd had of the small woman seemed to reveal a timid personality, not a violent one.

I finished just one shirt that evening. I still had many to sew before I could collect my fee from the reverend and make the final payment on Lizzie's music portfolio and series of lessons. I felt the Slough of Despond begin to fall over me, that blackness of mood that arrives from a sense of stagnation and hopelessness.

No, I told it. Soon it will be Christmas, and I am with my sister and writing stories and earning my living, and I will not give in to this. But the mood pushed back; it wrestled with me.

"Bedtime," said Lizzie at ten o'clock, folding her sewing into the basket. The hearth logs had burned down to embers and the sitting room was growing cold. "Will you come up, Louy?"

"I think I will write some first," I said, giving her a goodnight kiss on her forehead. "Sleep tight."

"Don't let the bedbugs bite," she finished.

I took a single candle up to my attic room and sat before the desk, wrapping a blanket around my shoulders for warmth. The wind whistled through loose boards; a flake or two found their way to my place and landed on my page, blurring a letter here and there. I sat shivering, rereading the pages of "Agatha's Confession." And a new thought came to me. The story was essentially about three people: Agatha, Philip, and Clara, for in a love triangle what other characters are required?

Ah. One other person is needed, always, someone who can secretly carry letters back and forth and make unseen arrangements. A maid. Suzie, a voice whispered in my head.

Suzie? I whispered back.

A cold draft made my candle flicker. Mrs. Percy could not have made herself clearer had she been trying, though of course it was but a draft that flickered the flame, and the next morning the Slough of Despond had been driven back by a new optimism that Suzie, whether she knew it or not, held the key to this mystery.

"You again," she said gloomily, when I pulled my chair up outside her cell the next day.

"I've brought you something," I said, holding out the raisin cake I had purchased at a little shop around the corner.

Suzie reached greedily for it through the bars and had to break it in half to pull it back through her barrier. She began to eat immediately, cramming her face as children do.

"The slops here is something awful," she said between mouthfuls.

"The menu and accommodations are not designed for comfort as much as for the encouragement of repentance, I agree. But are they treating you well enough?"

Suzie snorted and tossed back her disheveled hair. "I had a bath and a change of linen, if that's what you mean. Don't know as I'd call that well, since I didn't do nothing to be here."

"Miss Dear, it is nonsense to plead complete innocence of all that happened at Mrs. Percy's," I said gently. "Items of dubious provenance were found in your room, and I wonder if you might not have pickpocketed Mr. Phips's watch during the séance. It is missing, he says."

"It fell out of his pocket and I forgot to give it back to him." She studied the ceiling.

"Help me, now, Miss Dear, and I will speak on your behalf. Let us be honest with each other." I leaned closer.

"How honest?" asked she, also leaning closer.

"Completely. Let's begin with a simple question. How long were you employed by Mrs. Percy?"

"Six months."

"Was she a good employer?"

"She were fine. Paid well, not as demanding as some. Friendly sometimes. I think she'd been in service herself. Can always tell a woman who's come up the hard way. They aren't as bad as those born to it."

"And did you smoke opium with her?"

Suzie snorted again. "Hell—I mean heavens, no. My mother smoked the pipe and I saw what good it did her. And Mrs. Percy weren't no fiend, if that's what you're thinking. She smoked maybe once a month, no more. 'For sweet dreams,' she would say. Most the time she took one of those little brown pills. 'Not as hard to break the habit,' she said. 'The stomach dissipates the properties of addiction.' Them were her words. She were knowledgeable."

A guard came clanking down the hall toward us, his keys rattling on the large chain at his waist.

"Constable Cobban has said I might speak with the prisoner," I informed him somewhat prematurely, as I had not yet asked Cobban. The guard scratched his head and walked away, muttering something about ladies in the courthouse.

"Prisoner!" moaned Suzie.

"And for longer a prisoner if you don't answer all my questions," I warned her, for I could see that under that tough exterior she was truly frightened, and fear can be a great motivator for the truth. "Now tell me where you were that night before and the morning of Mrs. Percy's murder."

"With Eddie, the sod, the cad. I'll . . . I'll tear his hair, I will, when I get out of here, him leaving me high and dry like this." She made fists of her hands and banged them against her legs.

I abstained from reminding her that according to Constable Cobban's report she had already lightened Mr. Nichols of a chunk of hair and scalp.

"Say," she said, looking at me now with suspicion. "How did you know I was away that night?"

"Because your shoes were wet from having been walking in the snow. You hadn't had time to dry them before the fire. And your hair was patted flat from your hat. I thought at first you had been napping. I realized later you had been out, and just returned. Did you often spend nights with Mr. Nichols?"

"Often enough. Mrs. Percy knew. She didn't mind, long as the parlor got dusted. Like I said, she come up the hard way herself. She weren't a lady of pretension, like that Mrs. Deeds. I'll bet she's never had her hands in the washbasin, not even to scrub her own—"

"Miss Dear," I interrupted, "was Mr. Nichols with you all that night and morning, right up to the time of the séance?"

Suzie knit her brows again in concentration. "He went out an hour or so before I left his rooms. Said he were going for a pot o' tea and a bun. Never brought one back to me, though. He were a selfish man."

An hour or so. Could he have been to Mrs. Percy's home and arranged the murder in that short a time? For I was convinced the more I spoke with Suzie that she had not been involved in the murder, nor even at home when it would have occurred, else she would have gone to Mrs. Percy's defense.

She seemed fond enough of her employer to avoid easing her out of this life.

I leaned even closer, my face just a few inches away from the bars separating me from Suzie and Suzie from freedom. "Now think, Miss Dear. Mrs. Percy would have mentioned a name now and then, anything a little unusual or out of the ordinary."

Suzie groaned and grasped the sides of her iron cot and rocked back and forth a little, thinking. "So many names." She sighed. "Names were her business, weren't it?"

"Think," I prompted.

"Well, most names that come up were live people, you know, customers. But right before that last séance she talked a bit about a dead 'Emily' somebody. Would you bring me another cake? And a pork pie?"

"How do you know this Emily is dead?" I asked.

" 'Cause Mrs. Percy said so, and she went to visit her in the cemetery. Up in the Granary on Beacon Hill."

She will scour the cemeteries for information about her clients, Mrs. O'Connor had told me, when I first quizzed her about the ways of a crystal gazer.

"Do you remember a last name, Suzie?"

"It were Phips. Mr. Phips's wife."

My heart sank. Another dead end, I thought. Mrs. Percy had most likely visited the grave just to confirm dates of birth and death, to be able to quote the epitaph at the séance and make her performance more convincing.

"I will bring you two pork pies," I told Suzie Dear. "Now keep up your courage."

I thought to go to the Beacon Hill cemetery to see what Mrs. Percy had seen, but the wet weather had soaked my stockings and feet, thanks to my great hurry of the morning, which had led me to quit Auntie Bond's home without a layer of fresh and dry newspaper in my boots. Home I must return, or risk catching a cold, and then risk passing that cold on to Lizzie, whose constitution was not as strong as mine. So for Lizzie's sake I delayed that visit to the cemetery, a choice that was to prove ironic, indeed.

For when I arrived back at Auntie Bond's, the place was in an uproar!

"Oh, Louisa, you've a message from Reverend Gannett! And he sent it by messenger, not post! You know what that means!" Auntie Bond wrung her hands and hopped from foot to foot in nervousness. She held all reverends in very high esteem and feared their wrath and disapproval, and since I was living under her roof she felt she shared my guilt.

"He is out of patience," I guessed. I opened the envelope even before removing my hat and coat. "He is leaving Boston tomorrow to visit relatives, and wishes the shirts in the morning. If not, he cannot receive them, nor make payment for them, until February. Oh, my." Still in my damp coat and wet boots, I trudged in a daze to Auntie Bond's parlor and sat heavily in my favorite chair. There was the sewing basket next to me. There were the finished shirts (who knew where the missing finished one had gone?), and there were the others still waiting to be done. And next to that basket, the pieces for the ordered dozen spring shirts for the reverend, not even begun.

The spring order could and would wait. The winter order

could not, for with that payment I had planned to purchase the Faber pencils for Abby and the writing paper for Father and the warm coat for Marmee, and the music portfolio for Lizzie—and with that portfolio a chance in the drawing to work with Signor Massimo himself.

"Don't worry, Louy," said Lizzie, coming and sitting on the chair next to me. "We'll do it together."

"All in one day? Not even two people can do it, not if they are to be done well enough to ask payment for them," I said morosely, for the Slough of Despond that had been making my feet feel heavy and my spirits low sank me completely at that moment. I had failed.

Mrs. Percy's murderer was nowhere closer to apprehension than he had been the day of the murder. My logic and thinking had carried me in circles, and all I had to show for it were some pages of a very strange and morose story waiting on my attic desk, a story, moreover, that no sane editor would ever want to publish. Worse, I had failed to earn the income that had been the main purpose for living apart from my beloved family for these many months, and because I had not completed the work I could not give the Christmas presents I wished, with all my heart, to present to that beloved family.

The situation looked dark, indeed.

Why, then, was Lizzie beaming at me in that radiant fashion?

"Oh, you look so awful," she teased. "Like that very hot summer day you wanted to swim in Walden Pond but you had eaten four green apples and felt ill, so Marmee wouldn't let you. Do you remember?"

"I do remember," I said, and smiled despite the day because Lizzie's smile was impossible to ignore. "What amazes me is that you remember. You were so little then. The prettiest child." I touched her soft curls. Sweet, gentle, shy Lizzie. She was too good for this world. "But what am I to do, Lizzie? Oh, I had such plans for the money I was to earn!"

Reader, if you do not have one, I recommend you quickly acquire a little sister, for they are the most astonishing of creatures. My little sister's smile grew broader, and her eyes glistened with joy.

"I meant it as a surprise, but it had to come out sooner or later, and now seems the right time," said she, kneeling next to the sewing basket. "Did you think nothing strange about these shirts, Louy? I know you are preoccupied, but still your quick mind should have noticed."

"The fabric is lighter than it should be for winter shirts," I said, bemused.

"That," said Lizzie with a great deep breath of pride, "is because you have been sewing the spring shirts. I changed the baskets, and I myself have been sewing the winter shirts, so they might be done sooner. I know you wanted the money for Christmas, and since I cannot earn"—Lizzie was too fragile, too precious, for employment—"I thought to help you earn. And so, dear Louy, there is but one shirt to finish, and even that shirt needs only the buttonholes. There! I can finish the buttonholes before dinner, and we can have the shirts sent to the reverend this evening. Tomorrow morning you will do your Christmas shopping!"

She sat back on her heels and folded her arms over her chest.

"Oh, you darling!" I exclaimed, kneeling beside her and embracing her. "You have been earning the money for your own present!"

"No," said she, growing serious. "The gift I most desire I already have. And money cannot purchase a loving mother and father, and brood of sisters. You may whistle if you want, Louy."

I did not whistle. I wiped away a tear of joy and gratitude instead.

"Well, this would be a fine time for a glass of warm eggnog," said Auntie Bond, who had been watching and listening from the doorway.

"Come here, you good woman," I said, and she did, and the three of us embraced and performed an impromptu jig before the hearth in anticipation of the happy season to come.

And so that evening befell just as Lizzie predicted; Auntie Bond and I made a supper for us as Lizzie finished the buttonholes. Before we sat down to our soup and vegetables and bread and cheese, Auntie Bond sent the lad from next door to deliver the finished shirts to Reverend Ezra Gannett, and packed in with the shirts, well wrapped, was one of her own baked fruitcakes to brighten his season. One hour later, as we were drinking another glass of eggnog before the hearth and reading aloud to each other from Dickens's *Bleak House*, the lad returned with a fat envelope and my—our—payment. Half of it went to Lizzie, who was delighted with the feel of earned coins in her palm, and I still had enough left to realize my plans.

A fine job, Miss Alcott, fine indeed! the reverend wrote in a note included with the payment.

I hastily wrote a reply to his note: *I am pleased you are pleased, sir. Please know, though, that I cannot take credit, since much—most—of the stitching was accomplished by my sister Elizabeth, and she is, as you have noted, a fine seamstress. Merry Christmas, sir!*

Tomorrow, I thought, valuing that envelope more than wealth should be valued, I know. Tomorrow the shopkeepers shall be wrapping presents for the Alcott family.

I slept deeply that night, without a further thought for Mrs. Percy or Suzie Dear or Phineas Barnum, my vexed spirits giving themselves over to the joy of the season to come, to thoughts of trimming the Christmas tree and eating a roasted turkey with cranberries. But when I awoke on the morrow, two instant thoughts jarred me into the coming day: I would have to put aside money for a betrothal gift for Sylvia, I supposed, and I must visit the old Beacon Hill cemetery.

Neither thought was particularly pleasant. Sylvia lived in a headlong manner and often found herself in deep trouble because of her inability to look before leaping. As for visiting a cemetery to spend hours perusing tombstones—who would look forward to such a pastime?

Grimacing and muttering a little, I dressed in my plain brown workaday dress and tried to tame my willful hair into a tidy snood. Sparks flew about my face in the dim morning light as I sat before the dressing table mirror and gave my rebellious mane fifty strokes with the brush. My face looked back at me, pale and serious, the eyes darker and larger than usual. The goodwill of the evening before returned only when

I remembered that that morning I was to go make the final payment on Lizzie's music portfolio.

A knot of worry so filled my stomach, though, that I couldn't eat the bread and jam and bacon laid out for breakfast. Was the portfolio still waiting for me at Mr. Crowell's Music Store, or had I failed Lizzie?

CHAPTER FIFTEEN

A Discovery in the Cemetery

TREMONT STREET WAS thick with shoppers bustling on the walks and in the streets, a busy world filled with people wishing one another season's greetings and joy in the New Year to come as snow fell to remind us of winter's delight. Bakers' windows were filled with frosted fruitcakes, and cobblers displayed red silk dancing slippers for the balls and parties of the New Year; stationery windows boasted that new delight of the season, cards, already printed with best wishes for a happy holiday.

I headed directly for Mr. Crowell's Music Store. My heart was thudding painfully in my chest as I approached his window. But there, to my joy, was the last portfolio, still resting on its wooden stand, waiting for me!

Mr. Crowell beamed at me when I entered, holding up my purse to indicate I was there with coin in hand to finish payment.

"I knew you'd do it," he said, his smile so broad it filled

the bottom half of his face and set his side whiskers to twitching like a cat's. "A woman was in here yesterday looking at this, and I might have mentioned to her that the printing on this last set was not as good as the first. I might have mentioned that to discourage her, you know, though it's not true and I hope I'll be forgiven the exaggeration, but I did feel that Miss Elizabeth would sure enjoy receiving this for Christmas."

I was tempted to give Mr. Crowell a hug, but forbore to retain a semblance of dignity, though I was all but dancing with joy. "She will enjoy it, I am sure, Mr. Crowell," I agreed.

Carefully he removed the heavy portfolio from its place in the window, rested it on a piece of brown paper on the counter, and ran his hand over the red leather cover. The gold embossed lettering gleamed; the new leather gave off that glorious bookbinder's scent that promises everything, if you will but open to a page. Reverently Mr. Crowell opened the folio at random, and we beheld the strange cryptic art of the composer, those black staffs and dots climbing up and down the five-lined arbor of the musical score. "Beautiful." Mr. Crowell sighed, no doubt playing Liszt's music in his head and hearing the notes that were, for me, only black marks on an ivory page.

Almost with regret for his own loss, he carefully closed the heavy book, wrapped it in brown paper, and then gave it a second wrapping of a gay red-and-white-striped paper.

"The drawing for the lottery, for the lessons with Signor Massimo, will be this afternoon at three o'clock. Will you be here, Miss Alcott?" he asked.

Wild horses couldn't have kept me away!

"There will be punch and cookies," he said. "Mrs. Crowell insisted. Punch! In my store! Ay!" He pretended to hit himself in the head, but his pleasure was apparent in the wide grin beneath the gray-flecked mustache. "So come for punch and cookies, and let us see if little Elizabeth Alcott is to study with Signor Massimo!"

Feeling light as air, as happy as the dancing snowflakes, I finished my errands of the morning.

"A fad," said Mr. Giles of Giles Stationery, when I paused before his counter and examined the boxes of cards he had lined up next to the register. "Christmas cards won't last. People won't be content with sending a message someone else wrote for them." His white shirtsleeves were pushed up with black bands, displaying his thick wrists and the printer's ink staining his fingers, for in his back room Mr. Giles also had a small press with which he printed invitations to weddings and parties.

"They are a nice thought," I said, examining a box of cards and wondering if I might have enough money left over to purchase one so that I might send colorful greetings to my friends in Walpole and Concord.

"Some of Mr. Alcott's finest?" Mr. Giles asked, opening a drawer and, after putting on clean white gloves, taking out a ream of good, heavy writing paper.

"Two reams, please," I said. "Wrapped for Christmas, and sent to his address in Walpole. And this box of pencils for Abby, also to be sent to Walpole." I had selected the heaviest box that Faber made, filled with dozens of drawing pencils in every color of the rainbow, a true treasure trove for an artist.

"Excellent." Mr. Giles smiled and almost reached over to

pat my head—that was how long he had supplied Father's writing paper—and then thought better of it, since it was years since I had been a child. The doorbell jangled, and a brace of other customers entered, exclaiming over the display of Christmas cards.

At Mrs. Frank's Dress Shop I looked at Marmee's new coat one last time, felt its softness against my cheek, checked its weight by balancing a sleeve in my palm, then had it wrapped in white paper, boxed, and made ready for shipment to Walpole.

"It will be there in plenty of time for Christmas," assured Mrs. Frank. "And won't Mrs. Alcott look grand in it! She'll be warm, too. That coat is made of good, heavy wool, New England wool, none of that fancy import fabric."

"Thank you, Mrs. Frank," I said, giving her a hearty handshake. The spirit of Christmas had entered my heart. Marmee and Father and my other sisters wouldn't be with me in Boston, but just the same they were there with me. Always. Even now, kind reader. At the Boston Emporium I made the final payment on Anna's blue lace shawl, and arranged for that to be shipped to Syracuse. Auntie Bond's new white house cap embroidered with blue forget-me-nots I carried away with me, to put under the tree next week.

The world had grown softer, a little easier, friendlier, once I knew those gifts were on their way to Walpole, so it was with great reluctance that I met Sylvia for tea later that afternoon at our favorite tea shop, which, by coincidence, was just a few blocks away from the old Beacon Hill cemetery. The afternoon would not be as pleasant as the morning had been.

"Signor Massimo? I've heard of him. A tyrant of a teacher.

But a genius. Oh, I do hope Lizzie wins," said Sylvia. The tea shop was busy, and the clatter of china, the ringing of bells, the exclamations of friends and relatives meeting and greeting one another filled the small shop.

"I know only his reputation," I replied somewhat loudly, so that I might be heard over the bustle. "But if he is a tyrant, and Lizzie wins the lottery, she will vanquish him and make him as gentle as a house cat. She has such power to win people over. And you, Sylvia, have you conquered our young Constable Cobban?"

My closest friend in all the world raised her eyebrows, pursed her mouth, and studied the ceiling for a moment. "I truly don't know," she said finally. "He is a very stubborn and somewhat eccentric personality."

"Then you two have much in common. Another sesame bun?" I moved the plate closer to her.

"He is coming to dinner after the New Year. It will be a very small dinner, only he and I and Mother and you and Lizzie."

"Oh, no," I said. "Don't subject me to this. Your mother meeting as a possible son-in-law an officer of the law who wears plaid suits? I don't think I could, Sylvia. I am staunch, but even I have limits," I teased.

"You will come," Sylvia said with great confidence. "Because I will plead with you until you agree."

And that, of course, was true. "Lizzie won't come," I said. "Remember, she fled Walpole simply to avoid an afternoon dancing party."

"I have it all figured out," Sylvia answered, cutting the last sesame bun in half so that we might share it. "I will promise her anything she wants to eat. Lobsters, ice cream, pink cake. Anything. And music by candlelight, a pianist and violinist, but no dancing. She may simply sit and listen. And the music hour will suit Albert, as well."

"Is Constable Cobban a lover of music?" I asked, surprised.

"No." Sylvia grinned. "But it will mean an hour when he won't have to answer Mother's questions. He may nap, if he wishes."

The great throng that had gathered in the little tea shop for an eleven o'clock cup and bun had begun to thin; mothers with wailing children made their way out the double doors, and young girls gathered up the boxes and bags of their errands and straightened their hats before putting on their coats to return to their households and the afternoon's labor of French tutors or dancing classes or fancy sewing. The women of Boston returned to their schedule of activities, and Sylvia and I drained our teacups and also rose. Our chore for the afternoon was not as pleasant as conjugating verbs or embroidering shirts.

"Does Albert—Mr. Cobban—know the purpose of this little dinner party?" I asked Sylvia as we fetched our hats and coats from the rack near the door. Sylvia's coat was new, I noticed, and stylishly short, burgundy velvet trimmed with brown fur, stopping just at the hourglass indent of the waist so that the fullness of her skirt wasn't crushed. There was a new muffler to match. I admit to a thrill of pleasure, imagining the afternoons we might spend selecting Sylvia's trousseau, should this business with young Cobban transpire according to her plan. A love of fashion and handsome clothing may point to a certain lack of seriousness, but it was a harmless flaw in both Sylvia and myself that, as young women, we delighted in silk and lace and bright colors.

"Albert begins to suspect," Sylvia answered my question. "He is a little slow, though."

"Just as long as he doesn't think you are a little fast! You've known him such a short time."

"A year now. Almost. You still don't have gloves, Louy? You'll get chilblains. Here, take these. I have an extra pair of gloves in my muffler. Don't worry. They're old." She, with great nonchalance, reached into the fur-and-velvet muffler and brought out a pair of gloves of brown kidskin, lined with wool and finished with four buttons at the wrist.

"Sylvia, these are brand-new," I said.

"Are they? How forgetful I am. Well, consider them an early Christmas gift. Have you your package for Auntie Bond? You didn't leave it at the table? Yes? Then let's be on our way. But you owe me a favor, Louy."

"For the beautiful new gloves, Sylvia? Thank you."

"No, because I am coming with you this afternoon. I will spend an hour or two with you in the cemetery if you will spend an hour or two at Mother's table and in our music room after the New Year, when Albert comes."

"Agreed," I said. "You've won the match."

We crossed the Common, past the display of snowmen and snow angels; past the play area where mothers watched calmly or fearfully, according to temperament, as great snowball skirmishes took place; past the smokers' circle where men in greatcoats and tall hats paced and chatted, drawing on cigarettes or cigars; past the ice-skating pond and the new mansions of Boylston Street, barely visible over our left shoulders. Boston, my beloved Boston, but never so beloved as that sweet little town of Concord, for what place can ever be as sweet as the place where we dream our childhood dreams?

There was a cold wind off the Atlantic that afternoon, cold enough to make our teeth chatter and to tug and pull at our skirts, making the walk up Beacon Hill a difficult one.

The cemetery, the second-oldest one in Boston, was a forlorn place, filled with bare-branched winter trees, crypts and stone angels, and other, smaller monuments that had leaned and sunk with great age, their lettering no more than a suggestion of what once had been so meaningfully carved on the worn, lichen-covered stone.

The air smelled of pine and salt, of cold, of solitude, of mourning. The sky was leaden and overcast, burdened with a great weight of quickly moving clouds that could not shed their encumbrance of snow because it was too cold. The wind cut through us to the bone and howled through bare branches, rattling the few browned and withered leaves still clinging to them. We were in a small city of the dead, surrounded by bustling Boston.

"Creepy," said Sylvia, shivering. "What are we looking for, Louy?"

"A grave marker for Mrs. Emily Phips. Mrs. Percy visited her here. Maybe over there?" I pointed at a little bluff where the stones were still polished, where the granite angels had not yet lost their noses or the fingers with which they pointed to heaven.

We trudged through crusted snow that crackled underfoot, our eyes filled with the whiteness of winter and the gray stones of death, our faces red and chapped from the wind. I heard a twig snap behind me and turned in alarm, feeling the gooseflesh rise on my arms under the thick, heavy wool of my coat.

Suddenly I had the distinct sensation that we were not alone, that someone watched us. I turned in a circle and saw only desolate pine trees, stark oaks, and gray stone.

"What's wrong, Louy? Or perhaps I should ask what is right. I do not like this place." She huddled close at my side.

"Why, Sylvia." I forced lightness into my voice. "Dear friend, you started this business by insisting we attend Mrs. Percy's séance, and now you are afraid of a perfectly charming old cemetery?"

"A séance in a new and well-furnished parlor is one thing. This is quite another," she insisted. "I'm cold and I'm quite certain the air is bad here. I shall get malaria."

"Not in winter, you won't," I tried to reassure her.

Another twig snapped. Or was it other footsteps crunching in the snow? I took a deep breath, remembering the terrible fear I had felt when locked into that small room in Mrs. Percy's cellar. At least here I was in the open, in the cold air with the sky above me and all the room I could desire. Here, no walls closed in.

"Come," I said. "Let's get this done so we can go home to our warm hearths. You take that row, Sylvia. I'll start here."

We were in the newer section by then, where the memorials were larger, more ornate than those preferred by our forefathers and foremothers, whose graves were marked with simple stones. Some of the memorials in this section, with their weeping seated angels and aboveground chapels, were so large that for minutes at a time I lost sight of Sylvia in her new burgundy coat as we made our way down our assigned white and gray rows, reading epithets aloud to fill the cold silence: "'The hand of the Lord was upon me, and carried me out in the spirit of the Lord.'" "'Can these bones live? O Lord God, thou knowest.'" "'Beloved Mother.'" "'Here lies a daughter sorely missed.'" "'To an inheritance incorruptible and undefiled that fadeth not away.'" "'Behold a man raised up by Christ!'" On one grave I found one of Father's favorite passages from *Pilgrim's Progress*: "'The Pilgrim they laid in a large upper chamber, whose window opened towards the Sun rising; the name of the chamber was Peace.'"

"Ugh!" I heard Sylvia exclaim at one point.

"What is it?" I shouted in alarm.

"An empty grave. They must have dug it in the autumn, before the ground froze, and never filled it in. I wonder why?" she yelled.

"Let's hope it is a fortuitous sign," I answered. "The gravely ill patient recovered from his illness."

"Is this really a place for humor?" she shouted back in a peeved voice.

"Keep looking, Sylvia."

We finished that row and began another, leaving our footprints in the virgin snow as we moved past tombstone after tombstone. The wind howled even more fiercely and I shivered, more grateful than I could tell for the new warm gloves from Sylvia. My nose and forehead had grown numb from the cold. And still I had that sensation of being watched, yet when I looked up I saw no one except the flicker of Sylvia's vibrant coat as she moved down her row in a line parallel to my own.

An hour of this gruesome labor passed. The winter sun was slipping down the gray afternoon sky, casting vague shadows on the white snow, when I stopped before one modest grave site, marked by a simple stone flanked by two columns.

BELOVED WIFE, the epitaph read. MRS. WILLIAM PHIPS, NÉE EMILY SIDNEY GRAYLING. MERCY, MERCY, SAVE, FORGIVE. OH, WHO SHALL LOOK ON THEE AND LIVE? BORN APRIL 6, 1807, DIED JANUARY 14, 1853.

"Over here!" I called to Sylvia. "I've found it."

"She was not aged when she passed over," said Sylvia, after we had said a prayer over the grave.

"In her prime," I agreed, "and still much missed, it would seem. There are footsteps, masculine, I'd say, and newly made." The snow about the monument had been trampled. "Her husband still misses her and comes to pray here." Reader, it was wrong of me to make an assumption of that magnitude, I would soon learn.

We stood quietly before that grave, reflecting on life and death.

"It is two thirty, Louy," said Sylvia after a while, quietly, for the cemetery had sombered her. She replaced her timepiece into her reticule and gave me a meaningful glance.

"The lottery! We must hurry!" And like that, the mysteries of the grave were put aside so that I might attend to the living—to the drawing for the three lessons with Signor Massimo.

We arrived back at Mr. Crowell's shop at a quarter to

three, out of breath and laughing, since we had run almost all the way from Beacon Hill, but that mad race had been mostly downhill, and Sylvia had fallen right before the Common and bent her skirt hoop so that she now had a lopsided tilt to her costume.

Mr. Crowell, who had known both our families for many years, looked at us with affection, and this time did pat my head, though I was a grown woman.

"The young should amuse themselves," he said, helping to brush snow off Sylvia. "Old age comes soon enough, and the sadness."

"Hush, Mr. Crowell," said his wife, who had come out of her small office to help attend to the festivities. "This is no time to be talking of sadness. You'll bring bad luck on them." She looked at him with great tenderness even as she scolded, and I felt a sudden pang of homesickness for Marmee and Father.

Punch and tea cakes had been set out on a table in the middle of the little shop, and a handful of people had already gathered there, talking amongst themselves and eyeing the rows of music scores and books about the lives of the great composers.

"Where are you coming from in such a rush, Miss Alcott?" Mrs. Crowell asked, giving me a cup of ruby-colored punch.

"The old Beacon Hill cemetery. I went to see the grave of Emily Phips."

A shadow passed over Mrs. Crowell's face.

"Did you know her?" I asked.

"I did." Mrs. Crowell slowly, with an air of preoccupation, rearranged the biscuits on the platter. "A very unhappy woman. She purchased a parlor organ through us . . . oh, years ago, perhaps twenty or more. And then she came in once a month to buy music. Until she died, year before. Death was a kindness for her, I thought. She had no will to live."

"She played church hymns mostly," said Mr. Crowell. "And some Bach, of course. You have to respect a lady who takes the time to play Bach."

"She were a very sad woman," repeated Mrs. Crowell.

"Here now," said Mr. Crowell. "Don't go gossiping."

By unspoken arrangement Sylvia and Mrs. Crowell and I stood silent until the doorbells chimed again and the husband went to greet the next set of customers.

"Why sad?" I asked when we three had privacy.

"It is gossip; Mr. Crowell is correct," said the wife. "But since you visited her grave and did her that favor, I will tell you this much. There was gossip that her husband was unfaithful. Ach, men." She heaved a sigh of disapproval. "And it weren't a happy marriage to begin with, I fear. She still missed that first one, the boy she was engaged to when she were a girl. Can't think of his name. He weren't from round about these ways."

"Was there gossip about who the other woman was?" I asked.

"You might ask her brother, if it matters. He still has the old town house on Charles Street. Near the corner of Chestnut. Dilapidated old house, but he'll not move from it. Never married himself. He preferred Beethoven, as I recall. Ah! Miss Young is here! I must go see to her, Miss Alcott. Excuse me, please."

After Mrs. Crowell left us, Sylvia and I stood quietly for a moment, thinking. "Funny, isn't it?" she finally said. "You see an old gent with a soft smile and gray whiskers and you think, 'What a jovial fellow he looks!' But you never know what he gets up to behind closed doors. Do you think Albert will be faithless, Louy?"

"No," I said automatically, though I hadn't really considered this topic yet. A final customer came, jangling the doorbell, and I saw that everyone had gathered around the little table where Mr. Crowell had placed the punch, cakes, and a glass jar with our names on folded papers inside. I went to join them.

With silent prayers rising from me like heat rises from a cake just out of the oven, I watched as Mr. Crowell picked up the jar and gave it a sturdy shaking. Twelve little pieces of folded paper rattled up and down, back and forth, and then came to rest on the bottom of the jar.

"We need to do this fair and square. Jim!" He called to his assistant, a gangly lad in a striped wool shirt and trousers who looked like many awkward youths of fifteen but played like an angel, like a genius, when sitting before a piano. Jim played the pieces for those customers who could not read music well enough to play for themselves.

"Close your eyes and select a piece of paper," his employer told him.

Jim tugged at his brown hair, grinned, then put one long-fingered, slightly grimy hand over his eyes, and with the other felt for the opened jar, with its little bits of paper resting on the bottom.

We held our breaths and watched.

Please, I prayed to that beneficent being who watched over my family. And other families, I reminded myself. Other people want this as much as you, probably deserve it even more. Please, I said again. For sweet Lizzie. I had been dancing with joy a moment before. Now, watching Jim's hand flail in the jar, reaching, I felt heavy as lead, as if pressed to earth by an invisible hand.

Jim's fingers found one of the little papers. He grasped it between thumb and forefinger and brought his large hand out of that little jar.

"Do the honors, Jim," said Mr. Crowell, who looked as tense as I felt.

Jim, still grinning, unfolded the paper. His eyes moved back and forth. It seemed to take him forever to read the name.

"Miss Elizabeth Alcott," he finally announced.

Reader, I know we all wish to present a dignified, serious aspect of ourselves to a world that often judges harshly what it deems frivolous; but there are moments in life when one must jump for joy without further thought to reputation or judgment from others. I jumped for joy. So did elderly Mr. Crowell.

"I myself will write to Signor Massimo and ask for the first appointment time," said that fine man, after waltzing me about his store a bit. "Before Christmas or after, Miss Alcott? And don't be surprised if he serves a lunch for Lizzie. Noodles. I've had them myself. Not as hearty as a roast beef and slippery on the fork, but tasty, tasty."

"Ask for the lessons to begin immediately!" I said.

Congratulations were offered by the other eleven, at least

most of them, although some skulked out without a word, irked to have lost those coveted lessons with Signor Massimo.

Sylvia hugged me over and over, for she loved Lizzie almost as much as I did and that sad hour we had spent in the cemetery made us both thankful for the riches we shared in life: the love of those close to us.

"Are you going to tell Lizzie today, or wait?" Sylvia asked.

"She must wait awhile, yet," I said. "I have another errand, one more, and need your company for another hour."

"Where to this time, Louy? Is there a present you forgot to pick up?"

"No gift. But a visit. To a brother."

"I don't understand. How can Mrs. Phips's brother be involved with Mrs. Percy's death? It is still her death that interests you, is it not?"

"Of course. More than ever. Someday, Sylvia, I will tell you Mr. Emerson's theory of the universal mind. For now, let me say that there is an invisible connection between all beings, and sometimes those connections become visible. Mrs. Crowell gave us the next step in this investigation, without even intending to."

"What if he won't receive us?" asked Sylvia. "Then what?"

We bumped, literally, into Amelia Snodgrass coming down Charles Street. Her arms were full of bags and boxes and she was in very good spirits. She wore a bright blue day gown with a red cape over it, and a red-and-white-striped bow on her hat.

"Miss Alcott! Miss Shattuck!" she exclaimed joyfully. "How good to see you!"

She seemed to be quite a different person.

"She's awfully pleased about something," Sylvia whispered to me.

"I'm happy to see you in such high spirits," I said, a question in my voice.

"Ah. You wonder why. This terrible business with Mrs. Percy is just about over, don't you think? His accomplice is in jail and soon he himself will stand trial." There was a cruel gleam of satisfaction in her eye.

"You refer to Suzie Dear," I guessed.

"Yes, of course. And to that snake Eddie Nichols. Constable Cobban says he has been seen in Worcester and will be arrested by the Cleveland men any minute. Will he hang, do you think?" she asked eagerly.

I was, as you may guess, shocked by this extreme change in her feelings for the man; though he was a cad, she had once felt tenderly for him, I was certain.

"Let us be honest with each other," I began.

"Let us, Miss Alcott," she agreed, no longer smiling, "since if you spread any ill report of me, I'll have your father barred from every decent parlor in Boston."

"You don't have that power," I said, uncertain. Perhaps she did. "Even so, I would like to know this: Were you and Mr. Nichols more than friendly acquaintances? Did he steal the pearl necklace?"

"Yes. And yes. I was badly used by Mrs. Percy and her stepbrother. He betrayed me, and now he will pay. Louisa— may I call you Louisa?—Wilmot and I have decided not to wait the full year of mourning. We are to be married after the New Year. And then we shall go to Venice."

"My congratulations," I said.

"I will send you a card from Italy, since you are never likely to see the place yourself. Seamstresses can hardly afford to travel abroad."

That stung.

"Good day, Louisa. Sylvia." Miss Snodgrass, bearing her Christmas boxes, made her way down the sidewalk.

"I think if Eddie Nichols broke her heart, it was a rather temporary situation," said Sylvia, watching Miss Snodgrass's slender back grow smaller in the distance.

"I wonder," I said, "how far she would go for her revenge against him. And I wonder if she has yet told Mr. Wilmot Green that she cannot be married in her heirloom necklace."

CHAPTER SIXTEEN

A Brother's Anger and
a Wife's Disappointment

IT WAS, AS Mrs. Crowell had indicated, a very dilapidated
house that Emily's brother occupied, one of those sad abodes
all too obviously inhabited by one who has turned his back
on his fellow creatures, on all that is living and joyous. Once
it had been a grand, even splendiferous domicile, but houses,
like people, fall derelict if they fail to receive love and a certain amount of attention.

If anyone, I thought, knocking on that ancient, paint-
flaking door, is in need of speaking with the dead, it is this
house's inhabitant.

"What do you want?" An elderly woman, judging from
her apron and cap a servant, opened the creaking door only
halfway. She did not smile.

"To see Mr. Grayling," I said. "Please."

"He don't receive." She started to close the door but I
put my boot in the frame, preventing her. To do this I had to
move around an urn of dried and withered marigolds left

over from the summer, and their brown leaves crackled in protest.

"Please," I repeated. "It is about his sister, Emily, Mrs. Phips."

A man in a frayed silk dressing gown stepped into view. He was about sixty, with thin white hair sweeping unkempt to his shoulders, and spectacles slipping down his narrow nose. He wore a French military jacket over his nightshirt, and a three-cornered hat.

"May we come in, just for a moment?" I asked. The wind was blowing, and both Sylvia and I shivered from the cold.

We were allowed in, but barely, restrained to the threshold with the still-open door at our backs and the wind howling, and before us the dark, cold hall. I longed for a sitting room with a warm hearth. Mr. Grayling hopped from foot to foot, as children do, alternately grinning and frowning at us as he asked the purpose of our interruption of his day.

"The soldiers are lined up for the Battle of Waterloo," he said with a glower. "Do you think Napoleon will wait?" He clutched one of the little lead soldiers in his hand.

Sylvia stood very close at my side, saying nothing.

"Mrs. Percy is dead," I said, trying to think of a way to begin my questions. "Did you know?"

"No, I did not. Haven't read a newspaper in years. But if Mrs. Percy is gone, good, I say. And none too soon," replied he, grinning madly. "Are you here just to tell me that? Who are you?"

"Miss Louisa May Alcott. And my friend, Miss Sylvia Shattuck."

I extended my hand. He did not take it. "Was Mrs. Percy a friend of your sister's?" I asked.

He shook his shaggy head. "No. They never even met. But Mrs. Percy came asking questions about her a few months ago. Good-bye." He began to push us gently toward the still-open door.

"I should love to see the battle scene," I said.

"Truly? Then come in, come in."

The Battle of Waterloo took up the entire floor of the front parlor. All of the furniture had been taken out and the rug rolled up, so that Napoleon and his brigades, led by Grouchy, Vandamme, and Gerard in their tricornered hats, faced off across Blucher's Prussian army with their plumed helmets. I picked up one of the little soldiers to admire the fine detailing of the uniform.

"Put Ponsonby back down!" ordered Mr. Grayling, trembling with emotion. "Be useful, and if you must touch, bring up some of those cavalry. They are lagging behind." He saluted, as if he had just given an order in the field.

I crouched on the floor, trying to keep my heavy skirts from tipping over a regiment or two, and brought up the cavalry.

"Fine, fine." Mr. Grayling chuckled. "Napoleon will have a surprise or two this day."

"Mr. Grayling, what do you know of relations between your sister and Mrs. Percy?"

"Weren't no such thing," he said, tenderly brushing a mote of dust from a cunningly crafted figure of the well-known Marshal Ney. "After Emily's funeral Mrs. Percy came and asked questions and implied she was a good friend of William

Phips, knew about him in China, the old days. I had a sense of what she meant by *friend*. Mr. Phips was a disloyal husband. Over and over. He was a bounder, and those things often go together. Bring up more cavalry, quickly."

"Oh, my," spoke up Sylvia, who had been watching from the doorway.

"Are you certain?" I asked, pushing some of the cavalry closer to the center of the field. I tried to imagine courtly Mr. Phips and blowsy Mrs. Percy as illicit lovers, or indeed lovers of any kind, and admit that the effort was too much for my imagination. Certainly Mr. Grayling was wrong on that point; Mrs. Percy had been interested in Mr. Phips for reasons other than romance.

"I know a brute when I see one," said Mr. Grayling, crouching before a group of foot soldiers and readjusting their alignment. "I warned Emily not to marry him. Better to live with a broken heart, since August had died. But she didn't listen. Now August, there was a good lad. I never believed that story William told Emily, about August marrying a Chinese woman. Never believed it. Now she's dead and Mrs. Percy is murdered, and that was a job well-done. And now, I really must concentrate on the battle. Time to be off with you."

"Well," said Sylvia, having little else to say after we had been shown the door and that door slammed on our backs.

"Well, indeed," I said, somewhat stunned by this turn of events. I turned up my collar against the cold.

"Mr. Grayling doesn't seem the type to forgive a trespass against his sister."

"Worse," I said, "his last statement, 'a job well-done,' worries me. If he did not read the obituary, how did he know Mrs. Percy did not die a natural death? I wonder if brotherly love might extend as far as violence." Yet, worry as I might about the strength of a brother's passion to defend his sister from the woman he believed had wronged her, a dark light shone from the end of this tunnel: Perhaps Mr. Barnum was an innocent bystander after all.

"The situation grows ever more complicated," Sylvia said. "Truthfully, I'm having difficulty picturing Mr. Phips straying from his marital obligation."

"He would have been a younger man, Sylvia, and men do stray sometimes. Perhaps he attends séances because of his feelings of guilt. Isn't that what Mrs. Percy told him? 'I forgive you, William. I know there was another, but I forgive.'"

"Oh, Albert!" Sylvia sighed, looking ahead to dark days in her own marriage, days I hoped would never occur, for if ever a woman was meant for domestic happiness that woman was Sylvia.

"Constable Cobban seems the loyal type," I said. "One could even say dogged in his pursuits. Don't anticipate problems that will in all likelihood never arise," I recommended.

We walked with haste to our own abodes, the wind howling about our ears. The drifting snow blew so fiercely we could not speak, but only gasp for breath and lean forward, into the wind. A day that had begun with such promise, with payment for work and that glorious hour of buying presents for my darlings, with Lizzie's winning of the lottery and a friendly tea with Sylvia, was now ending very badly, with low spirits and more confusion, not less.

Martha, Auntie Bond's housekeeper, greeted me at her

door. "You look all done in, Miss Louisa. Come sit by the fire. Your aunt is in the parlor, with her guests."

I had forgotten she had a card party planned for that evening. "I am done in," I agreed, sitting heavily on a bench, untying my wet boots, and leaving them there in the hall on a piece of oilcloth so that they would not stain her rugs. My toes poked out of new holes in my knit stockings. I had hours of darning ahead of me, and nothing pushed me closer to the Slough of Despond than having to mend old stockings.

A quick thumbing through the day's mail from the tray by the door revealed no new letters from Marmee or Father, and my chest felt hollow with missing them. There was a quick note from Mrs. O'Connor, though, and this I tore open and read greedily, hoping for news of Meh-ki.

No word of her yet, dearie, but don't worry, she'll show up in someone's kitchen. A cook has got to cook, don't she, and I've ears in all the kitchens of Boston. We'll find her.

Feeling as heavy as one of Mr. Grayling's lead soldiers, I put the note in my pocket and wondered for the hundredth time: Why had Meh-ki fled Mrs. Percy's home in the middle of the night? What did she know about those strange events, or had she perhaps even witnessed the murder?

"What is it, dear? You are grimacing," said Lizzie, who had come downstairs to join me in our favorite chairs in front of the blazing fire. Auntie Bond believed in old-fashioned comfort, and her chairs were plumped with feather cushions, not the new kind built around creaking springs that almost made one seasick if one shifted too quickly. I was glad for this comfort, for the blazing hearth, for coming home to a friendly soul who would listen, for more than ever I missed Marmee—Marmee who, with her knowledge of human nature, would have made sense of all this.

"I am lost in a wood," I told Lizzie, putting my stockinged feet perilously close to the hearth. "I cannot find the path."

"You refer to Mrs. Percy," Lizzie guessed. "Louy, look at those holes in your stockings! They are whoppers!"

Auntie Bond came in just then to fetch another lamp for her card party visitors. "I knew this was going to be problematic as soon as you announced you were attending one of her séances," she said, having overheard us. "I've never, Louisa, never heard good of Mrs. Percy. I'm not surprised that even dead she is proving to be difficult."

"Who is being difficult?" asked Martha, gliding into the room and holding a tray with sliced bread, strawberry preserves, and two toasting forks. "Tea is coming as well, my dears." She put down the tray and returned to the kitchen.

"I'll put bread on the fork for you, Louy," offered Lizzie.

"Have you heard much at all about Mrs. Percy?" I asked Auntie Bond, pressing deeply into those old-fashioned feather cushions for warmth and comfort.

"Oh, all sorts of talk," she admitted, wiping a bit of dust from the lamp with her dress sleeve, "though I don't like to repeat gossip." She cleared her throat and pursed her mouth as if forbidding herself to say more.

"Gossip about affairs?" I asked.

"Who is having affairs?" Lizzie asked. Her face had flushed red from sitting close to the flames.

"You are too young, dear," said Auntie Bond.

"I'm twenty," retorted Lizzie, "and anything that concerns Louy also concerns me."

"That is the gossip I wished to avoid," admitted Auntie Bond. "Yes, affairs. And suspicions of other irregularities in her household. She was in Boston some years before, you know, and there were all sorts of rumors. Mrs. Percy was a very unhappy woman, I fear."

"Have you heard any reports about her cook, Meh-ki?" I asked, pushing my toasting fork closer to the flames. A little clot of flour on the crust sparked and flamed in a small explosion for a second, and I thought of Mr. Grayling and the ongoing Battle of Waterloo in his parlor, and the funny sounds I had heard men make when they played at war or described it, those pops and bangs, with a life ending with each one, though that was not discussed, not described.

"Nothing about the cook. Many people disapproved of her having a Chinawoman in the house, but she had to eat and sleep, didn't she? She needed a place, and to Mrs. Percy's credit she gave her one."

"Out of the kindness of her heart," I said softly, "though kindness does not seem to have been one of Mrs. Percy's virtues."

"I must return to my guests, Louy. Look, your toast is burning."

I plucked the bread from the toasting fork and spread jam thickly on it. "Happiness consists in virtue, not winning, Father always says."

"That would explain Mrs. Percy's lack of happiness," said Auntie Bond. "See you later, darlings. I must win at least one round before the evening is over or I shall be out of sorts all tomorrow." She left us to return to a new hand of cards. A moment later we heard laughter in the front parlor and then the buzz of voices spoken so as not to be overheard. I was sure that the older ladies playing at cards had plenty to say about Mrs. Percy that they did not want the "young" ladies to overhear. I speared another piece of bread with my fork.

I began to wonder—just wonder, mind you—if a life lived with something other than virtue as its premise might also have some rewards, adventure among them.

The doorbell rang. Martha padded lightly down the hall. She came into the sitting room a moment later.

"A gentleman here to see you, miss," she told me. "A Mr. Cobban. Should I bring him in?" Lizzie looked up, her eyes bright with interest.

"Ah." Constable Cobban was already standing behind her, in the hall, twisting his hat about in his hands and blushing fiery red. "I had hoped . . . had hoped I might find you alone," he said.

"What!" exclaimed a startled Lizzie, smiling.

"I mean . . . I mean . . . I had hoped for a few private words with Miss Alcott." I had never heard him stammer before. That was how I knew he was there to discuss Sylvia. He twisted his hat so furiously I was afraid it would be torn to shreds.

"Come," I said, rising. "We can speak openly before Lizzie."

He seemed much younger, boyish, since his visit was social rather than professional. Feeling almost sisterly, I poured him a cup of tea and gave him my toasted bread. He turned it this way and that and finally took a bite, then put the toast down on his tea saucer.

"It's about Miss Shattuck," he said finally.

"I know," I said. Lizzie hummed to herself and crouched close to the hearth, pretending to concentrate on her toast.

"You do?" He looked up in shocked surprise. Men can be so very slow-witted about these things.

"I . . . I . . . I would like to know the name of her fiancé."

"Fiancé?" I repeated, confused.

"Has Sylvia a fiancé?" asked Lizzie.

"She mentioned plans for a honeymoon in Niagara Falls. I distinctly heard her," he said.

"Oh! That!" How long ago it seemed, that afternoon when Mrs. Percy had first been discovered dead, with the Niagara Falls souvenir pillow on the floor next to her sofa. "I assure you, Mr. Cobban, she has not got a fiancé. She was just thinking of a possible future event."

He nodded, comprehending. "She intended me to feel jealous."

"She did. Did it work?"

"I . . . I . . ." The stammer had returned. "I have feelings for your friend, Miss Alcott. Do you mind?"

I put another piece of toasting bread on my fork, hesitating to answer. "It is not that I mind," I said after a while. "More that I don't understand."

"What is there to understand? She is kind and gentle and virtuous, is she not?" Cobban said.

"She has lovely hair," Lizzie agreed, twisting her fork in the flames.

"And a lively humor and disposition!" Cobban said, glad for an ally. "All in all she's a splendid girl, I think. First-rate. I could not ask for a finer friend in life."

"But I fear for the two of you," I said, deciding to speak openly. "Married life is very trying, and does need infinite patience and love as well as an eye to practical matters. Mother and Father taught me that much. You would both rebel if you were mated for life. You are too different and both too fond of freedom. Sylvia is . . . Well, she is not the kind to make a stew and boil lye soap for the laundry, if you see what I mean. She has never had to work in that manner."

"Do you imagine I haven't thought of that?" Cobban drank his tea in one gulp. "But I would help her. And she is quick. She could learn. And though I am penniless now, I am industrious. I have bought stock in the railroad and shares in a trading vessel. I plan to do quite well, Miss Alcott."

"I am certain you shall," I said, leaning back and studying his earnest, freckled face. It seemed I might be seeing Mr. Cobban on a regular basis in the future, and as a friend, not as an officer of the law. Suddenly I felt that this could be a pleasant situation, that he could provide the masculine comradeship I'd not had in a brother, if he were attached to my closest friend.

"I intend to speak with her mother," he said. "But, Miss Alcott, Sylvia is closer to you than anyone else in this world. If I should interfere with your friendship, I would feel like a cad."

His blue eyes were round with earnest sincerity. I took his hand in mine. "Mr. Cobban, if you make Sylvia happy, then you also add to my happiness."

"Thank you! Thank you!" Now he swallowed the toast in one bite. "I am so glad that barrier is removed. I dislike this kind of scene."

"But you handled it very well!" exclaimed Lizzie. "Oh, bravo!" She applauded.

"I would rather discuss Mrs. Percy," I agreed.

"Eddie Nichols is in Worcester, we believe, and Pinkerton's men are hot on his heels. It is just a question of time. Is there more toast, Miss Alcott? I haven't had supper."

"Martha will bring us more. You still think Eddie Nichols murdered Mrs. Percy?"

"All signs point to it. He had the reason to wish her dead and the morals that would allow him to take another life. Obviously they had a falling-out and he wished to be rid of her. She knew too much about him. More tea, too, please?"

"I have met the brother of Mrs. Phips," I said. "He also has a motive, though an old one, and I don't know if he is capable of murder. But he believes that Mrs. Percy once caused his sister great unhappiness, so much unhappiness that it added to her death."

"Then I shall speak with him, though I think it is a waste of time. Mr. Nichols is our man."

Was he?

Cobban left a few moments later, having achieved the purpose of his visit—that unsurprising announcement of his feelings for my friend Sylvia. I sat dreaming before the fire, still strangely at odds now that I had no labor to occupy my hands. It was weeks before the spring shirts would need to be finished. Lizzie, after a while, went to the old piano and began to play Christmas tunes, but my spirits stayed apathetic, wondering. She went up to bed at ten; at ten thirty Auntie Bond's guests began to leave and Mrs. Wallace, a woman I had met before, came in to say good evening. She was a kindly soul with a perpetual look of disappointment in her lovely blue eyes, as if life had never measured up to her expectations.

"Miss Bond tells me you have been asking about Mrs. Percy," she said quietly, taking a seat in the chair next to me.

"Did you know her?" I asked, sitting up.

"Yes. In our younger days, and I knew many of her friends, when she still had them. When you have lived in one place all your life acquaintances build up, rather like the nacre on a pearl, only of course some acquaintances aren't at all luminous." She paused, wondering if she should go on. She had her hat on, but carried her cloak. Obviously she was willing to spend a moment or two with me.

"Please tell me of whom you speak," I asked.

"Mr. Phips." Her tone was icy.

"You do not care for him."

"I do not. He was possessive, in the way that men who marry above themselves can be. He cut his wife off from her old acquaintances, and he was no gentleman, Miss Alcott; I will tell you that much. Poor Emily. She never really stopped grieving for August Pincher. His death just about destroyed her. And then William Phips came along, carrying words from her dead beloved, carrying that portrait, and he convinced her she would be happy with him. Oh, the promises men will make." Her voice trailed off.

"Were Emily and William well matched?" I asked, intensely disliking that I sounded much as Sylvia's mother would have sounded at that moment—but sometimes, patient reader, facts of finance are relevant.

Mrs. Wallace tucked a strand of her lovely white hair back into its snood and paused before answering, as if in reflection. "My dear, his father was a stable hand in Pennsylvania. Breeding tells, in the long run. I'm certain he married for wealth and position. And there was considerable wealth in that family. Don't let the brother's eccentricity fool you. The Grayling children each inherited a small fortune. Many a man marries for wealth, and learns to love his bride." Her voice grew very soft and she seemed to become distracted. Then she shook off the mood and continued her story. "I'm not certain Phips grew to love Emily, not in the way she deserved. His kindness certainly had limits. He told her once—and I'm certain he meant to give pain, to take revenge for some little domestic sin she had committed—that August Pincher had been unfaithful to her in Canton, that he had taken a Chinese bride. I think he invented it, Miss Alcott, to wound Emily."

"Yes, her brother had the same belief. Her beloved Mr. Pincher," I said, wondering. "I feel sorry for your friend, Mrs. Wallace. She was unable to find any man true and loyal." In fact, I felt sorry for both husband and wife—for Emily, who lost her true love and married for comfort, only to find marriage brought no guarantees of peace; and for William Phips, the son of a laborer who had dreams to better himself and who married well, but perhaps without that passion that inspires fidelity, perhaps knowing he was never truly loved, not as another had once been.

"Poor Emily wasted away in that house, in that marriage. She, who had once been so worthy of love. Good night, Louisa," said Mrs. Wallace. On impulse she bent and kissed my forehead, as Marmee would have, had she been there.

"Only a fool marries for something less than love," Marmee had often told me. "I hope my daughters never make such a mistake."

When the house was quiet and I was alone in my writing room, I thought again of Mr. Barnum, of the relief that had been evident in his manner when Mrs. Percy had been found dead. I thought of the many strange people that Sylvia's adventure into the world of séances had brought into my life: Mrs. Deeds with her greed for jewels, even or perhaps especially those belonging to other people; her meek husband, almost too meek, so that he seemed to be playing a role—perhaps he had resented that dangerous triangular friendship between his wife, Mrs. Percy, and Mr. Nichols? Amelia Snodgrass, betrothed to a gentleman from whom she kept secrets, and now facing long years of overcoming the regret and pain of her affair with another man who had betrayed her several times and involved Mrs. Percy in those betrayals.

Mr. Barnum. Mr. Phineas T. Barnum, the greatest showman of all time, now tottering on disgrace and bankruptcy, thanks to Mrs. Percy's ability to forge signatures. My heart sank as I thought of him, and I knew deep in my heart that he had wished her dead.

The maid, Suzie Dear, still in jail and with many years of jail ahead of her, most likely, for having been caught with stolen goods, and the unfairness of that —for all I knew the items had been given to her by Mrs. Percy, as bribery as well as payment. Could Suzie, that flighty young woman, have murdered? Had her mistress not been generous enough?

Mr. Phips, the son of a stable hand, a war hero who married well, very well, but did not keep his vows to his wife, who caused her so much unhappiness that she lost her desire to live.

And at the middle of so much unhappiness was Agatha

Percy. She was the connection, the universal theme that united them.

There had been another. Yes, the Chinese cook, Meh-ki, who had fled in the middle of the night, the night that Mrs. Percy had been murdered. What had been her role in all of this? Certainly her actions, that hasty flight, had brought suspicion upon her. Why had she fled, when I merely wished to speak with her? Because that is what immigrants do, a voice that sounded suspiciously like Marmee's said in my head. Imagine yourself in a new country filled with unfamiliar customs, a language you barely understand, and now imagine that a great crime has occurred and you will be suspected of involvement. You flee.

I sighed. So many unexplained events, so many people who were not what they seemed, who had secrets and buried passions, for money, for forgiveness, for freedom, or even simply for excitement. Mrs. Percy, I said in my head, what strange course of events did you set in action that your own death must follow?

The voice answered immediately, the woman's voice in my head that had been telling me the story of "Agatha's Confession":

> I listened to the evil demon that possessed me, and hardening my woman's heart, I vowed a solemn vow that she should never win the prize she sought, never, if I killed her to prevent it.
>
> And I muttered to myself, "Twice I have conquered my revengeful spirit, but to be more deeply wounded. Now I will yield to it, and if a word of mine could save her, I would not utter it."

And so Agatha allows her former friend, Clara, to be buried alive. Could a word, I wondered, have saved Mrs. Agatha Percy? What word, and from whom? My two Agathas, the one in my story and the real Mrs. Percy, I saw now shared a similar fatal flaw, the blind merging of the living with the dead, and both would pay heavily for this sin, my Agatha by losing, finally and forever, the love of her life, and Mrs. Agatha Percy with her own life.

CHAPTER SEVENTEEN

The Cook Reappears

THE NEXT MORNING dawned bright and fair with a cold winter sun gleaming off the icicles hanging from the eaves. I awoke to a clatter of pots and pans coming from the kitchen and pantry. Auntie Bond was baking her famous Christmas seed cake, for while the neighborhood bakery might make a fine queen's cake and lemon pound cake, no one baked as fine a seed cake as Auntie Bond.

"May I help?" I asked, when I had thrown on my workaday brown dress and gone downstairs.

"You might shell the walnuts, please," Auntie Bond proposed, handing me a bag of nuts. "There's just enough time before the holidays to bake and soak a batch of cakes to send to Walpole." She winked. The secret of Auntie Bond's seed cakes: She aged them in brandy!

"Did you win a round last night?" I asked, finding in the table drawer the little hammer she kept for nutcracking.

"Three rounds! I won twelve cents! Don't tell your father,

Louisa. I know how he disapproves of gambling. I'll give a dime to the missions to make up for my little sin."

I spent the morning chopping walnuts and hazelnuts and chatting pleasantly with Auntie Bond about the holidays. I forced myself to cease thinking about Mrs. Percy. I had done what I could, and asked all the questions I could think to ask, and had only found myself deeper and deeper in confusion. Many puzzles are like that—they make no sense until the very last piece has been put into place. Except how does one know what the last piece is?

In the morning mail was a note from Mr. Crowell, which I took hastily from the tray and opened in private, so that neither Lizzie nor Auntie Bond could read it over my shoulder:

Signor Massimo will meet with your sister Elizabeth at three o'clock this afternoon. Will that suit?

"Lizzie," I called into the parlor, where she sat at the piano. "Can you come with me on an errand this afternoon?"

"Yes, Louy!"

"Be sure and wear your best hat and gloves!"

"Why, Louy, where are we going?"

"A surprise," I told her. "Part of your Christmas present!"

Three o'clock would suit, I wrote back to Mr. Crowell.

I dressed in my best as well, my best at that time being another brown workaday dress, but a newer one without scorch holes from hearth sparks and with a touch of lace at the wrists and throat. Eager to make a good impression on the great maestro, I carefully brushed my thick chestnut hair

into its snood and put a dab of lavender water on my handkerchief; in my pocket I carried my notebook and a pencil. Who
knew when I might need an authentic description of a great
Italian musician for a story?

"Louy, your face is a study, but you look splendid," said
Lizzie, coming down the stairs to meet me. "And you smell
nice, too. Is that lavender water? Why, Louy, what is this
about?"

"A surprise," I said. "You'll have to wait and see. First, a
little walk, if you don't mind. Your warmest coat, dear."

"Must I be blindfolded? Is this to be another séance?"

"Neither, thankfully. I have no desire to sit in the dark
and play at ghosts, have you? I thought not. This will be much
more pleasant."

Signor Massimo had rented a little house on Tremont
Street just across from the Common, situated with a fine view
of the greenery in the park, which seemed even lovelier that
day with its adornment of snow and icicles. When his servant
opened the door to us I very carefully said that the Alcott ladies were there for their appointment, and to prolong the surprise, did not yet mention Signor Massimo's name. I was
relishing every moment, anticipating the delight that would
replace the puzzlement in my sister's eyes.

The maestro had taken the house furnished, for the set-
tees and lace curtains and thick, dutiful carpets all seemed
very Bostonian and not at all Roman. But he had added his
own thrilling touches: little statues of Apollo Belvedere and
Venus placed here and there where occasional sun might
shine on their white marble; bunches of glass grapes wreathed
about doorways; a good oil of Pompeii in the hall.

We were shown to a little sitting room appointed with a cleverly carved table whose legs ended in satyrs' bodies, a matching settee and four chairs, a carpet patterned with cherubs and grapevines (surely that was Roman rather than Bostonian!), and a chiseled and painted wooden rack filled with sheet music, which his visitors could pick up and read as if they were newspapers!

But Lizzie was far too nervous to read. She sat stiffly in a chair, hands folded in her lap, feet flat on the floor. "Why are we here, Louy? What a strange place this is."

"Isn't it grand?" I asked. "What is that smell, do you think? Garlic? How wonderful! I would love to taste some."

"Smells like plain onion to me," said Lizzie. "But you haven't said why we are here."

"Have you heard of Signor Massimo, Lizzie?" I forced nonchalance into my voice, but the suspense of this surprise was making my face feel warm. Would she be pleased?

"Why, who hasn't?" Lizzie said. "I've already inquired about tickets for his performances, but they are far too expensive. I should love to hear him play Liszt." Her eyes grew dreamy; her shoulders relaxed a little as she imagined that inaccessible music.

"You shall do better than hear him in a public hall," I said. "You shall hear a private concert and then have lessons with him besides."

"Why, how is that possible, Louy? We are as poor as church mice. Not that I'm complaining, mind you. I have Marmee and Father and you and Abby and Anna and couldn't want for much more than that. Perhaps a good piano someday." Her voice trailed off with a little sigh.

"We are poor as church mice, but much luckier! Look!" I held up the little scrap of paper with her name on it and told her about the purchase of the portfolio and the lottery, a lottery we had won, and now she would have lessons with Signor Massimo himself, on his own grand piano.

"Oh, Louy!" Her eyes shone so I feared she would faint, and that would be difficult, as I had no salts with me. But Lizzie had a staunch heart; she did not swoon but only looked at me with joy and love and wonder, and in her gaze was the true meaning of Christmas.

"The maestro is ready for the young lady," said the same servant who had opened the door to us. He was tall and dressed in expensive livery, yet when he bowed Lizzie into the hall there was a friendly sparkle in his eye.

"When shall I return for her?" I asked.

"At four thirty," said the servant in a beautifully accented voice. "And then you will both take a little supper with the maestro, if you please. The soprano, Maria Venturi, will join you as well."

"Oh, Louy!" Shy Lizzie clasped her hands with delight. "Maria Venturi!" The soprano was second only to Jenny Lind in fame; this was almost too much for me as well.

"We accept with gratitude," I managed to reply.

I watched as the servant, with elegantly outstretched palm, led Lizzie down the hall. She was a small delicate girl dressed in blue next to that tall, powerful man dressed in brown. I saw, or was reminded, how fragile my sister was. A maid showed me to the door, and I was free, with nothing to do for an hour and a half but ramble through the Common and wonder if Lizzie was enjoying her music lesson.

But pure enjoyment is not a gift to humans from the gods. Underneath my pleasure in Lizzie's pleasure was a new worry. Signor Massimo had been invited to the séance circle and had not come, I remembered; had there been some ill will between him and Mrs. Percy? Why had I not thought of it before? The shock was such that it brought me to a complete standstill on the sidewalk as people poured around me like a river around a stone.

Louisa, I told myself sternly, you have been too narrow in your thinking, considering only those who were at the séance, not those who disdained to come. But surely not? Mr. Crowell had spoken most warmly of Signor Massimo. But Mr. Crowell thinks only of musical talent, I thought, and does not consider other virtues or vices if the music be divine. Tomorrow I would have to begin all over again and see what could be discovered about Signor Massimo. I would say nothing to Lizzie. I wished, then, that I had waited for my sister in the sitting room.

Too late. Distracted and newly unhappy—how fleeting is joy!—I decided to visit a tea shop on Avery Street, two blocks from Signor Massimo's house, and wait there till it was time to go back for Lizzie. I would use the hour to make notes about the artwork in Signor's house.

The usually quiet tea shop was doing a thriving business that afternoon, and after I found one little table in the back and was served tea and a plate of pastries, I realized why. They had a new pastry cook, and the usually heavy, lardy cakes had been replaced by ones light and tender as angel's breath. Matrons, children, men of affairs in their top hats and capes, all stood or sat in groups gobbling with pleasure.

Mrs. O'Connor? I wondered. Is it possible? But the muf-
fins had candied orange peel in them, and that was one of the
Irishwoman's trademark recipes. I was correct. No sooner
had I finished my second raisin bun than I saw that friendly
and gifted cook waving at me over the little counter that separated the glass case from the table area.

"Louisa!" she called. "Miss Alcott! A word! How lucky
you came. How did you know to find me?" she asked, when I
had risen from my chair to struggle through the crowd and
meet her at the counter.

"I didn't. I was just walking in the area." An arm rose free
from the throng of customers behind me and almost knocked
my hat off before it disappeared back into the fidgeting mass.
I clutched my hat and reticule.

"Well. You do have a four-leaf clover in your pocket, then,
for I was just about to send a message to you, but I've been so
busy I couldn't find time to pick up a pencil. I know where
that Chinese woman is cooking, or at least how you might
find her. Do you like the lemon cake? I've put in some ginger
as well."

"It's a dream," I shouted over the clamoring customers,
who were ordering cookies and cakes and pastries by the
boxful. A little serving girl behind the counter, trying to keep
up with the orders, was panting from exertion. "But tell me
about Meh-ki! How did you find her?"

"Two pounds of poppy-seed roll," shouted a man behind
me, tired of waiting his turn with the counter girl.

"Here now, do I look like a cash register?" Mrs. O'Connor
shouted back. "Give your order to the girl over there. Like
this," she said, leaning in my direction. "I'm cooking a Christ-

mas dinner for Mrs. Simon on Boylston—you know the house, the one with the little trees in front trimmed to look like spirals and such? Imagine, so much money you can pay to barber a tree."

"Meh-ki," I reminded her.

"Meh-ki. And while I was at Mrs. Simon's, getting the menu from her, I saw that gent you told me about, that Mr. Barnum. He's a friend of the family, I think, been invited for the dinner, but he said he couldn't make it. Asked me if I'd ever done my cooking before a crowd, said it might draw people to see a soufflé done up."

"Meh-ki," I said again.

Mrs. O'Connor picked up the thread of her tale. "So I'm going to the butcher to pick up the turkey I ordered for her, a big fat one, will roast up just fine with a marmalade glaze. And there's another turkey there, scrawnier but still tasty-looking, tasty, and the butcher is complaining that it ain't been fetched yet, and he's tired of feeding it corn and having it torment his little dog. Been paid for, and reserved for an Italian big shot, some sort of artist, new in Boston, and guess who paid for it? A Chinese woman, he says. Well, there can't be that many, can there?" She smiled and folded her arms over her ample bosom.

"Well-done!" I said but I had insufficient time to ponder the full meaning of this, for I heard a voice behind me calling my name. I turned and saw Mr. Phips smiling and waving, his top hat frosted with snow and his long nose gleaming from the cold. He forced his way through the crowd to my side, muttering, "Beg pardon," and, "Sorry," as he pushed toward me.

"Have you come for the poppy-seed roll?" I asked, less

than delighted to see him, for once you have learned a man's imperfection—that he made his wife unhappy—it is difficult to feel a real warmth for him.

"Ha. A little joke. Poppy. Opium. Yes, you have humor, I see. No, I've come for a seed cake. And you?"

"Tea. I had an hour of free time."

"What a shame. I would have joined you if I'd known. A young woman alone for tea. Doesn't seem correct. You have ignored my invitation to tea." He peered down his red nose at me, offended.

"I have been so very busy," I said, not feeling at all deprived not to have spent the hour with him, for he had become, in my imagination, the Faithless Husband.

"I heard you talking about a turkey. Are you having a dinner?" Was there something pleading in his voice, a supplication for friendship despite all? He must be a very lonely man, I thought, relenting somewhat.

"Not I, but I believe the pianist Signor Massimo is planning one." I tried to add some warmth to my voice. "To be given by his new cook."

"New cook? Before the holidays?" said Mr. Phips. "I don't envy him. She'll have the kitchen topsy-turvy and his meals all backward before she knows what goes where."

"Worse, she'll serve him soup made from birds' nests. I've heard they do that," shouted Mrs. O'Connor. "He's hired Mrs. Percy's Chinese woman."

"Has he now? Well." Mr. Phips's eyes opened wide in surprise. "Well, I will pick up my cake and be on my way. Good day, Miss Alcott. Beware of foreigners, Miss Alcott. They can be a treacherous lot."

"Many share your opinion." I did not. "Good day, Mr. Phips." He tipped his hat. I gave a half smile, and we parted company. Well, I thought. Many a man committed sins in his youth. I must not judge. At the door he turned and gave me a last wave of his hand. He turned left out the door, going in the direction I had come from a moment before.

The more important thing now was to return to Signor Massimo's and see if I might speak with his new cook, Meh-ki, for it would be impossible for a Chinese woman working for an Italian artist, newly arrived in Boston, not to be Meh-ki, it seemed. I had remembered by then what Mr. Crowell had said of his supper with Signor Massimo: There had been noodles, and while Italians often eat macaroni, Chinese also cook noodles. Meh-ki was found. But what would she reveal about the murder of Mrs. Percy? Please, I prayed, don't let her tell me that it was Mr. Barnum who came that night, who quarreled with Mrs. Percy, terrified Meh-ki in the kitchen, and then left, a murderer hiding in shadow.

CHAPTER EIGHTEEN

The Deadly Dessert Knife

THERE WAS ANOTHER half hour before Lizzie's lesson would be finished, but I decided not to wait the full time. I finished my cup of tea and pushed away the half-full plate of pastries, having lost my appetite. Mrs. O'Connor's news had given me a fresh sense of urgency; for all I knew Meh-ki might disappear again, and she seemed to be the key to this puzzle. It was time, past time, to know the answer of the fate of Mrs. Percy, so that I might enjoy Christmas, truly celebrate with a lightness of spirit and confidence that there is good in the world, there is a possibility for justice—for until I knew all the truth of Mrs. Percy, too many secrets about our society would also be hidden, and what is kept in darkness can never be healed or corrected.

Mr. Emerson, I thought, putting on my old, worn cape and my new gloves from Sylvia, you told me about the Oversoul, the light within us all that can guide us to reason and faith and goodness, if we will but let it, if we will obey our own better instincts. Husbands who are unfaithful are disobeying their instinct to love and protect that chosen one; businessmen who seek revenge against betraying affiliations disobey that better instinct to learn and make wiser choices in the future; young women who forge alliances with untrustworthy men disobey their instinct to bestow affection only when and where it is earned. All of Mrs. Percy's customers and associates somehow disobeyed the Over-soul, and she paid the heaviest price for their collective guilt.

My steps grew rushed. The more I thought about Lizzie being in that house where Meh-ki had found new employment, the more worried I became.

Only two blocks away, but yet it seemed a tremendous distance. Had the crowd grown even thicker? I had to force myself past wide groups walking abreast on the sidewalk, through swarms of children with skates slung over their shoulders. It had begun to snow again, making the walks slippery, my footing unsure. My progress took on a dreamlike quality, when one flails and strives and yet the goal keeps receding into the distance, and the feet grow heavier and heavier till they can't be lifted at all.

Lizzie, I thought, swimming through the crowd, my arms pushing in a breaststroke through snow and thick humanity, trying to get to my beloved sister. Every instinct I had, every cell of my soul, said she was in danger and I had been foolish to leave her there.

Finally, after fifteen minutes that seemed to last a full day, I arrived back at Signor Massimo's front door. I pulled the bell cord; it chimed. The servant did not come. I pulled again, harder, and again. No servant. Something was very wrong, I was even more certain.

Tentatively I tried the door. It was unlocked and swung easily open, but stopped short of its swing and would not budge past halfway. Sliding through, crushing my hooped skirt and not giving a damn about it, I saw the blockage. Signor Massimo's servant was sprawled on the floor, unconscious, a wound on his head seeping red blood onto the white-tiled floor. I pushed up his shirt cuff and took his pulse. It was faint, but regular. There was time; he could survive without immediate ministration.

"Lizzie!" I shouted. There was no sound in the house. No piano, no voices. Nothing. "Lizzie!" I screamed, my heart rising into my throat. I raced up the stairs to the first floor, where Lizzie and I had waited for the appointment. No one was there. I ran down the hall, throwing open door after door, and finding no one. "Lizzie!" I kept shouting. "Where are you?" No one answered.

I flew back downstairs to the kitchen, to Meh-ki, for I sensed then that where Meh-ki was, my sister would also be. Somehow they had been united in a shared and dangerous destiny, my beautiful, fragile sister and Meh-ki.

Through the thick wooden door, designed to keep out all noise so that the gentlefolk would not be disturbed by the sounds of the kitchen, through that heavy door I pushed and stopped, frozen.

They were there in a terrifying tableau, at first incomprehensible to me: Meh-ki was in the wild embrace of Mr. Phips, half dead, it seemed, and Lizzie was at her side, pushing and pulling at Mr. Phips, who kicked and shoved at her with his shoulder.

Then I realized what was truly happening. Mr. Phips, his pale eyes huge with rage, his lips drawn back like a rabid dog's, held a knife to Meh-ki's throat, and Lizzie, little Lizzie, was beating at him with her fists, crying and shouting that he was to let the woman go. On the floor, unconscious, with blood seeping from a large gash in his forehead, was Signor Massimo.

"Louy!" Lizzie screamed. "Help! He's going to kill her!"

"She must die!" growled Mr. Phips. "She's going to ruin everything I've worked for. I worked hard; I deserve it. I put up with that family, with Emily's weeping and sighing all those years for another man, and now her wealth is mine and no one will take it from me! Life requires boldness!" His voice seemed barely human.

"Put it down," I told him, standing as still as does a doe who has sighted the hunter.

"She's going to ruin everything!" he said again, pressing the knife deeper into Meh-ki's throat. "Why did she come here? She wants to ruin me!" Little drops of blood ran down onto Meh-ki's white apron. Her eyes turned in my direction, pleading and at the same time surrendering, ready to die, hopeless. Never will I forget that gaze.

"Don't," I begged. "Don't add this crime to the others. It is too late, Mr. Phips." He did not release Meh-ki, but I had enough of his attention that he had stopped lurching and kicking at Lizzie, trying to drive her away.

"No!" he shouted, and I saw his arm twist slightly, saw the slight movement as he prepared to press the knife even deeper, saw Meh-ki go limp in his deadly embrace. And then Lizzie's slender arm in its girlish blue dress rose up over his head, holding something in the little fist, and came down again. I heard the thump of solid wood against flesh and bone, heard the strange slithering sound as Mr. Phips slid to the floor, unconscious, with Meh-ki still locked in his embrace.

"Oh, Louy!" said Lizzie. "I've murdered him!" And then Lizzie collapsed to the floor as well in a swoon.

THE REST OF the day was quite busy, as you can imagine, gentle reader. There was much cleaning up to do, much chafing of wrists, binding of wounds, explaining.

"Signor Massimo asked me to play something for him," said Lizzie, resting upon a divan with a compress to her forehead half an hour later. Constable Cobban, who to his credit had arrived within minutes of my sending for him, had helped me carry her to a sitting room. "I could not play; I was just frozen with fear," she said softly. "So I asked for a glass of water, and when the servant didn't come, I decided to get one for myself. But I got lost, you see! So many rooms! Signor Massimo found me and said he would show me the way. Oh, he is so kind. A true gentleman, Louy."

"At your service, kind lady," said Signor Massimo. He lay on a second divan, his head wrapped in white bandages, a glass of brandy in his trembling hands. Sylvia, who had arrived with Cobban, cradled Signor Massimo's bleeding head in her lap, oblivious to the damage to her new coat and frock. "An angel," muttered the delirious maestro, looking up at her.

"So we went to the kitchen together and saw Mr. Phips

there, threatening Meh-ki with a knife." Lizzie shook with fear, and I held her hands more tightly in mine, trying to comfort her. "Signor Massimo shouted that he was to leave."

"At your service, kind lady," repeated the maestro, nodding and gazing about, still very stunned, with half-closed dark eyes.

"Instead, Mr. Phips hit him on the head and knocked him out."

"With this." Cobban held up an old-fashioned cudgel, small enough to be hidden in the pocket of a man's greatcoat, but large enough to do great damage to the skull. "Same thing he used on the servant to get in."

"And the same instrument I used. You saw the rest, Louy. Oh, how did you know to come? My lesson was nowhere near the end." Lizzie sat up and rested her head on my shoulder.

"Dearest," I said, putting my arms tightly about her, "an instinct made me run to you. I saw Mr. Phips in the tearoom and the world just didn't seem right after that."

"Mr. Phips," said Cobban, still not quite believing, though he was the one who had bound and cuffed the murderer even as he lay unconscious from the blow Lizzie had given him. Mr. Phips, groaning in pain, had already been led away to the courthouse. "I never suspected the old gent," said Cobban.

"Nor did I, till it was almost too late," I said. "Now that I know, I'm surprised I didn't see it sooner. Is there a doctor on the way? There are several injuries to see to." While both the maestro and his servant had had their wounds bathed and bound and Meh-ki's throat had been bandaged, I knew that they would all three require more care and several days, if not weeks, of bedrest.

"He'll be here in a moment, Louy. But how did you see that it was Phips?" asked Sylvia, fanning Signor Massimo's feverish brow.

"Because of the connection," I said. "Phips's years in China, that glorious history of his that seemed, upon reflection, a little too glorious. Many cowards come home heroes, when the true heroes don't come home at all."

"Oh, I do wish I knew what you were talking about." Sylvia sighed, dabbing at the maestro's forehead with her lacy handkerchief.

"Ask Meh-ki," I said.

She sat in a chair, her foot on a stool, small as a child and pale as the moon. She was very calm. Resigned, I thought.

"Finally, it is over," she said. "Many years of sorrow. Of fear. My husband can harm me no more."

"Husband?" exclaimed Constable Cobban.

"Yes," I said, having guessed just minutes before. "Tell us," I asked Meh-ki.

She nodded, her eyes glistening. "I was a little girl in Canton. My mother was a servant for the Englishmen there. She cooked. She liked very much a man named August Pincher, who was kind to her, talked to her in nice way, not like the others. Said her food was very good and he talked to her about his fiancée, in America, the woman he loved very much. He had a friend who was not so nice. Phips. He talked cruel to the servants, made fun of them, slapped them whenever he could. But Phips liked me. Told my mother he would take me back to America as his wife, give me a good life there and send for her and my brothers."

Mehi-ki closed her eyes for a moment, remembering. "So

273

we were married, Phips and me. I was not happy, but that did not matter. I would be able to send money home when we came to America. He promised. But when Phips left China, he did not take me with him. He left me there in Canton, a wife without a husband, an outcast because I had married a foreigner, a white devil. But better without him, I thought. He was cruel. He always shout same thing, 'Life requires boldness,' and then he would hit me."

Meh-ki's eyes grew hard. She stopped talking.

"The brute!" said Cobban, giving Sylvia a protective glance.

"What happened to August Pincher, Emily Grayling's first fiancé?" I asked.

"Phips kill him. I see it," Meh-ki said. "When assassins come to murder the traders, I see a struggle in the hall outside where I sleep. It is Mr. Pincher and he is fighting with other man, but man not Chinese. It was Phips. He killed his friend, and then he left Canton."

Sylvia looked more perplexed than ever. "Mr. Phips killed Emily Grayling's fiancé and then came back to marry her himself," I said. "For her money. A fortune can be more of a curse than a blessing," I added.

Cobban blushed to the roots of his hair. "But Phips already had a wife," he said, beginning to understand. "And if that were known, he would lose everything, for a bigamist does not inherit," he said.

Meh-ki was growing sleepy. She sank deeply into the cushions of the chair, looking smaller than ever. Judging from the circles under her eyes and her thinness, she hadn't slept well for quite some time. I felt partially responsible for that, having confronted her in Mrs. Wilkinson's kitchen and terrified her so that she fled and spent some time unemployed and probably hungry as well as homeless, before gaining employment with the visiting artist Signor Massimo.

"Before you sleep, Meh-ki, tell me about Mrs. Percy," I asked her. "How did you meet her?"

"I come to America five years ago," said the Chinese woman. "Mother die, brothers marry, no home for me in Canton. I think I come here, never see Phips, he never find me because it is a big country. I think he has forgotten about me. So I sign paper to work and pay back my ticket price and go on boat to New York. I work hard and pay half my debt, but my employer die. Mrs. Percy find me, then, give me job."

"At your service, kind lady," said the delirious maestro, trying to rise. "I have another guest coming."

"Rest, Signor," said Sylvia, pressing her hand against his chest so that he fell back onto the divan.

"How did Mrs. Percy find you, Meh-ki?" I asked.

"After lose job when employer die I come to Boston. Too many Chinese cooks in New York already. But I find no work, and sleep in house for people with no money, no work. Bad house. Many rats. Mrs. Percy come one day, looking us over. 'Quaint,' she say, when see me. 'Chinese woman look very good in my séance parlor. Add atmosphere.' I did not understand what she meant, but she promise to pay my debt if I work for her."

"And somehow she got you to talk about Canton, and your marriage to the Englishman," I guessed.

"Talk, talk, talk," said Meh-ki with a half smile. "Mrs. Percy talk all the time. Make me talk, too."

"The rest is quite obvious," I said, seeing that Meh-ki was too exhausted to continue.

"Tell us anyway," said Sylvia, frowning.

"Well, when Meh-ki let Mrs. Percy know she had been married to an Englishman, Mrs. Percy did her research," I said. "She discovered that William Phips, the so-called hero of Canton, had returned to Boston and married an heiress, making him a bigamist, and that the heiress had died a short while ago, making him very, very wealthy. Luckily for her—rather ill-luckily, as it turned out—Mr. Phips lived right here in Boston. So she sent him an invitation to the séance."

"And threatened to expose him," Cobban guessed.

"A tragedy is made up of so many strange coincidences," I said, when a sleeping Meh-ki had been carried out. I sipped the rest of the sherry in the glass we had given her. It was warm and sweet and strength returned to me, for I, too, was exhausted now that the danger was over, now that Lizzie was again safe and Meh-ki's long years of danger and torment were behind her and Mrs. Percy's murderer had been revealed.

"What coincidences?" asked Sylvia, now going to Lizzie and pressing her hand to her forehead. "Have you a fever, Elizabeth?"

"Where has my angel gone?" muttered Signor Massimo, looking wildly about.

"I'm well, Sylvia. Thanks to Louisa." Lizzie beamed at me, pale but radiant.

"It was your sister who put you in such danger," I said ruefully.

"No, it was that very strange woman, Mrs. Percy," said Lizzie. "I never liked her, Louy, even though I never met her."

"Yoo-hoo!" A woman's lilting soprano voice floated up the stairs. "The door is open! Is anyone at home?"

"Yoo-hoo, darling!" called back the maestro in a weak voice. Light steps climbed the stairs. A pretty face framed with dark curls peeked in at us.

"I am here for supper," said the great soprano Maria Venturi. Her great black eyes took in the maestro, lolling on the divan with a bandage pressed to his head. "Am I to think it has been canceled?"

CHAPTER NINETEEN

A Farewell Dinner

"WE GRANT THAT human life is mean; but what is the ground of this uneasiness of ours, of this old discontent?" Mr. Emerson had asked me one afternoon years before, when he first spoke of the universal mind and of the connections between all of humanity. "Louisa, dear, what is the universal sense of want and ignorance, but the fine innuendo by which the soul makes its enormous claim? Within man is the soul of the whole; the wise silence; the universal beauty."

On a sunny winter afternoon three days after the events in Signor Massimo's home, I sat in a circle of friendship and felt the soul of the whole, now that the crimes had been revealed and several culprits brought to justice. We were again at MacIntyre's Inn on Boylston.

Lizzie, was there, dear, sweet Lizzie, and Sylvia and Cobban, and Mr. Barnum. We laughed easily among ourselves and goodwill flowed.

Fellowship, I thought to myself, looking with joy at the

friends gathered there. Surrounded by dear ones is when I best understand what Mr. Emerson was trying to teach me about our connectedness.

"You said, that dreadful day, that a tragedy was made up of so many coincidences," said Sylvia, peering intently at me. "What did you mean, Louy?" Sylvia was outfitted once again in her expensive silks and laces rather than cotton and wool; the bright green-and-pink outfit suited her fair complexion, and the choice of clothing, I thought, suited her impulse to honesty. She was no drudge, and could never be, not even to please a lover.

"The first coincidence," I said, "was that after so many years, Meh-ki would find employment with a woman who would try to earn money off of Meh-ki's misfortune. It's clear that Mrs. Percy emotionally forced that strange personal history out of Meh-ki and decided to make Mr. Phips pay for it. Pay in a material, not a moral manner," I clarified.

"I am familiar enough with Mrs. Percy's perfidy, having been a victim of it myself," said Mr. Barnum. He seemed in a pleasant humor, despite the unhappy occurrences of the past weeks, despite the betrayals and the bankruptcy and the public humiliation that bankruptcy brought. "I count myself fortunate, though. Tomorrow I leave for home, to return to Charity and my daughters. I'll start all over again and build another fortune. Having done it once, I know how to do it again. Champagne!" he called to a passing waiter.

"At three in the afternoon?" asked Cobban. That young man, as usual, wore his terribly bright plaid and a very serious face; if Sylvia could make him more lighthearted, he would benefit, I thought.

"A charming idea, champagne," said Sylvia with a slight reproof in her tone. "I approve."

"So do I!" said Lizzie with delight.

We had much to celebrate. Mr. Phips was in jail awaiting his time in court to answer for his cruel past as well as the untimely death of his once-friend, Mrs. Percy. Also in jail once again, Cobban had announced just moments before, was wily Edward Nichols, charged with fraud against Mr. Barnum. Mr. Barnum and I were reunited in friendship now that I knew he need not be feared—not as a homicidal maniac, in any case. The universal mind had prevailed and all the connections had been discovered, restoring me to friendship with a man I had previously and wrongly suspected.

Dishes and cutlery rattled in the background; outside the window a group of carolers had gathered and were beginning "Silent Night," and the afternoon was a very happy one.

"I'll need new attractions," Mr. Barnum said. "I hear you are an expert seamstress, my dear." He turned to Lizzie. "Have you ever considered, say, participating in a stitching contest, perhaps one or two or three other seamstresses before an audience, a kind of marathon of sewing? Always on the lookout for anything that might bring in a paying customer. Happily, there is always more wheat than there is chaff, and people always want to be entertained. I could bill you as 'The Musical Seamstress.' Is there any chance you could sew with one hand and play piano with the other? Do you speak any foreign languages?"

Lizzie and I exchanged glances and understanding smiles.

"Mr. Barnum, you are not aware of the circumstances

that brought Lizzie to my rooms in Boston in the first place," I said gently. "A relative had planned an afternoon party in her honor and Lizzie fled!"

"I am shy, sir," explained Lizzie.

"Ah, yes, most true gentlewomen are," he said, and looked at her with true affection. Reaching over the plate of raisin bread, he patted her hand. "My own dear Charity cannot bear a crowd. Forgive my impertinence."

"There is nothing to forgive, if you'll just order me a second piece of mince pie," requested Lizzie.

"More pie, please," the showman loudly called. "Hogwash, just bring out the whole thing!" Voices buzzed around us and I heard, "Say, isn't that . . ." and "That's Bar . . ." The recognition made him beam for a moment; then he lowered his voice and spoke as Mr. Barnum, a man wounded by fate but resilient. "I've five dollars in my pocket and a loving family waiting for me. I am a rich man," he said to us in a private tone.

When the pie had been delivered and the champagne poured, Cobban seemed to recall something and turned to me. "You said, Miss Louisa, that was the first coincidence. What were the others?" he asked.

"The other important one, of course, was that Mrs. O'Connor had been hired by Mrs. Wilkinson, who had also just employed Meh-ki. Were it not for that, we might never have found Meh-ki."

"Believe me, that is not such a strange coincidence," spoke up Sylvia, the wealthy heiress. "Households always need extra hands for the holidays, and neither Mrs. O'Connor nor Meh-ki is the type to fade into the Bostonian background.

And of course, Mrs. Wilkinson is a competitive soul who hires anyone, just anyone who is available in December, to create that huge Christmas buffet of hers. She pays the highest wages, at least in December."

We all fell silent for a moment, enjoying the champagne—such a rare treat for me!—and the company. Outside, the carolers were now singing "The First Noel," and sun shone on the white snow piled around the streetlamps, imbuing the late afternoon with a fairy-tale quality. I was quite, quite content.

I had received letters from Walpole that morning, from Father and Marmee and Abby and Uncle Benjamin, and they were all well and enjoying the holidays. My gifts to them had arrived and had been put on the table, in readiness for opening on Christmas morning. I would not be with them, but they were in my heart, would always be, no matter what changes time wrought.

It is love that binds a family, and that kind of binding can never be undone. All my life when I thought of Father I would remember his long, noble nose nodding over a book and his white hair, once as black and thick as Barnum's, falling to his shoulders; and of Marmee I would remember her voice, as beautiful as a lark's, and the gentle patience in her eyes; of Lizzie, I would remember her gentleness, her shyness, and her slender fingers always happily practicing a fingering exercise for the piano. Such memories are immune to time and death, and I knew even then that sometime in the future I would make them immortal, in a story not about jealous femme fatales or faithless lovers but about the joy of family life.

"Of course, the biggest coincidence was that Meh-ki ended up cooking for Signor Massimo," said Lizzie.

"It appears coincidence, but I believe it was not," I said. "I had unfortunately terrified Meh-ki when I discovered her in Mrs. Wilkinson's kitchen. She was already afraid for her life. She had seen Mr. Phips in Mrs. Percy's sitting room and recognized him the day of the first séance, but probably hoped, rightly at the time, that he had not seen her. But before the second séance, that evening, she heard the quarrel between Mrs. Percy and Mr. Phips. Mrs. Percy asked for money, of course, and Mr. Phips responded with violence. Meh-ki fled, fearing for her life. Imagine traveling so many miles, after so many years, only to end up yards away from the man she most dreaded."

"But how did she end up with Signor Massimo?" asked Lizzie.

"He was a stranger," I said, "a visitor who knew little of us and Boston and had not been reading the papers or following the gossip. She thought she could safely hide there. That's why that was not a coincidence but an act of reason and choice." Mr. Barnum poured me a second glass of champagne. I sipped very slowly, knowing it would be a long while before I tasted it again. Mr. Barnum had not touched his own glass. He was a teetotaler, yet he would buy champagne for the pleasure of his friends. He was that kind of person.

"The coincidence," said Sylvia, "is that Louy won the lottery, and you ended up in Signor Massimo's house. I suppose that Signor Massimo will not continue your lessons? Attempted murder can destroy enthusiasm for meeting strangers."

"Oh, he has been ever so kind!" said Lizzie, who had just finished her first lesson—it had been decided that the original lesson did not count, because of the many dangerous interruptions—with the maestro that afternoon. "He said it was a good adventure, except for the headache. It will be a good tale to tell of the Wild West when he returns to Rome. Boston has not been the western frontier for some centuries now, but I thought it rude to point that out to him."

"Very thoughtful, very thoughtful," said Mr. Barnum. "Shall we order a bowl of trifle as well?"

"I think there is enough on the table," I protested, laughing.

"My dear," he said, understanding I did not wish us to use up every penny in his pocket, "I started with nothing. I am once more nearly at the bottom of the ladder, and am about to begin in the world again. The situation is disheartening, but I have energy and hope."

"You do not know how disheartening it is to face a pile of sewing," spoke up Lizzie. "We still have half a dozen spring shirts to sew, Louy. Oh, if only we could afford a sewing machine!"

"A sewing machine," mused Mr. Barnum. "I suspect many women will be wanting one of the new contraptions." He thoughtfully scratched his chin. (And now, dear reader, I must jump forward two months into the future, when I received a note from my friend Mr. Barnum, telling us that he had purchased the Wheeler & Wilson Sewing Machine Company and moved it into his bankrupt clock factory in Bridgeport. The note was attached to a foot-pedaled sewing machine wrapped in a bright red bow with a card for Lizzie. Uncle Benjamin, who kept up with his club gossip, reported that Mr. Barnum was expected to earn back his fortune, and more, with the new factory. He did. But still in the distant future was the venture that would make him famous for all time: Barnum and Bailey's Circus, The Greatest Show on Earth!)

Let us return, dear reader, to MacIntyre's Inn on Boylston. I remember the crumb of raisin cake that fell onto Mr. Barnum's cravat and stayed there the length of that long and happy meal and how, when he finally brushed it away, his eyes gleamed as if he were still a boy not to be dismayed by crumbs or bankruptcy.

"Louy, what was not coincidence in these strange events?" protested Sylvia.

"Very little, as it turns out," I said. "Perhaps the one true coincidence occurred years before, when William Phips, son of a stable hand, met August Pincher, who showed him a portrait of the girl he loved. Phips, covetous by nature, as are most criminals, decided to take the girl and the fortune for himself, not for love but for greed and pride."

"And to think schoolboys grow up thinking of him as a hero," Mr. Barnum said sadly.

"After that original coincidence," I continued, "the consequences were almost destined, and Mrs. Percy planned the rest. Mrs. Percy was well rehearsed for her séances. I have it here, in my notebook, exactly what she said: 'Your wife knows your weakness.' I thought she meant Mrs. Emily Phips. She was referring to Meh-ki. And that statement sealed Agatha Percy's death warrant."

"Oh, Louy, you give me chills," Lizzie said.

"Between the first and second séances they must have had a meeting," Cobban guessed, "for he let several days go by before the murder."

"Perhaps he was thinking, meditating," I said. "Perhaps his soul was trying to find a way out of the situation without resorting to violence, and sadly could not. One may only hope that he at least hesitated before the crime."

"The night before the second séance, he acts." Cobban swung his hand through the air and added a melodramatic flair to his voice. Like me, he had a taste for the theater. "He finds her delirious from opium. Perhaps that was why he waited? For that once or twice a month when Mrs. Percy smoked her pipe. He finds her delirious and easily suffocates her."

"But how did he get into that locked room?" asked Sylvia.

"He came in through the large side window, breaking the pane and unlocking it," I said. "He made sure the door to the room was locked, and when he left, he relocked the broken window, to try to make it appear that her death had been a self-inflicted accident rather than murder, to make it seem that no one else could have been in the room. The broken glass would have been hidden by the heavy draperies."

"But the next day we heard him break the pane of glass," Sylvia said, frowning with confusion.

"Two panes had been broken," I said. "He merely broke a different pane so that we would hear the glass shatter."

"I hope I was never a suspect!" said Mr. Barnum, sitting up straighter and putting his thumbs behind his jacket lapels, preening as men sometimes do.

"Never," I lied. "Of course, what does disturb me is knowing that Mr. Phips must have been watching me, and I never noticed. I should have suspected him sooner. There was, for instance, the problem of the missing pipe."

"Missing pipe?" repeated Sylvia.

"Mrs. Percy's opium pipe. It was not in the room where she died. Days later, when I ran into Mr. Phips while buying a new pipe for Uncle Benjamin, Mr. Phips forgetfully confessed that he collected opium pipes. I did not make the connection then. Now it is obvious."

"Hindsight." Mr. Barnum sighed. "In hindsight, I never would have entered into business relations with that young cousin of mine, Eddie Nichols."

"Mr. Phips knew I was getting closer," I said. "It was no coincidence that he was at the Avery Street Bakery the same day and time as was I, no coincidence that he overheard my conversation with Mrs. O'Connor about Meh-ki's new employment." I pushed my cup away. "To think, he arrived at Signor Massimo's before I did and almost murdered again because I was finishing a cup of tea."

"The Christmas crowds," said Sylvia. "They could hide any number of assassins."

"Now there is a cheerful thought." Lizzie laughed. "So it was Mr. Phips who locked you in the cellar?"

"No," I said, wondering how much I should say about that matter. A woman's reputation is such a fragile thing. But these friends had been through much with me. They deserved the entire story. "It was Amelia Snodgrass. She knew that her stolen necklace had been returned to Mrs. Percy, and she was determined to find it. It was she in the house that afternoon, she who barred the door so that I could not interrupt her searching. She did not wish me harm; she wished only the return of her property. Though if she had asked, I would have helped her search for it. When Miss Amelia Snodgrass is wed to Mr. Wilmot Green, I am certain the society column will report that she was wearing a family heirloom, an ancient necklace of pearls and diamonds."

"She stole it back!" exclaimed Sylvia with delight. "Now there is justice!"

"And as you know from that dropped glove, Miss Louisa, I was also in the house that afternoon." Mr. Barnum blushed with shame, for while he may have stretched the truth a bit for entertainment purposes, he was by nature an honest and law-abiding man. "I had hoped to find examples of Mrs. Percy's attempts at forging my name. I must have arrived just after Amelia Snodgrass left."

"And you did me a good deed by alerting Mr. Cobban to my predicament," I said. "Miss Snodgrass gave me quite a fright, and unnecessarily so, when she bolted that door to protect her secret. I fear that every time she wears the necklace she will be forced to remember her disastrous affair with Eddie Nichols." The thought brought me a tiny amount of pleasure, I am sad to admit.

"Perhaps Mrs. Deeds has learned her lesson and will acquire her future jewels through more approved and legitimate means," said Constable Cobban. "I can charge her with nothing now, but I have her name, and she knows it."

Mrs. Deeds. Her greed had so offended me that I had hoped she would prove guilty of the murder. Well, there was time yet for destiny to deliver a cruel blow to a woman so covetous of the property of others.

The mince pie was finished, and the bottle of champagne. We all stirred, sensing that it was time to rise, to return to our homes, our lives, to put aside this grisly affair and enjoy all there was to be enjoyed, for life is too short to spend it brooding over crime. The universal mind, Mr. Emerson would have said, delights in delight and should not be left in darkness. Our best instinct is for happiness, and the real fault of crime is that it destroys happiness.

"Of course, the one person to whom restitution can never be made is Mr. Phips's wife, Emily," I said, pushing back my chair and rising. "She died believing that her first lover, her true love, had been unfaithful, because that was what Mr. Phips wished her to believe. How sad."

"Mr. Cobban, shall we fetch the ladies' wraps?" asked Mr. Barnum, and the two men headed for the coatroom.

"Now, Sylvia, tell me," I said when the gentlemen were gone. "Have you and Constable Cobban arrived at an understanding?"

"We have," she said, grinning. "We will wait a year before we talk more of this matter, and not rush in."

"How wise you've become!" I said with relief.

"It was Father's idea," she said.

I sighed. "You still believe you are in communication with his spirit?"

"I do," said my friend. "As is every child who feels a bond with a parent, be he present in life or not. Even if he speaks only in dreams, he is speaking, is he not?" Her eyes gleamed, and I saw that, indeed, she enjoyed something of the presence of the father she had never known, perhaps simply because she wished to.

"But what of the day that Mrs. Percy seemed to speak through you?" I asked. "That was no dream."

"I cannot explain," Sylvia said. "We must, I fear, leave that as a mystery."

"And now, home," said Lizzie, "to Auntie Bond's piano and my new Liszt music. I believe it has all been worth it."

I FINISHED "AGATHA'S CONFESSION" that evening in my little attic writing room. After her terrible crime of passion Agatha pleads with Philip to forgive her, to be merciful.

> *"I had suffered so much from her, and I could not give you up. Be merciful, and I will atone for it by a whole life of sacrifice and penitence—but do not cast me off," I cried, overcoming in my despair the horror and remorse that froze my blood.*
>
> *But he never heeded me, and his stern purpose never changed. He tore himself away, saying solemnly as he passed out into the night:*
>
> *"God pardon us both. Our sins have wrought out their own punishment and we must never meet again."*
>
> *We never have.*

As sorry as I was for Agatha Percy, she had sealed her own fate by choosing crime rather than repentance. We must never overcome horror and remorse, for sin found in a person can also be found in a society, and vice versa; we must root out the crime, not our penance. So Mr. Emerson and Father would say, and so say I, if people and nations are to be healed.

Read on for an excerpt from the
first Louisa May Alcott mystery,

Louisa and the Missing Heiress

Available from Obsidian.

Dunreath Place
Roxbury, Massachusetts
February 1887

Gentle Readers,

I had a letter from an old friend recently. She asked if I
remembered Dot and if I had ever thought of writing her
story. She is too kind to say outright but she gently
reminded me that youth is far behind and that what I am
going to write, I should perhaps write now, and quickly. The
letter seemed an omen, for that same day Father had sat up
in bed and asked if I had heard from Dorothy Brownly
recently. His mind wanders and he thought, that morning,
that I was perhaps on my way to one of those girlhood
afternoon activities that occupied my younger years.

In my youth, I struggled to write and publish stories.
Now I am known and I may even admit beloved. In the
streets of Concord I cannot even mail a letter or purchase
yarn without being recognized. That is one of the joys of age
and success, though I admit to occasionally yearning for
those younger days when I could walk the streets
anonymously. A certain anonymity no doubt assisted the
events of which I now wish to write. While I have never
shied away from telling my readers about my family and my
childhood, I have—in part because of the deepest personal
reservations—kept silent about many of what used to be
called my "adventures." In part from modesty, and a wish
not to hurt the living, I have kept secret many of the most

interesting years of my life, years in which I found myself in the curious role of lady detective.

I do find myself reticent, however, I who have already revealed so much of my life in my fictional works. What mother would wish to reveal to her sweet children that their beloved author, Louisa May Alcott, had knowledge of crime and criminals, and deeds so dastardly that if known they would require a night-light to burn in the hall? Yet knowledge of them I had. For many years of my life, I found myself surrounded by unexplained death and unexpected danger, as well as holding the unusual and unmerited position of being the only person able to reach a satisfactory conclusion to the mysterious events.

I have decided to go through my diaries and reconstruct the events of some of these years. These, then, are the other stories of my youth, of friends and foes who chanced across my path, sometimes gracing it, sometimes causing such distress I would fall into the Slough of Despond and doubt all, even the words on a white page. I begin with the story of my dear childhood friend Dot, and her untimely demise.

I trust you may gain some enjoyment through the reading of these tales.

Louisa May Alcott

Prologue

"Listen then," replied the count, "and perhaps you too may share in the excitement of those about you. That box belongs to Josephine. . . ."

I PAUSED, PEN in hand, and scratched out the name. It simply did not suit her. I considered following Shakespeare, knowing that my heroine would be as enticing with whatever name God gave her, until I realized that, surely, no reader would become entranced with the lady's plight were she named Maud or Jo.

"Josephine won't do," I said. "People would be calling her Jo, and this woman is most definitely not a Jo. Jo is a homespun name, tomboyish and striving, not given over to frivolity or melodrama. This woman needs a name that is more Italianate, more romantic. Beatrice. Yes, that's it. . . . And her rival shall be Therese."

"Nay, not so strange as one may fancy, Arthur," said his friend, "for it is whispered, and with truth, I fear, that she will bestow the hand so many have sought in vain upon the handsome painter yonder. He is a worthy person, but not a fitting husband for a truehearted woman like Beatrice; he is gay, careless, and fickle, too. I fear she is tender and confiding, loving with an Italian's passionate devotion, if he be true, and taking an Italian's quick revenge, if he prove false."

"And then what, Louisa? Does she give her hand to the faithless painter, Claude?" breathlessly asked Miss Sylvia Shattuck.

I stopped reading and began marking on the pages, crossing out some words and adding others. On some days the phrases came easily; on others each was a struggle. This day was a struggle, since I was already preoccupied with the events to come . . . though I could not yet know how truly and frighteningly eventful the afternoon would become.

Sylvia and I were in the attic writing room in my family's house on Pinckney Street. She stood beside my piles of manuscript wrapped in paper and string, leaning on the huge ancient desk at which I wrote. Behind her on a ledge stood my favorite, much-thumbed books: my father's gift, *Pilgrim's Progress*, and my secret thrill, an edition of Poe's *Murders in the Rue Morgue*. I have always adored Poe for his prose and the suspense and thrill of his writing. But, truth be told, not so much for the mystery of this story, which I solved long before Poe intended me to, an achievement I credit to my education in my father's philosophical methods and the influence of my mother's gift for insight. My parents' careful education in the ways of the world has made me particularly apt at arriving at answers to questions of human nature.

The one window in my garret was curtained with muslin, not lace—I prefer a gentle light when I work, and of course my family could not waste money on lace. The floor was bare but scrupulously clean. It was 1854, I was twenty-two, Mother had just lost her job with the charity agency, and Father . . . well, he had never had a talent for earning income. Those years of poverty bleed together in my memory, always overpowered by memories of more important problems. That was the year following the election of President Franklin Pierce, and Father, months later, still grumbled to himself about it. We would see him pottering from library to parlor, from parlor to dinner table, jabbing the air with his forefinger as he lectured President Pierce in absentia. Pierce was a will-o'-the-wisp, a moral deficient, willing to do anything for a vote, including support slavery.

That was also the year my beloved older sister, Anna, had gone to Syracuse to work as a governess. I missed her every day, every evening, and perhaps my friendship with Sylvia grew even deeper because of that longing for the wise, gentle, absent Anna.

That afternoon, as I finished my work, the slanted light coming through that window indicated it was close to three o'clock, the household dinner hour.

"Well," Sylvia said impatiently, reading over my shoulder. "Does she leave the stage and pledge herself to the faithless one?"

I considered Sylvia's question, replacing my pen in its tray. "She must, else there is no story, I fear. But it will not end happily."

"Claude will love another," Sylvia guessed, leaning forward eagerly.

"He will be absolutely unreliable," I admitted. "But Beatrice will have her revenge."

"How exciting, Louisa!"

"Do you think so, Sylvia? Is it, perhaps, too exciting?"

"Could there be such a thing as too exciting?"

I scratched my nose, leaving a smudge of ink behind, one of my bad habits, I'm afraid. I contemplated the quality of my writing. It was all blood and thunder. My natural ambition was, I suppose, for the lurid style. I could not help but indulge in gorgeous fancies. Perhaps there was no other way for me to write, I thought as I straightened the manuscript pages into a neat pile. Yet there was this impulse, deep inside, to tell a true story, not a fancy.

Even then, before I had published my first work, I sensed what would ultimately be the real value of my work. But that day there were three manuscripts on my desk: *The Flower Fables*, little stories I invented for the Emerson children and was now working into a children's book; my true short story, "How I Went Out to Service"; and my tale of Beatrice and Therese, which I had just named as "The Rival Prima Donnas." None had yet been published. Next to "How I Went Out to Service" was a rejection letter. I hadn't anticipated how much pain a simple envelope could carry. The rejection had suggested—no, stated—that I should pay more attention to domestic duties, as I had no talent as a writer. The story was one of my first "real" stories about real people, rather than inventions such as Beatrice and her fickle lover, Claude. In fact, it was about me, and the rejection had a double sting to

it, for it was my life, my experience that was rejected, as well as the story.

That name Josephine, though. That was not a blood-and-thunder name, nor was it a fairy name for the *Fables*. The name conjured up a fleeting image. A young woman, a character who sprawled on rugs rather than sitting primly in chairs, a woman who cherished books over new bonnets and rich husbands. Was this too ordinary a character for a novel? What would she say if she spoke? The seed that bloomed into Josephine took root that day . . . but I get ahead of myself.

Whilst some authors complain that they cannot work without perfect solitude, at this stage in my life I found being with Sylvia Shattuck more natural and more helpful than being alone. We had been friends since childhood, and we had arrived at that wonderful, intimate stage in which words are often unnecessary, so well does one know the other. Of a far less humble background than I, Sylvia was able to enjoy the frivolity that comes with wealth. Unlike so many members of "society," however, she possessed a deep conscience and dedication to help those less fortunate, and, for this and her sweetness, my parents had accepted her into the bosom of our family. "She can't help that she was born wealthy," Father often said, in the same tone in which another person might say, *He can't help that he was born lame*, or mute, or some other inescapable and unearned defect of nature.

And so Sylvia was allowed into my attic workroom. When Sylvia and I were alone, and not working for the poor, for women abandoned by their husbands, or for children desperate to learn, she helped me be less serious and indulge my fancies, my whims, my creativity. Looking back, I am certain that Sylvia was something of an inspiration for me. But I often wondered how we could be frivolous—even silly—when there was so much injustice in the world. Was it that Sylvia and I valued each other not for the fancies and fantasies we indulged, but for what was most subtle in the other's character, for that mysterious promise of what could be?

"What could be," I repeated aloud.

"Another gorgeous fancy?" Sylvia asked. Seeing the look on my face, she said, "Are you thinking again of that letter? You must not let it discourage you. Your writing is marvelous and success will come."

"Sylvia, you are a friend. Meanwhile I write my blood-and-thunders filled with moonlight in Rome, adulteresses with flashing black eyes, madwomen locked in attics, when real life needs to be written. If Father ever read this . . ." I riffled the pages on the desk.

"Now, Louy, you know your father never reads anything more entertaining than *Pilgrim's Progress*. And you may publish those *Flower Fables*, that sweet collection."

"Yes. A children's book. Closer to life, I hope."

"Louisa! Sylvia! It is almost time!" my mother's voice called up the narrow stairway.

I carefully placed the manuscript in a drawer, leaving Beatrice to her fate, and locked the drawer. I extinguished the lamp, for the attic was dark even in the afternoon, and stood.

"We must go, Sylvia. Time to face the terrible siblings and the Medusa."

"Poor Dottie," Sylvia said, also rising.

Dear reader, I must now explain this profusion of friends.

302

Mr. Hawthorne, in one of his calmer moments a few years before, had patiently explained to me the importance of pacing, of
allowing the characters time to speak, to be known by the
reader, before introducing the next. "Think of it as a play," he
had instructed, knowing I was stagestruck in my teens. "Characters appear one at a time, or in couples. Never all at once."

Suffice it to say that before Sylvia became my sole close
companion (for as much as I loved my younger sisters, Lizzie
and May, they were too young for the adult conversations I had
shared with Anna when she was at home), Dottie had also
been a close companion. She had, the year before, married Sylvia's cousin, Preston Wortham, and embarked on a honeymoon
visit to the capitals of Europe. For months Sylvia and I had
speculated on Dottie's daily activities (her visit to Italy had
inspired me to place my heroines in peril throughout the Apen-
nines and along the Bay of Naples), and the tea party was our
first chance to see her since her return to Boston. Unfortunately, as a price of seeing our friend, Sylvia and I would be
forced to endure a visit with Dottie's sisters, and her aunt, a
formidable creature we had nicknamed "the Medusa."

Mother waited for us at the bottom of the attic stairs, a
basket of just-baked rolls in her hands.

"Bring these for Dottie," she said. "She always liked my
raisin cakes. Just imagine, Dottie is a married woman now.
Seems like just yesterday she was still in short skirts and
afraid of the dark."

"Oh, Abba, with all you have to do," Sylvia said, accepting the basket and giving my mother a kiss on the cheek. Like
all of us, Sylvia called Mrs. Bronson Alcott by the familiar
name, Abba, short for Abigail. Mother usually had high spir-

its, but today she looked tired and worn. We worried that she bore too much responsibility on those frail shoulders. Yet she remained my rock, my deepest support in times of difficulty.

"A year seems a long time for a young woman to be away from home and friends." Abba sighed. "These new customs. Why, after your father and I married at King's Chapel we went back to his room at the boardinghouse, and after supper he wrote his lecture for the next day of school. We didn't make such a fuss of things."

"You and Father are the exception to all customs," I said, smiling.

"But to invite you for tea instead of supper," said Abba. "Well, it is time. Send Dottie my love."

In my mind's eye, I can still see us rushing out of the house, two pairs of neat, high-buttoned shoes clacking over the wooden floor and down the stairs, and our black cloaks making the whooshing sound of heavy flannel as we dressed for outdoors. I dashed out, chiming the doorbell as I left, both of us laughing with nervousness, dreading the ordeal to come.

Mother, with her housecap askew on her graying hair, waved from an upstairs window and shouted, "Louy, remember to bring back a cake of laundry soap. Now hurry along, or you'll be late! Don't keep Dottie waiting!"

"Oh, true and tender guide, we will not forget the soap!" I waved back a farewell. "And we won't keep Dottie—Mrs. Preston Wortham—waiting!"

Later, I would recall with great sadness the irony of those words.

© STEVE POLESKIE

About the Author

Anna Maclean is the pseudonym of Jeanne Mackin, an award-winning journalist and the author of several historical novels. She lives in the Finger Lakes area of New York with her husband, artist and writer Stephen Poleskie. Visit her Web site at www.annamaclean.net.

About the Author